INDIAN FAIRY TALES

PRINCESS LABAM

INDIAN FAIRY TALES

Selected and Edited by
JOSEPH JACOBS

Illustrated by
JOHN D. BATTEN

MANOHAR
2026

Due to the academic and scholarly importance of this volume, we are reprinting/republishing it from the original source without any modifications or changes. Therefore, some misprints and errors may occur.

First published 1912
Reprinted 2026

ISBN 978-93-6080-054-3 (hardbound)
ISBN 978-93-6080-633-0 (ebook)

Published by
Ajay Kumar Jain *for*
Manohar Publishers & Distributors
4753/23 Ansari Road, Daryaganj
New Delhi 110 002

Printed and bound in India

INDIAN FAIRY TALES

SELECTED AND EDITED BY

JOSEPH JACOBS

EDITOR OF "FOLK-LORE"

ILLUSTRATED BY

JOHN D. BATTEN

LONDON
DAVID NUTT, 57-59 LONG ACRE
NEW YORK: G. P. PUTNAM'S SONS
1912

TO

MY DEAR LITTLE PHIL

Preface

FROM the extreme West of the Indo-European world, we go this year to the extreme East. From the soft rain and green turf of Gaeldom, we seek the garish sun and arid soil of the Hindoo. In the Land of Ire, the belief in fairies, gnomes, ogres and monsters is all but dead; in the Land of Ind it still flourishes in all the vigour of animism.

Soils and national characters differ; but fairy tales are the same in plot and incidents, if not in treatment. The majority of the tales in this volume have been known in the West in some form or other, and the problem arises how to account for their simultaneous existence in farthest West and East. Some—as Benfey in Germany, M. Cosquin in France, and Mr. Clouston in England—have declared that India is the Home of the Fairy Tale, and that all European fairy tales have been brought from thence by Crusaders, by

Mongol missionaries, by Gipsies, by Jews, by traders, by travellers. The question is still before the courts, and one can only deal with it as an advocate. So far as my instructions go, I should be prepared, within certain limits, to hold a brief for India. So far as the children of Europe have their fairy stories in common, these—and they form more than a third of the whole—are derived from India. In particular, the majority of the Drolls or comic tales and jingles can be traced, without much difficulty, back to the Indian peninsula.

Certainly there is abundant evidence of the early transmission by literary means of a considerable number of drolls and folk-tales from India about the time of the Crusaders. The collections known in Europe by the titles of *The Fables of Bidpai*, *The Seven Wise Masters*, *Gesta Romanorum*, and *Barlaam and Josaphat*, were extremely popular during the Middle Ages, and their contents passed on the one hand into the *Exempla* of the monkish preachers, and on the other into the *Novelle* of Italy, thence, after many days, to contribute their quota to the Elizabethan Drama. Perhaps nearly one tenth of the main incidents of European folk-tales can be traced to this source.

There are even indications of an earlier literary contact between Europe and India, in the case of one branch of the folk-tale, the Fable or Beast Droll. In a somewhat elaborate discussion* I have come to the conclusion that a goodly number of the fables that pass under the name of the Samian slave, Æsop, were derived from India, probably from the same source whence the same tales were utilised in the Jatakas, or Birth-stories of Buddha. These Jatakas contain a large quantity of genuine early Indian folk-tales, and form the earliest collection of folk-tales in the world, a sort of Indian Grimm, collected more than two thousand years before the good German brothers went on their quest among the folk with such delightful results. For this reason I have included a considerable number of them in this volume; and shall be surprised if tales that have roused the laughter and wonder of pious Buddhists for the last two thousand years, cannot produce the same effect on English children. The Jatakas have been fortunate in their English translators, who render with vigour and point; and I rejoice in being able to publish the translation of two new Jatakas, kindly done into English for this volume by Mr. W. H. D. Rouse, of Christ's College, Cambridge. In one of these I think I have traced the source of the Tar Baby incident in "Uncle Remus."

Though Indian fairy tales are the earliest in existence, yet they are also from another point of view the youngest.

* "History of the Æsopic Fable," the introductory volume to my edition of Caxton's *Fables of Esope* (London, Nutt, 1889).

For it is only about twenty-five years ago that Miss Frere began the modern collection of Indian folk-tales with her charming "Old Deccan Days" (London, John Murray, 1868; fourth edition, 1889). Her example has been followed by Miss Stokes, by Mrs. Steel, and Captain (now Major) Temple, by the Pandit Natesa Sastri, by Mr. Knowles and Mr. Campbell, as well as others who have published folk-tales in such periodicals as the *Indian Antiquary* and *The Orientalist.* The story-store of modern India has been well dipped into during the last quarter of a century, though the immense range of the country leaves room for any number of additional workers and collections. Even so far as the materials already collected go, a large number of the commonest incidents in European folk-tales have been found in India. Whether brought there or born there, we have scarcely any criterion for judging; but as some of those still current among the folk in India can be traced back more than a millennium, the presumption is in favour of an Indian origin.

From all these sources—from the Jatakas, from the Bidpai, and from the more recent collections—I have selected those stories which throw most light on the origin of Fable and Folk-tales, and at the same time are most likely to attract English children. I have not, however, included too many stories of the Grimm types, lest I should repeat the contents of the two preceding volumes of this series. This has to some degree weakened the case for India as represented by this book. The need of catering for the young ones has restricted my selection from the well-named "Ocean of the Streams of Story," *Katha-Sarit Sagara* of Somadeva. The stories existing in Pali and Sanskrit I have taken from translations, mostly from the German of Benfey or the vigorous English of Professor Rhys-Davids, whom I have to thank for permission to use his versions of the Jatakas.

I have been enabled to make this book a representative collection of the Fairy Tales of Ind by the kindness of the original collectors or their publishers. I have especially to thank Miss Frere, who kindly made an exception in my favour, and granted me the use of that fine story, "Punchkin," and that quaint myth, "How Sun, Moon, and Wind went out to Dinner." Miss Stokes has been equally gracious in granting me the use of characteristic specimens from her "Indian Fairy Tales." To Major Temple I owe the advantage of selecting from his admirable *Wideawake Stories*, and Messrs. Kegan Paul, Trench & Co. have allowed me to use Mr. Knowles' "Folk-tales of Kashmir," in their Oriental Library; and Messrs. W. H. Allen have been equally obliging with regard to Mrs. Kingscote's "Tales of the Sun." Mr. M. L. Dames has enabled me to add to the published story-store of India by granting me the use of one from his inedited collection of Baluchi folk-tales.

I have again to congratulate myself on the co-operation of my friend Mr. J. D. Batten in giving beautiful or amusing form to the creations of the folk fancy of the Hindoos. It is no slight thing to embody, as he has done, the glamour and the humour both of the Celt and of the Hindoo. It is only a further proof that Fairy Tales are something more than Celtic or Hindoo. They are human.

JOSEPH JACOBS.

Contents

Contents

Full-page Illustrations

[Plates, vignettes, initials, and cuts are from "process" blocks supplied by Messrs. J. C. Drummond & Co. of Covent Garden.]

The Lion and the Crane

THE Bodhisatta was at one time born in the region of Himavanta as a white crane; now Brahmadatta was at that time reigning in Benares. Now it chanced that as a lion was eating meat a bone stuck in his throat. The throat became swollen, he could not take food, his suffering was terrible. The crane seeing him, as he was perched on a tree looking for food, asked, "What ails thee, friend?" He told him why. "I could free thee from that bone, friend, but dare not enter thy mouth for fear thou mightest eat me." "Don't be afraid, friend, I'll not eat thee; only save my life." "Very well," says he, and caused him to lie down on his left side. But thinking to himself, "Who knows what this fellow will do?" he placed a small stick upright between his two jaws that he could not close his mouth, and inserting his head inside his mouth struck one end of the bone with his beak. Whereupon the bone dropped and fell out. As soon as he had caused the bone to fall, he got out of the lion's mouth, striking the stick with his beak so that it fell out, and then settled on a branch. The lion gets well, and one day was eating a buffalo he had killed. The crane, thinking "I will sound him," settled on a branch just over him, and in conversation spoke this first verse:

"A service have we done thee
To the best of our ability,
King of the Beasts! Your Majesty!
What return shall we get from thee?"

In reply the Lion spoke the second verse:

"As I feed on blood,
And always hunt for prey,
'Tis much that thou art still alive
Having once been between my teeth."

Then in reply the crane said the two other verses:

"Ungrateful, doing no good,
Not doing as he would be done by,
In him there is no gratitude,
To serve him is useless.

"His friendship is not won
By the clearest good deed.
Better softly withdraw from him,
Neither envying nor abushing."

And having thus spoken the crane flew away.

And when the great Teacher, Gautama the Buddha, told this tale, he used to add: "Now at that time the lion was Devadatta the Traitor, but the white crane was I myself."

How the Raja's Son won the Princess Labam

IN A country there was a Raja who had an only son who every day went out to hunt. One day the Rani, his mother, said to him, "You can hunt wherever you like on these three sides; but you must never go to the fourth side." This she said because she knew if he went on the fourth side he would hear of the beautiful Princess Labam, and that then he would leave his father and mother and seek for the princess.

The young prince listened to his mother, and obeyed her for some time; but one day, when he was hunting on the three sides where he was allowed to go, he remembered what she had said to him about the fourth side, and he determined to go and see why she had forbidden him to hunt on that side. When he got there, he found himself in a jungle, and nothing in the jungle but a quantity of parrots, who lived in it. The young Raja shot at some of them, and at once they all flew away up to the sky. All, that is, but one, and this was their Raja, who was called Hiraman parrot.

When Hiraman parrot found himself left alone, he called out to the other parrots, " Don't fly away and leave me alone when the Raja's son shoots. If you desert me like this, I will tell the Princess Labam."

Then the parrots all flew back to their Raja, chattering. The prince was greatly surprised, and said, " Why, these birds can talk ! " Then he said to the parrots, " Who is the Princess Labam ? Where does she live ? " But the parrots would not tell him where she lived. " You can never get to the Princess Labam's country." That is all they would say.

The prince grew very sad when they would not tell him anything more ; and he threw his gun away and went home. When he got home, he would not speak or eat, but lay on his bed for four or five days, and seemed very ill.

At last he told his father and mother that he wanted to go and see the Princess Labam. " I must go," he said ; " I must see what she is like. Tell me where her country is."

" We do not know where it is," answered his father and mother.

" Then I must go and look for it," said the prince.

" No, no," they said, " you must not leave us. You are our only son. Stay with us. You will never find the Princess Labam."

" I must try and find her," said the prince. " Perhaps God will show me the way. If I live and I find her, I will come back to you ; but perhaps I shall die, and then I shall never see you again. Still I must go."

So they had to let him go, though they cried very much at parting with him. His father gave him fine clothes to wear, and a fine horse. And he took his gun, and his bow and arrows, and a great many other weapons ; " for," he said, "I may want them." His father, too, gave him plenty of rupees.

Then he himself got his horse all ready for the journey, and he said good-bye to his father and mother; and his mother took her handkerchief and wrapped some sweetmeats in it, and gave it to her son. "My child," she said to him, "when you are hungry eat some of these sweetmeats."

He then set out on his journey, and rode on and on till he came to a jungle in which were a tank and shady trees. He bathed himself and his horse in the tank, and then sat down under a tree. "Now," he said to himself, "I will eat some of the sweetmeats my mother gave me, and I will drink some water, and then I will continue my journey." He opened his handkerchief and took out a sweetmeat. He found an ant in it. He took out another. There was an ant in that one too. So he laid the two sweetmeats on the ground, and he took out another, and another, and another, until he had taken them all out; but in each he found an ant. "Never mind," he said, "I won't eat the sweetmeats; the ants shall eat them." Then the Ant-Raja came and stood before him and said, "You have been good to us. If ever you are in trouble, think of me and we will come to you."

The Raja's son thanked him, mounted his horse and continued his journey. He rode on and on until he came to another jungle, and there he saw a tiger who had a thorn in his foot, and was roaring loudly from the pain.

"Why do you roar like that?' said the young Raja. "What is the matter with you?"

"I have had a thorn in my foot for twelve years," answered the tiger, "and it hurts me so; that is why I roar."

"Well," said the Raja's son, "I will take it out for you.

But perhaps, as you are a tiger, when I have made you well, you will eat me?"

"Oh no," said the tiger, "I won't eat you. Do make me well."

Then the prince took a little knife from his pocket and cut the thorn out of the tiger's foot; but when he cut, the tiger roared louder than ever—so loud that his wife heard him in the next jungle, and came bounding along to see what was the matter. The tiger saw her coming, and hid the prince in the jungle, so that she should not see him.

"What man hurt you that you roared so loud?" said the wife.

"No one hurt me," answered the husband; "but a Raja's son came and took the thorn out of my foot."

"Where is he? Show him to me," said his wife.

"If you promise not to kill him, I will call him," said the tiger.

" I won't kill him ; only let me see him," answered his wife.

Then the tiger called the Raja's son, and when he came the tiger and his wife made him a great many salaams. Then they gave him a good dinner, and he stayed with them for three days. Every day he looked at the tiger's foot, and the third day it was quite healed. Then he said good-bye to the tigers, and the tiger said to him, " If ever you are in trouble, think of me, and we will come to you."

The Raja's son rode on and on till he came to a third jungle. Here he found four fakirs whose teacher and master had died, and had left four things,—a bed, which carried whoever sat on it whithersoever he wished to go ; a bag, that gave its owner whatever he wanted, jewels, food or clothes ; a stone bowl that gave its owner as much water as he wanted, no matter how far he might be from a tank ; and a stick and rope, to which its owner had only to say, if any one came to make war on him, " Stick, beat as many men and soldiers as are here," and the stick would beat them and the rope would tie them up

The four fakirs were quarrelling over these four things. One said, " I want this ; " another said, " You cannot have it, for I want it ; " and so on.

The Raja's son said to them, " Do not quarrel for these things. I will shoot four arrows in four different directions. Whichever of you gets to my first arrow, shall have the first thing—the bed. Whosoever gets to the second arrow, shall have the second thing—the bag. He who gets to the third arrow, shall have the third thing—the bowl. And he who gets to the fourth arrow, shall have the last things—the stick and rope." To this they agreed. And the prince shot off his first arrow. Away raced the fakirs to get it. When they brought it back to him he shot off the second, and when they had found and brought it to him he shot off his third, and when they had brought him the third he shot off the fourth.

While they were away looking for the fourth arrow the Raja's son let his horse loose in the jungle and sat on the bed, taking the bowl, the stick and rope, and the bag with him. Then he said, "Bed, I wish to go to the Princess Labam's country." The little bed instantly rose up into the air and began to fly, and it flew and flew till it came to the Princess Labam's country, where it settled on the ground. The Raja's son asked some men he saw, "Whose country is this?"

"The Princess Labam's country," they answered. Then the prince went on till he came to a house where he saw an old woman.

"Who are you?" she said. "Where do you come from?"

"I come from a far country," he said; "do let me stay with you to-night."

"No," she answered, "I cannot let you stay with me; for our king has ordered that men from other countries may not stay in his country. You cannot stay in my house."

"You are my aunty," said the prince; "let me remain with you for this one night. You see it is evening, and if I go into the jungle, then the wild beasts will eat me."

"Well," said the old woman, "you may stay here to-night; but to-morrow morning you must go away, for if the king hears you have passed the night in my house, he will have me seized and put into prison."

Then she took him into her house, and the Raja's son was

very glad. The old woman began preparing dinner, but he stopped her. "Aunty," he said, "I will give you food." He put his hand into his bag, saying, "Bag, I want some dinner," and the bag gave him instantly a delicious dinner, served up on two gold plates. The old woman and the Raja's son then dined together.

When they had finished eating, the old woman said, "Now I will fetch some water."

"Don't go," said the prince. "You shall have plenty of water directly." So he took his bowl and said to it, "Bowl, I want some water," and then it filled with water. When it was full, the prince cried out, "Stop, bowl!" and the bowl stopped filling. "See, aunty," he said, "with this bowl I can always get as much water as I want."

By this time night had come. "Aunty," said the Raja's son, "why don't you light a lamp?"

"There is no need," she said. "Our king has forbidden the people in his country to light any lamps; for, as soon as it is dark, his daughter, the Princess Labam, comes and sits on her roof, and she shines so that she lights up all the country and our houses, and we can see to do our work as if it were day."

When it was quite black night the princess got up. She dressed herself in her rich clothes and jewels, and rolled up her hair, and across her head she put a band of diamonds and pearls. Then she shone like the moon and her beauty made night day. She came out of her room and sat on the roof of her palace. In the daytine she never came out of her house; she only came out at night. All the people in her father's country then went about their work and finished it.

The Raja's son watched the princess quietly, and was very happy. He said to himself, "How lovely she is!"

At midnight, when everybody had gone to bed, the princess came down from her roof and went to her room; and when she was in bed and asleep, the Raja's son got up softly and sat on his bed. "Bed," he said to it, "I want to go to the Princess Labam's bed-room." So the little bed carried him to the room where she lay fast asleep.

The young Raja took his bag and said, "I want a great deal of betel-leaf," and it at once gave him quantities of betel-leaf. This he laid near the princess's bed, and then his little bed carried him back to the old woman's house.

Next morning all the princess's servants found the betel-leaf, and began to eat it. "Where did you get all that betel-leaf?" asked the princess.

"We found it near your bed," answered the servants. Nobody knew the prince had come in the night and put it all there.

In the morning the old woman came to the Raja's son. "Now it is morning," she said, "and you must go; for if the king finds out all I have done for you, he will seize me."

"I am ill to-day, dear aunty," said the prince; "do let me stay till to-mororw morning."

"Good," said the old woman. So he stayed, and they took their dinner out of the bag, and the bowl gave them water.

When night came the princess got up and sat on her roof, and at twelve o'clock, when every one was in bed, she went to her bed-room, and was soon fast asleep. Then the Raja's son sat on his bed, and it carried him to the princess. He took his bag and said, "Bag, I want a most lovely shawl." It gave him a splendid shawl, and he spread it over the princess as she lay asleep. Then he went back to the old woman's house and slept till morning.

In the morning, when the princess saw the shawl she was delighted. "See, mother," she said; "Khuda must have given me this shawl, it is so beautiful." Her mother was very glad too.

"Yes, my child," she said; "Khuda must have given you this splendid shawl."

When it was morning the old woman said to the Raja's son, "Now you must really go."

"Aunty," he answered, "I am not well enough yet. Let me stay a few days longer. I will remain hidden in your house, so that no one may see me." So the old woman let him stay.

When it was black night, the princess put on her lovely clothes and jewels and sat on her roof. At midnight she went to her room and went to sleep. Then the Raja's son sat on his bed and flew to her bed-room. There he said to his bag, "Bag, I want a very, very beautiful ring." The bag gave him a glorious ring. Then he took the Princess Labam's hand gently to put on the ring, and she started up very much frightened.

"Who are you?" she said to the prince. "Where do you come from? Why do you come to my room?"

"Do not be afraid, princess," he said; "I am no thief. I am a great Raja's son. Hiraman parrot, who lives in the jungle where I went to hunt, told me your name, and then I left my father and mother and came to see you."

"Well," said the princess, "as you are the son of such a

great Raja, I will not have you killed, and I will tell my father and mother that I wish to marry you."

The prince then returned to the old woman's house; and when morning came the princess said to her mother, "The son of a great Raja has come to this country, and I wish to marry him." Her mother told this to the king.

"Good," said the king; "but if this Raja's son wishes to marry my daughter, he must first do whatever I bid him. If he fails I will kill him. I will give him eighty pounds weight of mustard seed, and out of this he must crush the oil in one day. If he cannot do this he shall die."

In the morning the Raja's son told the old woman that he intended to marry the princess. "Oh," said the old woman, "go away from this country, and do not think of marrying her. A great many Rajas and Rajas' sons have come here to marry her, and her father has had them all killed. He says whoever wishes to marry his daughter must first do whatever he bids him. If he can, then he shall marry the princess; if he cannot, the king will have him killed. But no one can do the things the king tells him to do; so all the Rajas and Rajas' sons who have tried have been put to death. You will be killed too, if you try. Do go away." But the prince would not listen to anything she said.

The king sent for the prince to the old woman's house, and his servants brought the Raja's son to the king's court-house to the king. There the king gave him eighty pounds of mustard seed, and told him to crush all the oil out of it that day, and bring it next morning to him to the court-house. "Whoever wishes to marry my daughter," he said to the prince, "must first do all I tell him. If he cannot, then I have him killed. So if you cannot crush all the oil out of this mustard seed you will die."

The prince was very sorry when he heard this. "How can I crush the oil out of all this mustard seed in one day?" he said to himself; "and if I do not, the king will kill me." He took the mustard seed to the old woman's house, and did not know what to do. At last he remembered the Ant-Raja, and the moment he did so, the Ant-Raja and his ants came to him. "Why do you look so sad?" said the Ant-Raja.

The prince showed him the mustard seed, and said to him, "How can I crush the oil out of all this mustard seed in one day? And if I do not take the oil to the king to-morrow morning, he will kill me."

"Be happy," said the Ant-Raja; "lie down and sleep; we will crush all the oil out for you during the day, and to-morrow morning you shall take it to the king." The Raja's son lay down and slept, and the ants crushed out the oil for him. The prince was very glad when he saw the oil.

The next morning he took it to the court-house to the king. But the king said, "You cannot yet marry my daughter. If you wish to do so, you must first fight with my two demons, and kill them." The king a long time ago had caught two demons, and then, as he did not know what to do with them, he had shut them up in a cage. He was afraid to let them loose for fear they would eat up all the people in his country; and he did not know how to kill them. So all the kings and kings' sons who wanted to marry the Princess Labam had to fight with these demons; "for," said the king to himself, "perhaps the demons may be killed, and then I shall be rid of them."

When he heard of the demons the Raja's son was very sad. "What can I do?" he said to himself. "How can I fight with these two demons?" Then he thought of his tiger: and the tiger and his wife came to him and said, "Why are you so sad?" The Raja's son answered, "The king has ordered me to fight with his two demons and kill

them. How can I do this?" "Do not be frightened," said the tiger. "Be happy. I and my wife will fight with them for you."

Then the Raja's son took out of his bag two splendid coats. They were all gold and silver, and covered with pearls and diamonds. These he put on the tigers to make them beautiful, and he took them to the king, and said to him, "May these tigers fight your demons for me?" "Yes," said the king, who did not care in the least who killed his demons, provided they were killed. "Then call your demons," said the Raja's son, "and these tigers will fight them." The king did so, and the tigers and the demons fought and fought until the tigers had killed the demons.

"That is good," said the king. "But you must do something else before I give you my daughter. Up in the sky I have a kettle-drum. You must go and beat it. If you cannot do this, I will kill you."

The Raja's son thought of his little bed; so he went to the old woman's house and sat on his bed. "Little bed," he said, "up in the sky is the king's kettle-drum. I want to go to it." The bed flew up with him, and the Raja's son beat the drum, and the king heard him. Still, when he came down, the king would not give him his daughter. "You have," he said to the prince, "done the three things I told you to do; but you must do one thing more." "If I can, I will," said the Raja's son.

Then the king showed him the trunk of a tree that was lying near his court-house. It was a very, very thick trunk. He gave the prince a wax hatchet, and said, "To-morrow morning you must cut this trunk in two with this wax hatchet."

The Raja's son went back to the old woman's house. He was very sad, and thought that now the Raja would certainly kill him. "I had his oil crushed out by the ants," he said to himself. "I had his demons killed by the tigers. My bed helped me to beat his kettle-drum. But now what can I do? How can I cut that thick tree-trunk in two with a wax hatchet?"

At night he went on his bed to see the princess. "To

morrow," he said to her, " your father will kill me." " Why ? " asked the princess.

" He has told me to cut a thick tree-trunk in two with a wax hatchet. How can I ever do that ? " said the Raja's son. " Do not be afraid," said the princess ; " do as I bid you, and you will cut it in two quite easily."

Then she pulled out a hair from her head and gave it to the prince. " To-morrow," she said, " when no one is near you, you must say to the tree-trunk, 'The Princess Labam commands you to let yourself be cut in two by this hair. Then stretch the hair down the edge of the wax hatchet's blade."

The prince next day did exactly as the princess had told him ; and the minute the hair that was stretched down the edge of the hatchet-blade touched the tree-trunk it split into two pieces.

The king said, " Now you can marry my daughter." Then the wedding took place. All the Rajas and kings of the countries round were asked to come to it, and there were great rejoicings. After a few days the prince's son said to his wife, " Let us go to my father's country." The Princess Labam's father gave them a quantity of camels and horses and rupees and servants ; and they travelled in great state to the prince's country, where they lived happily.

The prince always kept his bag, bowl, bed, and stick ; only, as no one ever came to make war on him, he never needed to use the stick.

The Lambikin

ONCE upon a time there was a wee wee Lambikin, who frolicked about on his little tottery legs, and enjoyed himself amazingly.

Now one day he set off to visit his Granny, and was jumping with joy to think of all the good things he should get from her, when who should he meet but a Jackal, who looked at the tender young morsel and said: "Lambikin! Lambikin! I'll EAT YOU!"

But Lambikin only gave a little frisk, and said:

"To Granny's house I go,
Where I shall fatter grow,
Then you can eat me so."

The Jackal thought this reasonable, and let Lambikin pass.

By-and-by he met a Vulture, and the Vulture, looking hungrily at the tender morsel before him, said: "Lambikin! Lambikin! I'll EAT YOU!"

But Lambikin only gave a little frisk, and said:

"To Granny's house I go,
Where I shall fatter grow
Then you can eat me so."

The Vulture thought this reasonable, and let Lambikin pass.

And by-and-by he met a Tiger, and then a Wolf, and a Dog, and an Eagle; and all these, when they saw the tender little morsel, said: "Lambikin! Lambikin! I'll EAT YOU!"

But to all of them Lambikin replied, with a little frisk:

"To Granny's house I go,
Where I shall fatter grow,
Then you can eat me so."

At last he reached his Granny's house, and said, all in a great hurry, "Granny dear, I've promised to get very fat; so, as people ought to keep their promises, please put me into the corn-bin *at once.*"

So his Granny said he was a good boy, and put him into the corn-bin, and there the greedy little Lambikin stayed for seven days, and ate, and ate, and ate, until he could scarcely waddle, and his Granny said he was fat enough for anything, and must go home. But cunning little Lambikin said that would never do, for some animal would be sure to eat him on the way back, he was so plump and tender.

"I'll tell you what you must do," said Master Lambikin; "you must make a little drumikin out of the skin of my little brother who died, and then I can sit inside and trundle along nicely, for I'm as tight as a drum myself.'

So his Granny made a nice little drumikin out of his brother's skin, with the wool inside, and Lambikin curled himself up snug and warm in the middle, and trundled away gaily. Soon he met with the Eagle, who called out:

> "Drumikin! Drumikin!
> Have you seen Lambikin?"

And Mr. Lambikin, curled up in his soft warm nest, replied:

> "Fallen into the fire, and so will you
> On little Drumikin. Tum-pa, tum-too!"

"How very annoying!" sighed the Eagle, thinking regretfully of the tender morsel he had let slip.

Meanwhile Lambikin trundled along, laughing to himself, and singing:

> "Tum-pa, tum-too;
> Tum-pa, tum-too!"

Every animal and bird he met asked him the same question:

> "Drumikin! Drumikin!
> Have you seen Lambikin?"

And to each of them the little slyboots replied:

> "Fallen into the fire, and so will you
> On little Drumikin. Tum-pa, tum-too;
> Tum-pa, tum-too; Tum-pa, tum-too!"

Then they all sighed to think of the tender little morsel they had let slip.

At last the Jackal came limping along, for all his sorry looks as sharp as a needle, and he too called out:

> "Drumikin! Drumikin!
> Have you seen Lambikin?"

And Lambikin, curled up in his snug little nest, replied gaily:

> "Fallen into the fire, and so will you
> On little Drumikin! Tum-pa——"

But he never got any further, for the Jackal recognised his voice at once, and cried: "Hullo! you've turned yourself inside out, have you? Just you come out of that!"

Whereupon he tore open Drumikin and gobbled up Lambikin.

Punchkin

ONCE upon a time there was a Raja who had seven beautiful daughters. They were all good girls; but the youngest, named Balna, was more clever than the rest. The Raja's wife died when they were quite little children, so these seven poor Princesses were left with no mother to take care of them.

The Raja's daughters took it by turns to cook their father's dinner every day, whilst he was absent deliberating with his Ministers on the affairs of the nation.

About this time the Prudhan died, leaving a widow and one daughter; and every day, every day, when the seven

Princesses were preparing their father's dinner, the Prudhan's widow and daughter would come and beg for a little fire from the hearth. Then Balna used to say to her sisters, "Send that woman away; send her away. Let her get the fire at her own house. What does she want with ours? If we allow her to come here, we shall suffer for it some day."

But the other sisters would answer, "Be quiet, Balna; why must you always be quarrelling with this poor woman? Let her take some fire if she likes." Then the Prudhan's widow used to go to the hearth and take a few sticks from it; and whilst no one was looking, she would quickly throw some mud into the midst of the dishes which were being prepared for the Raja's dinner.

Now the Raja was very fond of his daughters. Ever since their mother's death they had cooked his dinner with their own hands, in order to avoid the danger of his being poisoned by his enemies. So, when he found the mud mixed up with his dinner, he thought it must arise from their carelessness, as it did not seem likely that any one should have put mud there on purpose; but being very kind he did not like to reprove them for it, although this spoiling of the curry was repeated many successive days.

At last, one day, he determined to hide, and watch his daughters cooking, and see how it all happened; so he went into the next room, and watched them through a hole in the wall.

There he saw his seven daughters carefully washing the rice and preparing the curry, and as each dish was completed, they put it by the fire ready to be cooked. Next he noticed the Prudhan's widow come to the door and beg for a few sticks from the fire to cook her dinner with. Balna turned to her angrily and said, "Why don't you keep fuel in your own house, and not come here every day and take ours? Sisters, don't give this woman any more wood; let her buy it for herself."

Then the eldest sister answered, "Balna, let the poor woman take the wood and the fire; she does us no harm." But Balna replied, "If you let her come here so often, maybe she will do us some harm, and make us sorry for it some day."

The Raja then saw the Prudhan's widow go to the place where all his dinner was nicely prepared, and, as she took the wood, she threw a little mud into each of the dishes.

At this he was very angry, and sent to nave the woman seized and brought before him. But when the widow came, she told him that she had played this trick because she wanted to gain an audience with him; and she spoke so cleverly, and pleased him so well with her cunning words, that, instead of punishing her, the Raja married her, and made her his Ranee, and she and her daughter came to live in the palace.

Now the new Ranee hated the seven poor Princesses, and wanted to get them, if possible, out of the way, in order that her daughter might have all their riches, and live in the palace as Princess in their place; and instead of being grateful to them for their kindness to her, she did all she could to make them miserable. She gave them nothing but bread to eat, and very little of that, and very little water to drink; so these seven poor little Princesses, who had been accustomed to have everything comfortable about them, and good food and good clothes all their lives long, were very miserable and unhappy; and they used to go out every day and sit by their dead mother's tomb and cry—and say:

"Oh mother, mother, cannot you see your poor children, how unhappy we are, and how we are starved by our cruel step-mother?"

One day, whilst they were thus sobbing and crying, lo and behold! a beautiful pomelo-tree grew up out of the grave, covered with fresh ripe pomeloes, and the children satisfied their hunger by eating some of the fruit; and every day after this, instead of trying to eat the bad dinner their step-mother provided for them, they used to go out to their mother's grave and eat the pomeloes which grew there on the beautiful tree.

Then the Ranee said to her daughter, "I cannot tell how it is, every day those seven girls say they don't want any dinner, and won't eat any; and yet they never grow thin nor look ill; they look better than you do. I cannot tell how it is." And she bade her watch the seven Princesses, and see if any one gave them anything to eat.

So next day, when the Princesses went to their mother's grave, and were eating the beautiful pomeloes, the Prudhan's daughter followed them and saw them gathering the fruit.

Then Balna said to her sisters, "Do you not see that girl watching us? Let us drive her away, or hide the pomeloes, else she will go and tell her mother all about it, and that will be very bad for us."

But the other sisters said, "Oh no, do not be unkind, Balna. The girl would never be so cruel as to tell her mother. Let us rather invite her to come and have some of the fruit."

And calling her to them, they gave her one of the pomeloes.

No sooner had she eaten it, however, than the Prudhan's daughter went home and said to her mother, "I do not wonder the seven Princesses will not eat the dinner you prepare for them, for by their mother's grave there grows a beautiful pomelo-tree, and they go there every day and eat the pomeloes. I ate one, and it was the nicest I have ever tasted."

The cruel Ranee was much vexed at hearing this, and all next day she stayed in her room, and told the Raja that she had a very bad headache. The Raja was deeply grieved, and said to his wife, "What can I do for you?" She answered, "There is only one thing that will make my headache well. By your dead wife's tomb there grows a fine pomelo-tree; you must bring that here and boil it, root and branch, and put a little of the water in which it has been boiled on my forehead, and that will cure my headache." So the Raja sent his servants, and had the beautiful pomelo-tree pulled up by the roots, and did as the Ranee desired; and when some of the water in which it had been boiled was put on her forehead, she said her headache was gone and she felt quite well.

Next day, when the seven Princesses went as usual to the grave of their mother, the pomelo-tree had disappeared. Then they all began to cry very bitterly.

Now there was by the Ranee's tomb a small tank, and as they were crying they saw that the tank was filled with a rich cream-like substance, which quickly hardened into a thick white cake. At seeing this all the Princesses were very glad, and they ate some of the cake and liked it; and next day the same thing happened, and so it went on for many days. Every morning the Princesses went to their mother's grave, and found the little tank filled with the nourishing cream-like cake. Then the cruel step-mother said to her daughter: "I cannot tell how it is, I have had the pomelo-tree which used to grow by the Ranee's grave destroyed, and yet the Princesses grow no thinner, nor look more sad, though they never eat the dinner I give them. I cannot tell how it is!"

And her daughter said, "I will watch."

Next day, while the Princesses were eating the cream-cake, who should come by but their step-mother's daughter. Balna saw her first, and said, "See, sisters, there comes that girl again. Let us sit round the edge of the tank and not allow her to see it, for if we give her some of our cake, she will go and tell her mother, and that will be very unfortunate for us.

The other sisters, however, thought Balna unnecessarily suspicious, and, instead of following her advice, they gave the Prudhan's daughter some of the cake, and she went home and told her mother all about it.

The Ranee, on hearing how well the Princesses fared, was exceedingly angry, and sent her servants to pull down the dead Ranee's tomb and fill the little tank with the ruins. And not content with this, she next day pretended to be very, very ill—in fact, at the point of death—and when the Raja was much grieved, and asked her whether it was in his power to procure her any remedy, she said to him: "Only one thing can save my life, but I know you will not do it." He replied, "Yes, whatever it is, I will do it." She then said, "To save my life, you must kill the seven daughters of your first wife, and put some of their blood on my forehead and on the palms of my hands, and their death will be my life." At these words the Raja was very sorrowful; but because he feared to break his word, he went out with a heavy heart to find his daughters.

He found them crying by the ruins of their mother's grave.

Then, feeling he could not kill them, the Raja spoke kindly to them, and told them to come out into the jungle with him; and there he made a fire and cooked some rice, and gave it to them. But in the afternoon, it being very hot, the seven Princesses all fell asleep, and when he saw they were fast asleep, the Raja, their father, stole away and left them (for he feared his wife), saying to himself: "It is better my poor daughters should die here than be killed by their step-mother."

He then shot a deer, and returning home, put some of its blood on the forehead and hands of the Ranee, and she thought then that he had really killed the Princesses, and said she felt quite well.

Meantime the seven Princesses awoke, and when they found themselves all alone in the thick jungle they were much frightened, and began to call out as loud as they could, in hopes of making their father hear; but he was by that time far away, and would not have been able to hear them even had their voices been as loud as thunder.

It so happened that this very day the seven young sons of a neighbouring Raja chanced to be hunting in that same jungle, and as they were returning home, after the day's sport was over, the youngest Prince said to his brothers: "Stop, I think I hear some one crying and calling out.

Do you not hear voices ? Let us go in the direction of the sound, and find out what it is."

So the seven Princes rode through the wood until they came to the place where the seven Princesses sat crying and wringing their hands. At the sight of them the young Princes were very much astonished, and still more so on learning their story; and they settled that each should take one of these poor forlorn ladies home with him and marry her.

So the first and eldest Prince took the eldest Princess home with him and married her.

And the second took the second;

And the third took the third;

And the fourth took the fourth;

And the fifth took the fifth;

And the sixth took the sixth;

And the seventh, and the handsomest of all, took the beautiful Balna.

And when they got to their own land there was great rejoicing throughout the kingdom at the marriage of the seven young Princes to seven such beautiful Princesses.

About a year after this Balna had a little son, and his uncles and aunts were so fond of the boy that it was as if he had seven fathers and seven mothers. None of the other Princes and Princesses had any children, so the son of the seventh Prince and Balna was acknowledged their heir by all the rest.

They had thus lived very happily for some time, when one fine day the seventh Prince (Balna's husband) said he would go out hunting, and away he went; and they waited long for him, but he never came back.

Then his six brothers said they would go and see what had become of him; and they went away, but they also did not return.

And the seven Princesses grieved very much, for they feared that their kind husbands must have been killed.

One day, not long after this had happened, as Balna was rocking her baby's cradle, and whilst her sisters were working in the room below, there came to the palace door a man in a long black dress, who said that he was a Fakir, and came to beg. The servants said to him, "You cannot go into the palace—the Raja's sons have all gone away; we think they must be dead, and their widows cannot be interrupted by your begging." But he said, "I am a holy man, you must let me in." Then the stupid servants let him walk through the palace, but they did not know that this was no Fakir, but a wicked Magician named Punchkin.

Punchkin Fakir wandered through the palace, and saw many beautiful things there, till at last he reached the room where Balna sat singing beside her little boy's cradle. The Magician thought her more beautiful than all the other beautiful things he had seen, insomuch that he asked her to go home with him and to marry him. But she said, "My husband, I fear, is dead, but my little boy is still quite young; I will stay here and teach him to grow up a clever man, and when he is grown up he shall go out into the world, and try and learn tidings of his father. Heaven forbid that I should ever leave him, or marry you." At these words the Magician was very angry, and turned her into a little black dog, and led her away, saying, "Since you will not come with me of your own free will, I will make you." So the poor Princess was dragged away, without any power of effecting an escape or of letting her sisters know what had become of her. As Punchkin passed through the palace gate the servants said to him, "Where did you get that pretty little dog?" And he answered, "One of the Princesses gave it to me as a present." At hearing which they let him go without further questioning.

Soon after this, the six elder Princesses heard the little baby, their nephew, begin to cry, and when they went upstairs they were much surprised to find him all alone, and Balna nowhere to be seen. Then they questioned the servants, and when they heard of the Fakir and the little black dog, they guessed what had happened, and sent in every direction seeking them, but neither the Fakir nor the dog were to be found. What could six poor women do? They gave up all hopes of ever seeing their kind husbands, and their sister, and her husband, again, and devoted themselves thenceforward to teaching and taking care of their little nephew.

Thus time went on, till Balna's son was fourteen years old. Then, one day, his aunts told him the history of the family; and no sooner did he hear it than he was seized with a great desire to go in search of his father and mother and uncles, and if he could find them alive to bring them home again. His aunts, on learning his determination, were much alarmed, and tried to dissuade him, saying, "We have lost our husbands and our sister and her husband, and you are now our sole hope; if you go away, what shall we do?" But he replied, "I pray you not to be discouraged; I will return soon, and if it is possible bring my father and mother and uncles with me." So he set out on his travels;

but for some months he could learn nothing to help him in his search.

At last, after he had journeyed many hundreds of weary miles, and become almost hopeless of ever hearing anything further of his parents, he one day came to a country that seemed full of stones, and rocks, and trees, and there he saw a large palace with a high tower; hard by which was a Malee's little house.

As he was looking about, the Malee's wife saw him, and ran out of the house and said, "My dear boy, who are you that dare venture to this dangerous place?" He answered, "I am a Raja's son, and I come in search of my father, and my uncles, and my mother, whom a wicked enchanter bewitched."

Then the Malee's wife said, "This country and this palace belong to a great enchanter; he is all-powerful, and if any one displeases him he can turn them into stones and trees. All the rocks and trees you see here were living people once, and the Magician turned them to what they now are. Some time ago a Raja's son came here, and shortly afterwards came his six brothers, and they were all turned into stones and trees; and these are not the only unfortunate ones, for up in that tower lives a beautiful Princess, whom the Magician has kept prisoner there for twelve years, because she hates him and will not marry him."

Then the little Prince thought, "These must be my parents and my uncles. I have found what I seek at last." So he told his story to the Malee's wife, and begged her to help him to remain in that place awhile and inquire further concerning the unhappy people she mentioned; and she promised to befriend him, and advised his disguising himself lest the Magician should see him, and turn him likewise into stone. To this the Prince agreed. So the Malee's wife dressed him up in a saree, and pretended that he was her daughter.

One day, not long after this, as the Magician was walking in his garden he saw the little girl (as he thought) playing about, and asked her who she was. She told him she was the Malee's daughter, and the Magician said, " You are a pretty little girl, and to-morrow you shall take a present of flowers from me to the beautiful lady who lives in the tower.

The young Prince was much delighted at hearing this, and went immediately to inform the Malee's wife; after consultation with whom he determined that it would be more safe for him to retain his disguise and trust to the chance of a favourable opportunity for establishing some communication with his mother, if it were indeed she.

Now it happened that at Balna's marriage her husband had given her a small gold ring on which her name was engraved, and she had put it on her little son's finger when he was a baby, and afterwards when he was older his aunt had had it enlarged for him, so that he was still able to wear it. The Malee's wife advised him to fasten the well-known treasure to one of the bouquets he presented to his mother, and trust to her recognising it. This was not to be done without difficulty, as such a strict watch was kept over the poor Princess (for fear of her ever establishing communication with her friends) that, though the supposed Malee's daughter was permitted to take her flowers every day, the Magician or one of his slaves was always in the room at the time. At last one day, however, opportunity favoured him, and when no one was looking, the boy tied the ring to a nosegay and threw it at Balna's feet. It fell with a clang on the floor, and Balna, looking to see what made the strange sound, found the little ring tied to the flowers. On recognising it, she at once believed the story her son told her of his long search, and begged him to advise her as to what she had better do; at the same time entreating him on no account to endanger his life by trying to rescue her. She told him that for twelve long years the Magician had kept her shut up in the tower because she refused to marry him, and she was so closely guarded that she saw no hope of release.

Now Balna's son was a bright, clever boy, so he said, "Do not fear, dear mother; the first thing to do is to discover how far the Magician's power extends, in order that we may be able to liberate my father and uncles, whom he has imprisoned in the form of rocks and trees. You have spoken to him angrily for twelve long years; now rather speak kindly. Tell him you have given up all hopes of again seeing the husband you have so long mourned, and say you are willing to marry him. Then endeavour to find out what his power consists in, and whether he is immortal, or can be put to death."

Balna determined to take her son's advice; and the next day sent for Punchkin, and spoke to him as had been suggested.

The Magician, greatly delighted, begged her to allow the wedding to take place as soon as possible.

But she told him that before she married him he must allow her a little more time. in which she might make his acquaintance, and that, after being enemies so long, their friendship could but strengthen by degrees. "And do tell me," she said, "are you quite immortal? Can death never touch you? And are you too great an enchanter ever to feel human suffering?"

"Why do you ask?" said he.

"Because," she replied, "if I am to be your wife, I would fain know all about you, in order, if any calamity threatens you, to overcome, or if possible to avert it."

"It is true," he added, "that I am not as others. Far, far away, hundreds of thousands of miles from this, there lies a desolate country covered with thick jungle. In the midst of the jungle grows a circle of palm trees, and in the centre of the circle stand six chattees full of water, piled one above another: below the sixth chattee is a small cage which contains a little green parrot; on the life of the parrot depends my life; and if the parrot is killed I must die. It is, however," he added, "impossible that the parrot should sustain any injury, both on account of the inaccessibility of the country, and because, by my appointment, many thousand genii surround the palm-trees, and kill all who approach the place."

Balna told her son what Punchkin had said; but at the same time implored him to give up all idea of getting the parrot.

The Prince, however, replied, "Mother, unless I can get hold of that parrot, you, and my father, and uncles, cannot be liberated: be not afraid, I will shortly return. Do you meantime, keep the Magician in good humour—still putting off your marriage with him on various pretexts; and before he finds out the cause of delay, I will be here." So saying, he went away.

Many, many weary miles did he travel, till at last he came to a thick jungle; and, being very tired, sat down under a tree and fell asleep. He was awakened by a soft rustling sound, and looking about him, saw a large serpent which was making its way to an eagle's nest built in the tree under which he lay, and in the nest were two young eagles. The Prince seeing the danger of the young birds, drew his sword and killed the serpent; at the same moment a rushing sound was heard in the air, and the two old eagles, who had been out hunting for food for their young ones, returned. They quickly saw the dead serpent and the young Prince standing over it; and the old mother eagle said to him, "Dear boy, for many years all our young ones have been devoured by that cruel serpent; you have now saved the lives of our children; whenever you are in need therefore, send to us and we will help you; and as for these little eagles, take them, and let them be your servants."

At this the Prince was very glad, and the two eaglets crossed their wings, on which he mounted; and they carried him far, far away over the thick jungles, until he came to the place where grew the circle of palm-trees, in the midst of which stood the six chattees full of water. It was the middle of the day, and the heat was very great. All round the trees were the genii fast asleep; nevertheless, there were such countless thousands of them, that it would have been quite impossible for anyone to walk through their ranks to the place; down swooped the strong-winged eaglets —down jumped the Prince; in an instant he had overthrown the six chattees full of water, and seized the little green parrot, which he rolled up in his cloak; while, as he mounted again into the air, all the genii below awoke, and finding their treasure gone, set up a wild and melancholy howl.

Away, away flew the little eagles, till they came to their home in the great tree; then the Prince said to the old eagles, "Take back your little ones; they have done me good service; if ever again I stand in need of help, I will not fail to come to you." He then continued his journey on foot till he arrived once more at the Magician's palace, where he sat down at the door and began playing with the parrot. Punchkin saw him, and came to him quickly, and said, "My boy, where did you get that parrot? Give it to me, I pray you."

But the Prince answered, "Oh no, I cannot give away my parrot, it is a great pet of mine; I have had it many years."

Then the Magician said, "If it is an old favourite, I can understand you not caring to give it away; but come, what will you sell it for?"

"Sir," replied the Prince, "I will not sell my parrot."

Then Punchkin got frightened, and said, "Anything, anything; name what price you will, and it shall be yours." The Prince answered, "Let the seven Raja's sons whom you turned into rocks and trees be instantly liberated."

"It is done as you desire," said the Magician, "only give me my parrot." And with that, by a stroke of his wand, Balna's husband and his brothers resumed their natural shapes. "Now, give me my parrot," repeated Punchkin.

"Not so fast, my master," rejoined the Prince; "I must first beg that you will restore to life all whom you have thus imprisoned."

The Magician immediately waved his wand again; and

PUNCHKIN'S PRISONERS ARE SET FREE —

whilst he cried, in an imploring voice, " Give me my parrot ! " the whole garden became suddenly alive : where rocks, and stones, and trees had been before, stood Rajas, and Punts, and Sirdars, and mighty men on prancing horses, and jewelled pages, and troops of armed attendants.

" Give me my parrot ! " cried Punchkin. Then the boy took hold of the parrot, and tore off one of its wings ; and as he did so the Magician's right arm fell off.

Punchkin then stretched out his left arm, crying, " Give me my parrot ! " The Prince pulled off the parrot's second wing, and the Magician's left arm tumbled off.

" Give me my parrot ! " cried he, and he fell on his knees. The Prince pulled off the parrot's right leg, the Magician's right leg fell off : the Prince pulled off the parrot's left leg, down fell the Magician's left.

Nothing remained of him save the limbless body and the head ; but still he rolled his eyes, and cried, " Give me my parrot ! " " Take your parrot, then," cried the boy, and with that he wrung the bird's neck and threw it at the Magician ; and, as he did so, Punchkin's head twisted round, and, with a fearful groan, he died !

Then they let Balna out of the tower ; and she, her son, and the seven Princes went to their own country, and lived very happily ever afterwards. And as to the rest of the world, every one went to his own house.

The Broken Pot

THERE lived in a certain place a Brahman, whose name was Svabhavak*ri*pa*n*a, which means "a born miser." He had collected a quantity of rice by begging, and after having dined off it, he filled a pot with what was left over. He hung the pot on a peg on the wall, placed his couch beneath, and looking intently at it all the night, he thought, "Ah, that pot is indeed brimful of rice. Now, if there should be a famine, I should certainly make a hundred rupees by it. With this I shall buy a couple of goats. They will have young ones every six months, and thus I shall have a whole herd of goats. Then, with the goats, I shall buy cows. As soon as they have calved, I shall sell the calves. Then, with the calves, I shall buy buffaloes; with the buffaloes, mares. When the mares have foaled, I shall have plenty of horses; and when I sell them, plenty of gold. With that gold I shall get a house with four wings. And then a Brahman will come to my house, and will give me his beautiful daughter, with a large dowry. She will have a son, and I shall call him Somasarman

When he is old enough to be danced on his father's knee, I shall sit with a book at the back of the stable, and while I am reading, the boy will see me, jump from his mother's lap, and run towards me to be danced on my knee. He will come too near the horse's hoof, and, full of anger, I shall call to my wife, 'Take the baby; take him!' But

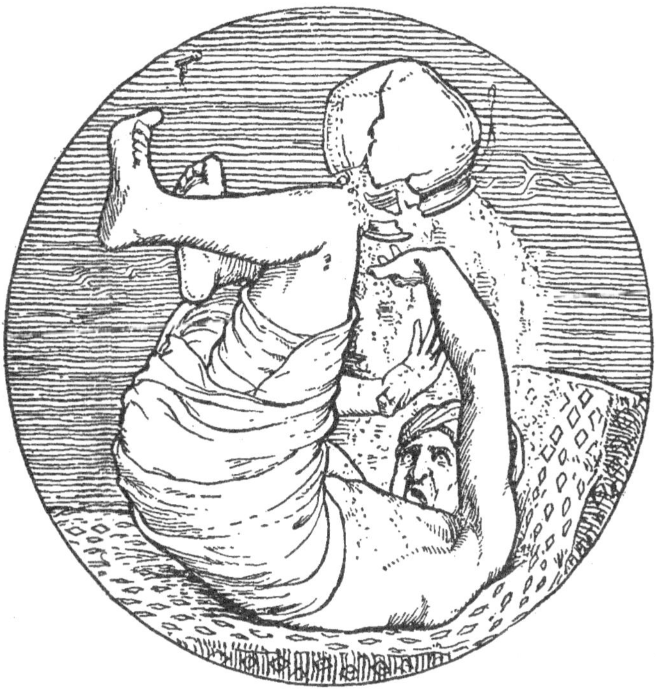

she, distracted by some domestic work, does not hear me. Then I get up, and give her such a kick with my foot." While he thought this, he gave a kick with his foot, and broke the pot. All the rice fell over him, and made him quite white. Therefore, I say, "He who makes foolish plans for the future will be white all over, like the father of Somaśarman."

The Magic Fiddle

ONCE upon a time there lived seven brothers and a sister. The brothers were married, but their wives did not do the cooking for the family. It was done by their sister, who stopped at home to cook. The wives for this reason bore their sister-in-law much ill-will, and at length they combined together to oust her from the office of cook and general provider, so that one of themselves might obtain it. They said, "She does not go out to the fields to work, but remains quietly at home, and yet she has not the meals ready at the proper time." They then called upon their Bonga, and vowing vows unto them they secured his good-will and assistance; then they said to the Bonga, "At midday, when our sister-in-law goes to bring water, cause it thus to happen, that on seeing her pitcher, the water shall vanish, and again slowly reappear. In this way she will be delayed. Let the water not flow into her pitcher, and you may keep the maiden as your own."

At noon, when she went to bring water, it suddenly dried up before her, and she began to weep. Then after a while the water began slowly to rise. When it reached her ankles she tried to fill her pitcher, but it would not go under the water. Being frightened, she began to wail and cry to her brother:

"Oh! my brother, the water reaches to my ankles,
Still, Oh! my brother, the pitcher will not dip."

The water continued to rise until it reached her knee, when she began to wail again:

"Oh! my brother, the water reaches to my knee,
Still, Oh! my brother, the pitcher will not dip."

The water continued to rise, and when it reached her waist, she cried again:

"Oh! my brother, the water reaches to my waist,
Still, Oh! my brother, the pitcher will not dip."

The water still rose, and when it reached her neck she kept on crying:

"Oh! my brother, the water reaches to my neck,
Still, Oh! my brother, the pitcher will not dip."

At length the water became so deep that she felt herself drowning, then she cried aloud:

"Oh! my brother, the water measures a man's height,
Oh! my brother, the pitcher begins to fill."

The pitcher filled with water, and along with it she sank and was drowned. The Bonga then transformed her into a Bonga like himself, and carried her off.

After a time she reappeared as a bamboo growing on the embankment of the tank in which she had been drowned. When the bamboo had grown to an immense size, a Jogi, who was in the habit of passing that way, seeing it, said to himself, "This will make a splendid fiddle." So one day he brought an axe to cut it down; but when he was about to begin, the bamboo called out, "Do not cut at the root, cut higher up." When he lifted his axe to cut high up the stem, the bamboo cried out, "Do not cut near the top, cut at the root." When the Jogi again prepared himself to cut at the root as requested, the bamboo said, "Do not cut at the root, cut higher up;" and when he was about to cut higher up, it again called out to him, "Do not cut high up, cut at the root." The Jogi by this time felt sure that a Bonga was trying to frighten him, so becoming angry he cut down the bamboo at the root, and taking it away made a fiddle out of it. The instrument had a superior tone and delighted all who heard it. The Jogi carried it with him when he went a-begging, and through the influence of its sweet music he returned home every evening with a full wallet.

He now and then visited, when on his rounds, the house of the Bonga girl's brothers, and the strains of the fiddle affected them greatly. Some of them were moved even to tears, for the fiddle seemed to wail as one in bitter anguish. The elder brother wished to purchase it, and offered to support the Jogi for a whole year if he would consent to part with his wonderful instrument. The Jogi, however, knew its value, and refused to sell it.

It so happened that the Jogi some time after went to the house of a village chief, and after playing a tune or two on his fiddle asked for something to eat. They offered to buy his fiddle and promised a high price for it, but he refused to sell it, as his fiddle brought to him his means of livelihood. When they saw that he was not to be prevailed upon, they gave him food and a plentiful supply of liquor. Of the latter he drunk so freely that he presently became intoxicated. While he was in this condition, they took away his fiddle, and substituted their own old one for it. When the Jogi recovered, he missed his instrument, and suspecting that it had been stolen asked them to return it to him. They denied having taken it, so he had to depart leaving his fiddle behind him. The chief's son, being a musician, used to play on the Jogi's fiddle, and in his hands the music it gave forth delighted the ears of all who heard it.

When all the household were absent at their labours in the fields, the Bonga girl used to come out of the bamboo fiddle, and prepared the family meal. Having eaten her own share, she placed that of the chief's son under his bed, and covering it up to keep off the dust, re-entered the fiddle. This happening every day, the other members of the household thought that some girl friend of theirs was in this manner showing her interest in the young man, so they did not trouble themselves to find out how it came about. The young chief, however, was determined to watch, and see which of his girl friends was so attentive to his comfort. He said in his own mind, "I will catch her to-day, and give her a sound beating; she is causing me to be ashamed before the others." So saying, he hid himself in a corner in a pile of firewood. In a short time the girl came out of the bamboo fiddle and began to dress her hair. Having completed her toilet, she cooked the meal of rice as usual, and having eaten some herself, she placed the young man's portion under his bed, as before, and was about to enter the fiddle again, when he, running out from his hiding-place, caught her in his arms. The Bonga girl exclaimed, "Fie! Fie! you may be a Don, or you may be a Hadi of some other caste with whom I cannot marry." He said, "No. But from to-day, you and I are one." So they began lovingly to hold converse with each other. When the others returned home in the evening, they saw that she was both a human being and a Bonga, and they rejoiced exceedingly.

Now in course of time the Bonga girl's family became very poor, and her brothers on one occasion came to the chief's house on a visit.

The Bonga girl recognised them at once, but they did not know who she was. She brought them water on their arrival, and afterwards set cooked rice before them. Then sitting down near them, she began in wailing tones to upbraid them on account of the treatment she had been subjected to by their wives. She related all that had befallen her, and wound up by saying, "You must have known it all, and yet you did not interfere to save me." And that was all the revenge she took.

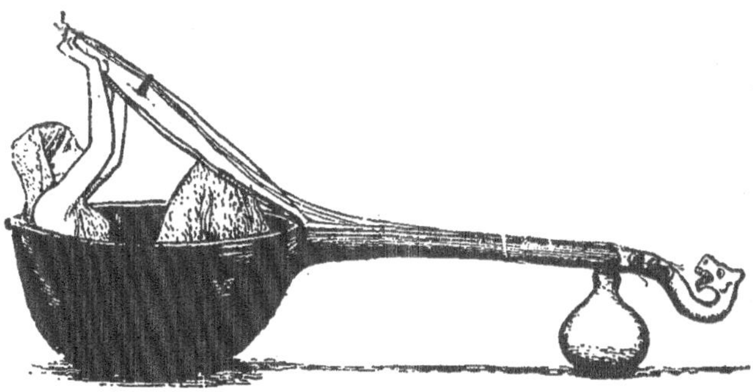

The Cruel Crane Outwitted

LONG ago the Bodisat was born to a forest life as the genius of a tree standing near a certain lotus pond.

Now at that time the water used to run short at the dry season in a certain pond, not over large, in which there were a good many fish. And a crane thought on seeing the fish :

" I must outwit these fish somehow or other and make a prey of them."

And he went and sat down at the edge of the water, thinking how he should do it.

When the fish saw him, they asked him, " What are you sitting there for, lost in thought ? "

" I am sitting thinking about you," said he.

" Oh, sir ! what are you thinking about us ? " said they.

"Why," he replied, "there is very little water in this pond, and but little for you to eat; and the heat is so great! So I was thinking, 'What in the world will these fish do now?'"

"Yes, indeed, sir! what *are* we to do?" said they.

"If you will only do as I bid you, I will take you in my beak to a fine large pond, covered with all the kinds of lotuses, and put you into it," answered the crane.

"That a crane should take thought for the fishes is a thing unheard of, sir, since the world began. It's eating us, one after the other, that you're aiming at."

"Not I! So long as you trust me, I won't eat you. But if you don't believe me that there is such a pond, send one of you with me to go and see it."

Then they trusted him, and handed over to him one of their number — a big fellow, blind of one eye, whom they thought sharp enough in any emergency, afloat or ashore.

Him the crane took with him, let him go in the pond, showed him the whole of it, brought him back, and let him go again close to the other fish. And he told them all the glories of the pond.

And when they heard what he said, they exclaimed, "All right, sir! You may take us with you."

Then the crane took the old purblind fish first to the bank of the other pond, and alighted in a Varana-tree growing on the bank there. But he threw it into a fork of the tree, struck it with his beak, and killed it; and then ate its flesh, and threw its bones away at the foot of the tree. Then he went back and called out:

"I've thrown that fish in; let another one come."

And in that manner he took all the fish, one by one, and ate them, till he came back and found no more!

But there was still a crab left behind there; and the crane thought he would eat him too, and called him out:

"I say, good crab, I've taken all the fish away, and put them into a fine large pond. Come along. I'll take you too!"

"But how will you take hold of me to carry me along?"

"I'll bite hold of you with my beak."

"You'll let me fall if you carry me like that. I won't go with you!"

"Don't be afraid! I'll hold you quite tight all the way."

Then said the crab to himself, "If this fellow once got hold of fish, he would never let them go in a pond! Now if he should really put me into the pond, it would be capital; but if he doesn't—then I'll cut his throat, and kill him!" So he said to him:

"Look here, friend, you won't be able to hold me tight enough; but we crabs have a famous grip. If you let me catch hold of you round the neck with my claws, I shall be glad to go with you."

And the other did not see that he was trying to outwit him, and agreed. So the crab caught hold of his neck with his claws as securely as with a pair of blacksmith's pincers and called out, "Off with you, now!"

And the crane took him and showed him the pond, and then turned off towards the Varana-tree.

"Uncle!" cried the crab, "the pond lies that way, but you are taking me this way!"

"Oh, that's it, is it?" answered the crane. "Your dear little uncle, your very sweet nephew, you call me! You mean me to understand, I suppose, that I am your slave, who has to lift you up and carry you about with him! Now cast your eye upon the heap of fish-bones lying at the root of yonder Varana-tree. Just as I have eaten those fish, every one of them, just so I will devour you as well!"

"Ah! those fishes got eaten through their own stupidity," answered the crab; "but I'm not going to let you eat *me*. On the contrary, it is *you* that I am going to destroy. For you in your folly have not seen that I was outwitting you. If we die, we die both together; for I will cut off this head of yours, and cast it to the ground!" And so saying, he gave the crane's neck a grip with his claws, as with a vice.

Then gasping, and with tears trickling from his eyes, and trembling with the fear of death, the crane beseeched him, saying, "O my lord! Indeed I did not intend to eat you. Grant me my life!"

"Well, well! step down into the pond, and put me in there."

And he turned round and stepped down into the pond, and placed the crab on the mud at its edge. But the crab cut through its neck as clean as one would cut a lotus-stalk with a hunting-knife, and then only entered the water!

When the Genius who lived in the Varana-tree saw this strange affair, he made the wood resound with his plaudits, uttering in a pleasant voice the verse:

"The villain, though exceeding clever,
Shall prosper not by his villainy.
He may win indeed, sharp-witted in deceit,
But only as the Crane here from the Crab!"

Loving Laili

ONCE there was a king called King Dantal, who had a great many rupees and soldiers and horses. He had also an only son called Prince Majnun, who was a handsome boy with white teeth, red lips, blue eyes, red cheeks, red hair, and a white skin. This boy was very fond of playing with the Wazir's son, Husain Mahamat, in King Dantal's garden, which was very large and full of delicious fruits and flowers and trees. They used to take their little knives there and cut the fruits and eat them. King Dantal had a teacher for them to teach them to read and write.

One day, when they were grown two fine young men, Prince Majnun said to his father, " Husain Mahamat and I should like to go and hunt." His father said they might go, so they got ready their horses and all else they wanted for their hunting, and went to the Phalana country, hunting all the way, but they only found jackals and birds.

The Raja of the Phalana country was called Munsuk Raja, and he had a daughter named Laili, who was very beautiful; she had brown eyes and black hair.

One night, some time before Prince Majnun came to her father's kingdom, as she slept, Khuda sent to her an angel in the form of a man who told her that she should marry Prince Majnun and no one else, and that this was Khuda's command to her. When Laili woke she told her father of the angel's visit to her as she slept; but her father paid no attention to her story. From that time she began repeating, "Majnun, Majnun; I want Majnun," and would say nothing else. Even as she sat and ate her food she kept saying, "Majnun, Majnun; I want Majnun." Her father used to get quite vexed with her. "Who is this Majnun? who ever heard of this Majnun?" he would say.

"He is the man I am to marry," said Laili. "Khuda has ordered me to marry no one but Majnun." And she was half mad.

Meanwhile, Majnun and Husain Mahamat came to hunt in the Phalana country; and as they were riding about, Laili came out on her horse to eat the air, and rode behind them. All the time she kept saying, "Majnun, Majnun; I want Majnun." The prince heard her, and turned round. "Who is calling me?" he asked. At this Laili looked at him, and the moment she saw him she fell deeply in love with him, and she said to herself, "I am sure that is the Prince Majnun that Khuda says I am to marry." And she went home to her father and said, "Father, I wish to marry the prince who has come to your kingdom; for I know he is the Prince Majnun I am to marry."

"Very well, you shall have him for your husband," said Munsuk Raja. "We will ask him to-morrow." Laili consented to wait, although she was very impatient. As it happened, the prince left the Phalana kingdom that night, and when Laili heard he was gone, she went quite mad. She would not listen to a word her father, or her mother, or her servants said to her, but went off into the jungle, and wandered from jungle to jungle, till she got farther and farther away from her own country. All the time she kept saying, "Majnun, Majnun; I want Majnun;" and so she wandered about for twelve years.

At the end of the twelve years she met a fakir—he was really an angel, but she did not know this—who asked her, "Why do you always say, 'Majnun, Majnun; I want Majnun'?" She answered, "I am the daughter of the king of the Phalana country and I want to find Prince Majnun; tell me where his kingdom is."

"I think you will never get there," said the fakir, "for it is very far from hence, and you have to cross many rivers to reach it." But Laili said she did not care; she must see Prince Majnun. "Well," said the fakir, "when you come to the Bhagirathi river you will see a big fish, a Rohu; and you must get him to carry you to Prince Majnun's country, or you will never reach it."

She went on and on, and at last she came to the Bhagirathi river. There was a great big fish called the Rohu fish. It was yawning just as she got up to it, and she instantly jumped down its throat into its stomach. All the time she kept saying, "Majnun, Majnun!" At this the Rohu fish was greatly alarmed and swam down the river as fast as he could. By degrees he got tired and went slower, and a crow came and perched on his back, and said "Caw, caw." "Oh, Mr. Crow," said the poor fish, "do see what is in my stomach that makes such a noise."

"Very well," said the crow, "open your mouth wide, and

I'll fly down and see." So the Rohu opened his jaws and the crow flew down, but he came up again very quickly. "You have a Rakshas in your stomach," said the crow, and he flew away. This news did not comfort the poor Rohu, and he swam on and on till he came to Prince Majnun's country. There he stopped. And a jackal came down to

the river to drink. "Oh, jackal," said the Rohu, "do tell me what I have inside me."

"How can I tell?" said the jackal. "I cannot see unless I go inside you." So the Rohu opened his mouth wide, and the jackal jumped down his throat; but he came up very quickly, looking much frightened and saying, "You have a Rakshas in your stomach, and if I don't run away quickly, I am afraid it will eat me." So off he ran. After the jackal came an enormous snake. "Oh," says the fish, "do tell me what I have in my stomach, for it rattles about so, and keeps saying, "Majnun, Majnun; I want Majnun."

The snake said, "Open your mouth wide, and I'll go down and see what it is." The snake went down: when he returned he said, "You have a Rakshas in your stomach, but if you will let me cut you open, it will come out of you." "If you do that, I shall die," said the Rohu. "Oh no," said the snake, "you will not, for I will give you a medicine that will make you quite well again." So the fish agreed, and the snake got a knife and cut him open, and out jumped Laili.

She was now very old. Twelve years she had wandered about the jungle, and for twelve years she had lived inside her Rohu; and she was no longer beautiful, and had lost her teeth. The snake took her on his back and carried her into the country, and there he put her down, and she wandered on and on till she got to Majnun's court-house, where King Majnun was sitting. There some men heard her crying, "Majnun, Majnun; I want Majnun," and they asked her what she wanted. "I want King Majnun," she said.

So they went in and said to Prince Majnun, "An old woman outside says she wants you." "I cannot leave this place," said he; "send her in here." They brought her in and the prince asked what she wanted. "I want to marry you," she answered. "Twenty-four years ago you came to my father the Phalana Raja's country, and I wanted to marry you then; but you went away without marrying me. Then I went mad, and I have wandered about all these years looking for you." Prince Majnun said, "Very good."

"Pray to Khuda," said Laili, "to make us both young again, and then we shall be married." So the prince prayed to Khuda, and Khuda said to him, "Touch Laili's clothes and they will catch fire, and when they are on fire she and you will become young again." When he touched Laili's clothes they caught fire, and she and he became young again. And there were great feasts, and they were married, and travelled to the Phalana country to see her father and mother.

Now Laili's father and mother had wept so much for their daughter that they had become quite blind, and her father kept always repeating, "Laili, Laili, Laili." When Laili saw their blindness, she prayed to Khuda to restore their sight to them, which he did. As soon as the father and mother saw Laili, they hugged her and kissed her, and then they had the wedding all over again amid great rejoicings. Prince Majnun and Laili stayed with Munsuk Raja and his wife for three years, and then they returned to King Dantal, and lived happily for some time with him.

They used to go out hunting, and they often went from country to country to eat the air and amuse themselves.

One day Prince Majnun said to Laili, "Let us go through this jungle." "No, no," said Laili; "if we go through this jungle, some harm will happen to me." But Prince Majnun laughed, and went into the jungle. And as they were going through it, Khuda thought, "I should like to know how much Prince Majnun loves his wife. Would he be very sorry if she died? And would he marry another wife? I will see." So he sent one of his angels in the form of a fakir into the jungle; and the angel went up to Laili, and threw some powder in her face, and instantly she fell to the ground a heap of ashes.

Prince Majnun was in great sorrow and grief when he saw his dear Laili turned into a little heap of ashes; and he went straight home to his father, and for a long, long time he would not be comforted. After a great many years he grew more cheerful and happy, and began to go again into his father's beautiful garden with Husain Mahamat. King Dantal wished his son to marry again. "I will only have Laili for my wife; I will not marry any other woman," said Prince Majnun.

"How can you marry Laili? Laili is dead. She will never come back to you," said the father.

"Then I'll not have any wife at all," said Prince Majnun.

Meanwhile Laili was living in the jungle where her husband had left her a little heap of ashes. As soon as Majnun had gone, the fakir had taken her ashes and made them quite clean, and then he had mixed clay and water with the ashes, and made the figure of a woman with them, and so Laili regained her human form, and Khuda sent life into it. But Laili had become once more a hideous old woman, with a long, long nose, and teeth like tusks; just such an old woman, excepting her teeth, as she had been when she came out of the Rohu fish; and she lived in the jungle, and neither ate nor drank, and she kept on saying, "Majnun, Majnun; I want Majnun."

At last the angel who had come as a fakir and thrown the powder at her, said to Khuda, "Of what use is it that this woman should sit in the jungle crying, crying for ever,

'Majnun, Majnun; I want Majnun,' and eating and drinking nothing? Let me take her to Prince Majnun." "Well," said Khuda, "you may do so; but tell her that she must not speak to Majnun if he is afraid of her when he sees her; and that if he is afraid when he sees her, she will become a little white dog the next day. Then she must go to the palace, and she will only regain her human shape when Prince Majnun loves her, feeds her with his own food, and lets her sleep in his bed."

So the angel came to Laili again as a fakir and carried her to King Dantal's garden. "Now," he said, "it is Khuda's command that you stay here till Prince Majnun comes to walk in the garden, and then you may show yourself to him. But you must not speak to him, if he is afraid of you; and should he be afraid of you, you will the next day become a little white dog." He then told her what she must do as a little dog to regain her human form.

Laili stayed in the garden, hidden in the tall grass, till Prince Majnun and Husain Mahamat came to walk in the garden. King Dantal was now a very old man, and Husain Mahamat, though he was really only as old as Prince Majnun, looked a great deal older than the prince, who had been made quite young again when he married Laili.

As Prince Majnun and the Wazir's son walked in the garden, they gathered the fruit as they had done as little children, only they bit the fruit with their teeth; they did not cut it. While Majnun was busy eating a fruit in this way, and was talking to Husain Mahamat, he turned towards him and saw Laili walking behind the Wazir's son.

"Oh, look, look!" he cried, "see what is following you; it is a Rakshas or a demon, and I am sure it is going to eat us." Laili looked at him beseechingly with all her eyes, and trembling with age and eagerness; but this only frightened Majnun the more. "It is a Rakshas, a Rakshas!" he cried, and he ran quickly to the palace with the Wazir's son; and as they ran away, Laili disappeared into the jungle. They ran to King Dantal, and Majnun told him there was a Rakshas or a demon in the garden that had come to eat them.

"What nonsense!" said his father. "Fancy two grown men being so frightened by an old ayah or a fakir! And if it had been a Rakshas, it would not have eaten you." Indeed King Dantal did not believe Majnun had seen anything at all, till Husain Mahamat said the prince was speaking the exact truth. They had the garden searched for the terrible old woman, but found nothing, and King Dantal told his son he was very silly to be so much frightened. However, Prince Majnun would not walk in the garden any more.

The next day Laili turned into a pretty little dog; and in this shape she came into the palace, where Prince Majnun soon became very fond of her. She followed him everywhere, went with him when he was out hunting, and helped him to catch his game, and Prince Majnun fed her with milk, or bread, or anything else he was eating, and at night the little dog slept in his bed.

But one night the little dog disappeared, and in its stead there lay the little old woman who had frightened him so much in the garden; and now Prince Majnun was quite sure she was a Rakshas, or a demon, or some such horrible thing come to eat him; and in his terror he cried out, "What do you want? Oh, do not eat me; do not eat me!" Poor Laili answered, "Don't you know me? I am your wife Laili, and I want to marry you. Don't you remember how you would go through that jungle, though I begged and begged you not to go, for I told you that harm would happen to me, and then a fakir came and threw powder in my face, and I became a heap of ashes. But Khuda gave me my life again, and brought me here, after I had stayed a long, long while in the jungle crying for you, and now I am obliged to be a little dog; but if you will marry me, I shall not be a little dog any more." Majnun, however, said, "How can I marry an old woman like you? how can you be Laili? I am sure you are a Rakshas or a demon come to eat me," and he was in great terror.

In the morning the old woman had turned into the little dog, and the prince went to his father and told him all that had happened. "An old woman! an old woman! always an old woman!" said his father. "You do nothing but think of old women. How can a strong man like you be so easily frightened?" However, when he saw that his son was really in great terror, and that he really believed the old woman would come back at night, he advised him to say to her, "I will marry you if you can make yourself a young girl again. How can I marry such an old woman as you are?"

That night as he lay trembling in bed the little old woman lay there in place of the dog, crying, "Majnun, Majnun, I want to marry you. I have loved you all these long, long years. When I was in my father's kingdom a young girl, I knew of you, though you knew nothing of me, and we should have been married then if you had not gone away so suddenly, and for long, long years I followed you." "Well," said Majnun, "if you can make yourself a young girl again, I will marry you."

Laili said, "Oh, that is quite easy. Khuda will make me a young girl again. In two days' time you must go into the garden, and there you will see a beautiful fruit. You must gather it and bring it into your room and cut it open yourself very gently, and you must not open it when your father or anybody else is with you, but when you are quite alone; for I shall be in the fruit quite naked, without any clothes at all on." In the morning Laili took her little dog's form and disappeared in the garden.

Prince Majnun told all this to his father, who told him to do all the old woman had bidden him. In two days' time he and the Wazir's son walked in the garden, and there they saw a large, lovely red fruit. "Oh!" said the prince, "I wonder shall I find my wife in that fruit." Husain Mahamat wanted him to gather it and see, but he would not till he had told his father, who said, "That must be the fruit; go and gather it." So Majnun went back and broke the fruit off its stalk; and he said to his father, "Come with me to my room while I open it; I am afraid to open it alone, for perhaps I shall find a Rakshas in it that will eat me."

"No," said King Dantal; "remember, Laili will be naked; you must go alone and do not be afraid if, after all, a Rakshas is in the fruit, for I will stay outside the door, and you have only to call me with a loud voice, and I will come to you, so the Rakshas will not be able to eat you."

Then Majnun took the fruit and began to cut it open

tremblingly, for he shook with fear; and when he had cut it, out stepped Laili, young and far more beautiful than she had ever been. At the sight of her extreme beauty, Majnun fell backwards fainting on the floor.

Laili took off his turban and wound it all round herself like a sari (for she had no clothes at all on), and then she called King Dantal, and said to him sadly, "Why has Majnun fallen down like this? Why will he not speak to me? He never used to be afraid of me; and he has seen me so many, many times."

King Dantal answered, "It is because you are so beautiful. You are far, far more beautiful than you ever were. But he will be very happy directly." Then the King got some water, and they bathed Majnun's face and gave him some to drink, and he sat up again.

Then Laili said, "Why did you faint? Did you not see I am Laili?"

"Oh!" said Prince Majnun, "I see you are Laili come back to me, but your eyes have grown so wonderfully beautiful that I fainted when I saw them." Then they were all very happy, and King Dantal had all the drums in the place beaten, and had all the musical instruments played on, and they made a grand wedding feast, and gave presents to the servants, and rice and quantities of rupees to the fakirs.

After some time had passed very happily, Prince Majnun and his wife went out to eat the air. They rode on the same horse, and had only a groom with them. They came to another kingdom, to a beautiful garden. "We must go into that garden and see it," said Majnun.

"No, no," said Laili; "it belongs to a bad Raja, Chumman Basa, a very wicked man." But Majnun insisted on going in, and in spite of all Laili could say, he got off the horse to look at the flowers. Now, as he was looking at the flowers, Laili saw Chumman Basa coming towards them, and she read in his eyes that he meant to kill her husband and seize her. So she said to Majnun, "Come, come, let us go; do not go near that bad man. I see in his eyes, and I feel in my heart, that he will kill you to seize me."

"What nonsense!" said Majnun. "I believe he is a very good Raja. Anyhow, I am so near to him that I could not get away."

"Well," said Laili, "it is better that you should be killed than I, for if I were to be killed a second time, Khuda would not give me my life again; but I can bring you to life if you are killed." Now Chumman Basa had come quite near, and seemed very pleasant, so thought Prince Majnun; but when he was speaking to Majnun, he drew his scimitar and cut off the prince's head at one blow.

Laili sat quite still on her horse, and as the Raja came towards her she said, "Why did you kill my husband?"

"Because I want to take you," he answered.

"You cannot," said Laili.

"Yes, I can," said the Raja.

"Take me then," said Laili to Chumman Basa; so he came quite close and put out his hand to take hers to lift her off her horse. But she put her hand in her pocket and pulled out a tiny knife, only as long as her hand was broad, and this knife unfolded itself in one instant till it was such a length! and then Laili made a great sweep with her arm and her long, long knife, and off came Chumman Basa's head at one touch.

Then Laili slipped down off her horse, and she went to Majnun's dead body, and she cut her little finger inside her hand straight down from the top of her nail to her palm, and out of this gushed blood like healing medicine. Then she put Majnun's head on his shoulders, and smeared her healing blood all over the wound, and Majnun woke up and said, "What a delightful sleep I have had! Why, I feel as if I had slept for years!" Then he got up and saw the Raja's dead body by Laili's horse.

"What's that?" said Majnun.

"That is the wicked Raja who killed you to seize me, just as I said he would."

"Who killed him?" asked Majnun.

"I did," answered Laili, "and it was I who brought you to life."

"Do bring the poor man to life if you know how to do so," said Majnun.

"No," said Laili, "for he is a wicked man, and will try to do you harm." But Majnun asked her for such a long time, and so earnestly, to bring the wicked Raja to life, that at last she said, "Jump up on the horse, then, and go far away with the groom."

"What will you do," said Majnun, "if I leave you? I cannot leave you."

"I will take care of myself," said Laili; "but this man is so wicked, he may kill you again if you are near him." So Majnun got up on the horse, and he and the groom went a long way off and waited for Laili. Then she set the wicked Raja's head straight on his shoulders, and she

How Loving Laili Became young again

squeezed the wound in her finger till a little blood-medicine came out of it. Then she smeared this over the place where her knife had passed, and just as she saw the Raja opening his eyes, she began to run, and she ran, and ran so fast, that she outran the Raja, who tried to catch her; and she sprang up on the horse behind her husband, and they rode so fast, so fast, till they reached King Dantal's palace.

There Prince Majnun told everything to his father, who was horrified and angry. "How lucky for you that you have such a wife," he said. "Why did you not do what she told you? But for her, you would be now dead." Then he made a great feast out of gratitude for his son's safety, and gave many, many rupees to the fakirs. And he made so much of Laili. He loved her dearly; he could not do enough for her. Then he built a splendid palace for her and his son, with a great deal of ground about it, and lovely gardens, and gave them great wealth, and heaps of servants to wait on them. But he would not allow any but their servants to enter their gardens and palace, and he would not allow Majnun to go out of them, nor Laili; "for," said King Dantal, "Laili is so beautiful, that perhaps some one may kill my son to take her away."

The Tiger, the Brahman, and the Jackal

ONCE upon a time, a tiger was caught in a trap. He tried in vain to get out through the bars, and rolled and bit with rage and grief when he failed.

By chance a poor Brahman came by. "Let me out of this cage, oh pious one!" cried the tiger.

"Nay, my friend," replied the Brahman mildly, "you would probably eat me if I did."

"Not at all!" swore the tiger with many oaths; "on the contrary, I should be for ever grateful, and serve you as a slave!"

Now when the tiger sobbed and sighed and wept and swore, the pious Brahman's heart softened, and at last he consented to open the door of the cage. Out popped the tiger, and, seizing the poor man, cried, "What a fool you are! What is to prevent my eating you now, for after being cooped up so long I am just terribly hungry!"

In vain the Brahman pleaded for his life; the most he could gain was a promise to abide by the decision of the first three things he chose to question as to the justice of the tiger's action.

So the Brahman first asked a *pipal* tree what it thought of the matter, but the *pipal* tree replied coldly, "What have you to complain about? Don't I give shade and shelter to every one who passes by, and don't they in return tear down my branches to feed their cattle? Don't whimper—be a man!"

Then the Brahman, sad at heart, went further afield till he saw a buffalo turning a well-wheel; but he fared no better from it, for it answered, "You are a fool to expect gratitude! Look at me! Whilst I gave milk they fed me on cotton-seed and oil-cake, but now I am dry they yoke me here, and give me refuse as fodder!"

The Brahman, still more sad, asked the road to give him its opinion.

"My dear sir," said the road, "how foolish you are to expect anything else! Here am I, useful to everybody, yet all, rich and poor, great and small, trample on me as they go past, giving me nothing but the ashes of their pipes and the husks of their grain!"

On this the Brahman turned back sorrowfully, and on the way he met a jackal, who called out, "Why, what's the matter, Mr. Brahman? You look as miserable as a fish out of water!"

The Brahman told him all that had occurred. "How very confusing!" said the jackal, when the recital was ended;

"would you mind telling me over again, for everything has got so mixed up?"

The Brahman told it all over again, but the jackal shook his head in a distracted sort of way, and still could not understand.

"It's very odd," said he, sadly, "but it all seems to go in at one ear and out at the other! I will go to the place where it all happened, and then perhaps I shall be able to give a judgment."

So they returned to the cage, by which the tiger was waiting for the Brahman, and sharpennig his teeth and claws.

"You've been away a long time!" growled the savage beast, "but now let us begin our dinner."

"*Our* dinner!" thought the wretched Brahman, as his knees knocked together with fright; "what a remarkably delicate way of putting it!"

"Give me five minutes, my lord!" he pleaded, "in order that I may explain matters to the jackal here, who is somewhat slow in his wits."

The tiger consented, and the Brahman began the whole story over again, not missing a single detail, and spinning as long a yarn as possible.

"Oh, my poor brain! oh, my poor brain!" cried the jackal, wringing its paws. "Let me see! how did it all begin? You were in the cage, and the tiger came walking by——"

"Pooh!" interrupted the tiger, "what a fool you are! *I* was in the cage."

"Of course!" cried the jackal, pretending to tremble with fright; "yes! I was in the cage—no I wasn't—dear!

dear! where are my wits? Let me see—the tiger was in the Brahman, and the cage came walking by——no, that's not it, either! Well, don't mind me, but begin your dinner, for I shall never understand!"

"Yes, you shall!" returned the tiger, in a rage at the jackal's stupidity; "I'll *make* you understand! Look here—I am the tiger——"

"Yes, my lord!"

"And that is the Brahman——"

"Yes, my lord!"

"And that is the cage——"

"Yes, my lord!"

"And I was in the cage—do you understand?"

"Yes—no—— Please, my lord——"

"Well?" cried the tiger impatiently.

"Please, my lord!—how did you get in?"

"How!—why in the usual way, of course!"

"Oh, dear me!—my head is beginning to whirl again! Please don't be angry, my lord, but what is the usual way?"

At this the tiger lost patience, and, jumping into the cage, cried, "This way! Now do you understand how it was?"

"Perfectly!" grinned the jackal, as he dexterously shut the door, "and if you will permit me to say so, I think matters will remain as they were!"

The Soothsayer's Son

A SOOTHSAYER when on his deathbed wrote out the horoscope of his second son, whose name was Gangazara, and bequeathed it to him as his only property, leaving the whole of his estate to his eldest son. The second son thought over the horoscope, and said to himself:

"Alas! am I born to this only in the world? The sayings of my father never failed. I have seen them prove true to the last word while he was living; and how has he fixed my horoscope! **'From my birth, poverty!'** Nor is that my only fate. **'For ten years, imprisonment'**—a fate harder than poverty; and what comes next? **'Death on the sea-shore'**; which means that I must die away from home, far from friends and relatives on a sea-coast. Now comes the most curious part of the horoscope, that I am to **'have some happiness afterwards!'** What this happiness is, is an enigma to me."

Thus thought he, and after all the funeral obsequies of his father were over, took leave of his elder brother, and started for Benares. He went by the middle of the Deccan avoiding both the coasts, and went on journeying and journeying for weeks and months, till at last he reached the Vindhya mountains. While passing that desert he had to journey for a couple of days through a sandy plain, with no signs of life or vegetation. The little store of provision with which he was provided for a couple of days, at last was exhausted. The chombu, which he carried always full, filling it with the sweet water from the flowing rivulet or plenteous tank, he had exhausted in the heat of the desert. There was not a morsel in his hand to eat; nor a drop of water to drink. Turn his eyes wherever he might he found a vast desert, out of which he saw no means of escape. Still he thought within himself, "Surely my father's prophecy never proved untrue. I must survive this calamity to find my death on some sea-coast." So thought he, and this thought gave him strength of mind to walk fast and try to find a drop of water somewhere to slake his dry throat.

At last he succeeded; heaven threw in his way a ruined well. He thought he could collect some water if he let down his chombu with the string that he always carried noosed to the neck of it. Accordingly he let it down; it went some way and stopped, and the following words came from the well: "Oh, relieve me! I am the king of tigers, dying here of hunger. For the last three days I have had nothing. Fortune has sent you here. If you assist me now you will find a sure help in me throughout your life. Do not think that I am a beast of prey. When you have become my deliverer I will never touch you. Pray, kindly lift me up." Gangazara thought: "Shall I take him out or not? If I take him out he may make me the first morsel of his hungry mouth. No; that he will not do. For my father's prophecy never came untrue. I must die on a sea-coast, and not by a tiger." Thus thinking, he asked the tiger-king to hold tight to the vessel, which he accordingly did, and he lifted him up slowly. The tiger reached the top of the well and felt himself on safe ground. True to his word, he did no harm to Gangazara. On the other hand, he walked round his patron three times, and standing before him, humbly spoke the following words: "My life-giver, my benefactor! I shall never forget this day, when I regained my life through your kind hands. In return for this kind assistance I pledge my oath to stand by you in all calamities. Whenever you are in any difficulty just think of me. I am there with you ready to oblige you by all the means that I can. To tell you briefly how I came in here: Three days ago I was roaming in yonder forest, when I saw a goldsmith passing through it. I chased him. He, finding it impossible to escape my claws, jumped into this well, and is living to this moment in the very bottom

of it. I also jumped in, but found myself on the first ledge of the well; he is on the last and fourth ledge. In the second lives a serpent half-famished with hunger. On the third lies a rat, also half-famished, and when you again begin to draw water these may request you first to release them. In the same way the goldsmith also may ask you. I beg you, as your bosom friend, never assist that wretched man, though he is your relation as a human being. Goldsmiths are never to be trusted. You can place more faith in me, a tiger, though I feast sometimes upon men, in a serpent, whose sting makes your blood cold the very next moment, or in a rat, which does a thousand pieces of mischief in your house. But never trust a goldsmith. Do not release him; and if you do, you shall surely repent of it one day or other." Thus advising, the hungry tiger went away without waiting for an answer.

Gangazara thought several times of the eloquent way in which the tiger spoke, and admired his fluency of speech. But still his thirst was not quenched. So he let down his vessel again, which was now caught hold of by the serpent, who addressed him thus: "Oh, my protector! Lift me up. I am the king of serpents, and the son of Adisesha, who is now pining away in agony for my disappearance. Release me now. I shall ever remain your servant, remember your assistance, and help you throughout life in all possible ways. Oblige me: I am dying." Gangazara, calling again to mind the "**death on the sea-shore**" of the prophecy lifted him up. He, like the tiger-king, walked round him thrice, and prostrating himself before him spoke thus: "Oh, my life-giver, my father, for so I must call you, as you have given me another birth. I was three days ago basking myself in the morning sun, when I saw a rat running before me. I chased him. He fell into this well. I followed him, but instead of falling on the third storey where he is now lying, I fell into the second. I am going away now to see my father. Whenever you are in any difficulty just think of me. I will be there by your side to assist you by all possible means" So saying, the Nagaraja glided away in zigzag movements, and was out of sight in a moment.

The poor son of the Soothsayer, who was now almost dying of thirst, let down his vessel for a third time. The rat caught hold of it, and without discussing he lifted up the poor animal at once. But it would not go away without showing its gratitude: "Oh, life of my life! My benefactor! I am the king of rats. Whenever you are in any calamity just think of me. I will come to you, and assist you. My keen ears overheard all that the tiger-king told you about the goldsmith, who is in the fourth storey. It is nothing but a sad truth that goldsmiths ought never to be trusted. Therefore, never assist him as you have done to us all. And if you do, you will suffer for it. I am hungry; let me go for the present." Thus taking leave of his benefactor, the rat, too, ran away.

Gangazara for a while thought upon the repeated advice given by the three animals about releasing the goldsmith: "What wrong would there be in my assisting him? Why should I not release him also?" So thinking to himself, Gangazara let down the vessel again. The goldsmith caught hold of it, and demanded help. The Soothsayer's son had no time to lose; he was himself dying of thirst. Therefore he lifted the goldsmith up, who now began his story. "Stop for a while," said Gangazara, and after quenching his thirst by letting down his vessel for the fifth time, still fearing that some one might remain in the well and demand his assistance, he listened to the goldsmith, who began as follows: "My dear friend, my protector, what a deal of nonsense these brutes have been talking to you about me; I am glad you have not followed their advice. I am just now dying of hunger. Permit me to go away. My name is Manikkasari. I live in the East main street of Ujjaini, which is twenty kas to the south of this place, and so lies on your way when you return from Benares. Do not forget to come to me and receive my kind remembrances of your assistance, on your way back to your country." So saying, the goldsmith took his leave, and Gangazara also pursued his way north after the above adventures.

He reached Benares, and lived there for more than ten years, and quite forgot the tiger, serpent, rat, and goldsmith. After ten years of religious life, thoughts of home and of his brother rushed into his mind. "I have secured enough merit now by my religious observances. Let me return home." Thus thought Gangazara within himself, and very soon he was on his way back to his country. Remembering the prophecy of his father he returned by the same way by which he went to Benares ten years before. While thus retracing his steps he reached the ruined well where he had released the three brute kings and the goldsmith. At once the old recollections rushed into his mind, and he thought of the tiger to test his fidelity. Only a moment passed, and the tiger-king came running before him carrying a large crown in his mouth, the glitter of the diamonds of which for a time outshone even the bright rays of the sun. He dropped the crown at his life-giver's feet, and, putting aside all his pride, humbled himself like a pet cat to the strokes of his protector, and began in the following words: "My life-giver! How is it that you have forgotten me, your poor servant, for such a long time? I am glad to find that I still occupy a corner in your mind. I can never forget the day when I owed my life to your lotus hands. I have several jewels with me of little value. This crown, being the best of all, I have brought here as a single ornament of great value, which you can carry with you and dispose of in your own country." Gangazara looked at the crown, examined it over and over, counted and recounted the gems, and thought within himself that he would become the richest of men by separating the diamonds and gold, and selling them in his own country. He took leave of the tiger-king, and after his disappearance thought of the kings of serpents and rats, who came in their turn with their presents, and after the usual greetings and exchange of words took their leave. Gangazara was extremely delighted at the faithfulness with which the brute beasts behaved, and went on his way to the south. While going along he spoke to himself thus: "These beasts have been very faithful in their assistance. Much more, therefore, must Manikkasari be faithful. I do not want anything from him now. If I take this crown with me as it is, it occupies much space in my bundle. It may also excite the curiosity of some robbers on the way. I will go now to Ujjaini on my way. Manikkasari requested me to see him without failure on my return journey. I shall do so, and request him to have the crown melted, the diamonds and gold separated. He must do that kindness at least for me. I shall then roll up these diamonds and gold ball in my rags, and wend my way homewards." Thus thinking and thinking, he reached Ujjaini. At once he inquired for the house of his goldsmith friend, and found him without difficulty. Manikkasari was extremely delighted to find on his threshold him who ten years before, notwithstanding the advice repeatedly given him by the sage-looking tiger, serpent, and rat, had relieved him from the pit of death. Gangazara at once showed him the crown that he received from the tiger-king, told him how he got it, and requested his kind assistance to separate the gold and diamonds. Manikkasari agreed to do so, and meanwhile asked his friend to rest himself for a while to have his bath and meals ; and Gangazara, who was very observant of his religious ceremonies, went direct to the river to bathe.

How came the crown in the jaws of the tiger? The king of Ujjaini had a week before gone with all his hunters on a hunting expedition. All of a sudden the tiger-king started from the wood, seized the king, and vanished.

When the king's attendants informed the prince about the death of his father he wept and wailed, and gave notice that he would give half of his kingdom to any one who should bring him news about the murderer of his father. The goldsmith knew full well that it was a tiger that killed the king, and not any hunter's hands, since he had heard from Gangazara how he obtained the crown. Still, he resolved to denounce Gangazara as the king's murderer, so, hiding the crown under his garments, he flew to the palace. He went before the prince and informed him that the assassin was caught, and placed the crown before him. The prince took it into his hands, examined it, and at once gave half the kingdom to Manikkasari, and then inquired about the murderer. "He is bathing in the river, and is of such and such appearance," was the reply. At once four armed soldiers flew to the river, and bound the poor Brahman hand and foot, while he, sitting in meditation, was without any knowledge of the fate that hung over him. They brought Gangazara to the presence of the prince, who turned his face away from the supposed murderer, and asked his soldiers to throw him into a dungeon. In a minute, without knowing the cause, the poor Brahman found himself in the dark dungeon.

It was a dark cellar underground, built with strong stone walls, into which any criminal guilty of a capital offence was ushered to breathe his last there without food and drink. Such was the cellar into which Gangazara was thrust. What were his thoughts when he reached that place? "It is of no use to accuse either the goldsmith or the prince now. We are all the children of fate. We must obey her commands. This is but the first day of my father's prophecy. So far his statement is true. But how am I going to pass ten years here? Perhaps without anything to sustain life I may drag on my existence for a day or two. But how pass ten years? That cannot be, and I must die. Before death comes let me think of my faithful brute friends."

So pondered Gangazara in the dark cell underground, and at that moment thought of his three friends. The tiger-king, serpent-king, and rat-king assembled at once with their armies at a garden near the dungeon, and for a while did not know what to do. They held their council, and decided to make an underground passage from the inside of a ruined well to the dungeon. The rat raja issued an order at once to that effect to his army. They, with their teeth, bored the ground a long way to the walls of the prison. After reaching it they found that their teeth could not work on the hard stones. The bandicoots were then specially ordered for the business; they, with their hard teeth, made a small slit in the wall for a rat to pass and repass without difficulty. Thus a passage was effected.

The rat raja entered first to condole with his protector on his misfortune, and undertook to supply his protector with provisions. "Whatever sweetmeats or bread are prepared in any house, one and all of you must try to bring whatever you can to our benefactor. Whatever clothes you find hanging in a house, cut down, dip the pieces in water, and bring the wet bits to our benefactor. He will squeeze them and gather water for drink! and the bread and sweetmeats shall form his food." Having issued these orders, the king of the rats took leave of Gangazara. They, in obedience to their king's order, continued to supply him with provisions and water.

The snake-king said: "I sincerely condole with you in your calamity; the tiger-king also fully sympathises with you, and wants me to tell you so, as he cannot drag his huge body here as we have done with our small ones. The king of the rats has promised to do his best to provide you with food. We would now do what we can for your release. From this day we shall issue orders to our armies to oppress all the subjects of this kingdom. The deaths by snake-bite and tigers shall increase a hundredfold from this day, and day by day it shall continue to increase till your release. Whenever you hear people near you, you had better bawl out so as to be heard by them: 'The wretched prince imprisoned me on the false charge of having killed his father, while it was a tiger that killed him. From that day these calamities have broken out in his dominions. If I were released I would save all by my powers of healing poisonous wounds and by incantations.' Some one may repart this to the king, and if he knows it, you will obtain your liberty." Thus comforting his protector in trouble, he advised him to pluck up courage, and took leave of him. From that day tigers and serpents, acting under the orders of their kings, united in killing as many persons and cattle as possible. Every day people were carried away by tigers or bitten by serpents. Thus passed months and years. Gangazara sat in the dark cellar, without the sun's light falling upon him, and feasted upon the breadcrumbs and sweetmeats that the rats so kindly supplied him with. These delicacies had completely changed his body into a red, stout, huge, unwieldy mass of flesh. Thus passed full ten years, as prophesied in the horoscope.

Ten complete years rolled away in close imprisonment. On the last evening of the tenth year one of the serpents got into the bed-chamber of the princess and sucked her life. She breathed her last. She was the only daughter of the king. The king at once sent for all the snake-bite curers. He promised half his kingdom and his daughter's hand to him who would restore her to life. Now a servant of the king who had several times overheard Gangazara's cries, reported the matter to him. The king at once ordered the cell to be examined. There was the man sitting in it. How had he managed to live so long in the cell? Some whispered that he must be a divine being. Thus they discussed, while they brought Gangazara to the king.

The king no sooner saw Gangazara than he fell on the ground. He was struck by the majesty and grandeur of his person. His ten years imprisonment in the deep cell underground had given a sort of lustre to his body. His hair had first to be cut before his face could be seen. The king begged forgiveness for his former fault, and requested him to revive his daughter.

"Bring me within an hour all the corpses of men and cattle, dying and dead, that remain unburnt or unburied within the range of your dominions; I shall revive them all," were the only words that Gangazara spoke.

Cartloads of corpses of men and cattle began to come in every minute. Even graves, it is said, were broken open, and corpses buried a day or two before were taken out and sent for their revival. As soon as all were ready, Gangazara took a vessel full of water and sprinkled it over them all, thinking only of his snake-king and tiger-king. All rose up as if from deep slumber, and went to their respective homes. The princess, too, was restored to life. The joy of the king knew no bounds. He cursed the day on which he imprisoned him, blamed himself for having believed the word of a goldsmith, and offered him the hand of his daughter and the whole kingdom, instead of half, as he promised. Gangazara would not accept anything, but asked the king to assemble all his subjects in a wood near the town. "I shall there call in all the tigers and serpents, and give them a general order."

When the whole town was assembled, just at the dusk of evening, Gangazara sat dumb for a moment, and thought upon the Tiger King and the Serpent King, who came with all their armies. People began to take to their heels at the sight of tigers. Gangazara assured them of safety, and stopped them.

The grey light of the evening, the pumpkin colour of

Gangazara, the holy ashes scattered lavishly over his body, the tigers and snakes humbling themselves at his feet, gave him the true majesty of the god Gangazara. For who else by a single word could thus command vast armies of tigers and serpents, said some among the people. "Care not for it; it may be by magic. That is not a great thing. That he revived cartloads of corpses shows him to be surely Gangazara," said others.

"Why should you, my children, thus trouble these poor subjects of Ujjaini? Reply to me, and henceforth desist from your ravages." Thus said the Soothsayer's son, and the following reply came from the king of the tigers: "Why should this base king imprison your honour, believing the mere word of a goldsmith that your honour killed his father? All the hunters told him that his father was carried away by a tiger. I was the messenger of death sent to deal the blow on his neck. I did it, and gave the crown to your honour. The prince makes no inquiry, and at once imprisons your honour. How can we expect justice from such a stupid king as that? Unless he adopt a better standard of justice we will go on with our destruction."

The king heard, cursed the day on which he believed in the word of a goldsmith, beat his head, tore his hair, wept and wailed for his crime, asked a thousand pardons, and swore to rule in a just way from that day. The serpent-king and tiger-king also promised to observe their oath as long as justice prevailed, and took their leave. The goldsmith fled for his life. He was caught by the soldiers of the king, and was pardoned by the generous Gangazara, whose voice now reigned supreme. All returned to their homes.

The king again pressed Gangazara to accept the hand of

his daughter. He agreed to do so, not then, but some time afterwards. He wished to go and see his elder brother first, and then to return and marry the princess. The king agreed; and Gangazara left the city that very day on his way home.

It so happened that unwittingly he took a wrong road, and had to pass near a sea-coast. His elder brother was also on his way up to Benares by that very same route. They met and recognised each other, even at a distance. They flew into each other's arms. Both remained still for a time almost unconscious with joy. The pleasure of Gangazara was so great that he died of joy.

The elder brother was a devout worshipper of Ganesa. That was a Friday, a day very sacred to that god. The elder brother took the corpse to the nearest Ganesa temple and called upon him. The god came, and asked him what he wanted. "My poor brother is dead and gone; and this is his corpse. Kindly keep it in your charge till I finish worshipping you. If I leave it anywhere else the devils may snatch it away when I am absent worshipping you; after finishing the rites I shall burn him." Thus said the elder brother, and, giving the corpse to the god Ganesa, he went to prepare himself for that deity's ceremonials. Ganesa made over the corpse to his Ganas, asking them to watch over it carefully. But instead of that they devoured it.

The elder brother, after finishing the puja, demanded his brother's corpse of the god. The god called his Ganas, who came to the front blinking, and fearing the anger of their master. The god was greatly enraged. The elder brother was very angry. When the corpse was not forthcoming he cuttingly remarked, "Is this, after all, the return for my deep belief in you? You are unable even to return my brother's corpse." Ganesa was much ashamed at the remark. So he, by his divine power, gave him a living Gangazara instead of the dead corpse. Thus was the second son of the Soothsayer restored to life.

The brothers had a long talk about each other's adventures They both went to Ujjaini, where Gangazara married the princess, and succeeded to the throne of that kingdom. He reigned for a long time, conferring several benefits upon his brother. And so the horoscope was fully fulfilled.

Harisarman

THERE was a certain Bráhman in a certain village, named Harisarman. He was poor and foolish and in evil case for want of employment, and he had very many children, that he might reap the fruit of his misdeeds in a former life. He wandered about begging with his family, and at last he reached a certain city, and entered the service of a rich householder called Sthuladatta. His sons became keepers of Sthuladatta's cows and other property, and his wife a servant to him, and he himself lived near his house, performing the duty of an attendant. One day there was a feast on account of the marriage of the daughter of Sthuladatta, largely attended by many friends of the bridegroom, and merry-makers. Harisarman hoped that he would be able to fill himself up to the throat with ghee and flesh and other dainties, and get the same for his family, in the house of his patron. While he was anxiously expecting to be fed, no one thought of him.

Then he was distressed at getting nothing to eat, and he said to his wife at night, "It is owing to my poverty and stupidity that I am treated with such disrespect here; so I will pretend by means of an artifice to possess a knowledge of magic, so that I may become an object of respect to this Sthuladatta; so, when you get an opportunity, tell him that I possess magical knowledge." He said this to her, and after turning the matter over in his mind, while people were

asleep he took away from the house of Sthuladatta a horse on which his master's son-in-law rode. He placed it in concealment at some distance, and in the morning the friends of the bridegroom could not find the horse, though they searched in every direction. Then, while Sthuladatta was distressed at the evil omen, and searching for the thieves who had carried off the horse, the wife of Harisarman came and said to him; "My husband is a wise man, skilled in astrology and magical sciences; he can get the horse back for you; why do you not ask him?"

When Sthuladatta heard that, he called Harisarman, who said, "Yesterday I was forgotten, but to-day, now the horse is stolen, I am called to mind," and Sthuladatta then propitiated the Brahman with these words—"I forgot you, forgive me"—and asked him to tell him who had taken away their horse. Then Harisarman drew all kinds of pretended diagrams, and said: "The horse has been placed by thieves on the boundary line south from this place. It is concealed there, and before it is carried off to a distance, as it will be at close of day, go quickly and bring it." When they heard that, many men ran and brought the horse quickly, praising the discernment of Harisarman. Then Harisarman was honoured by all men as a sage, and dwelt there in happiness, honoured by Sthuladatta.

Now, as days went on, much treasure, both of gold and jewels, had been stolen by a thief from the palace of the king. As the thief was not known, the king quickly summoned Harisarman on account of his reputation for knowledge of magic. And he, when summoned, tried to gain time, and said, "I will tell you to-morrow," and then he was placed in a chamber by the king, and carefully guarded. And he was sad because he had pretended to have knowledge. Now in that palace there was a maid named Jihva (which means Tongue), who, with the assistance of her brother, had stolen that treasure from the interior of the palace. She, being alarmed at Harisarman's knowledge, went at night and applied her ear to the door of that chamber in order to find out what he was about. And Harisarman, who was alone inside, was at that very moment blaming his own tongue, that had made a vain assumption of knowledge. He said: "O Tongue, what is this that you have done through your greediness? Wicked one, you will soon receive punishment in full." When Jihva heard this, she thought, in her terror, that she had been discovered by this wise man, and she managed to get in where he was, and falling at his feet, she said to the supposed wizard: "Brahman, here I am, that Jihva whom you have discovered to be the thief of the treasure, and after I took it I buried it in the earth in a garden behind the palace, under a pomegranate tree. So spare me, and receive the small quantity of gold which is in my possession."

When Harisarman heard that, he said to her proudly: "Depart, I know all this; I know the past, present and future; but I will not denounce you, being a miserable creature that has implored my protection. But whatever gold is in your possession you must give back to me." When he said this to the maid, she consented, and departed quickly. But Harisarman reflected in his astonishment: "Fate brings about, as if in sport, things impossible, for when calamity was so near, who would have thought chance would have brought us success? While I was blaming my jihva, the thief Jihva suddenly flung herself at my feet. Secret crimes manifest themselves by means of fear." Thus thinking, he passed the night happily in the chamber. And in the morning he brought the king, by some skilful parade of pretended knowledge into the garden, and led him up to the treasure, which was buried under the pomegranate tree, and said that the thief had escaped with a part of it. Then the king was pleased, and gave him the revenue of many villages.

But the minister, named Devajnanin, whispered in the king's ear: "How can a man possess such knowledge unattainable by men, without having studied the books of magic; you may be certain that this is a specimen of the way he makes a dishonest livelihood, by having a secret intelligence with thieves. It will be much better to test him by some new artifice." Then the king of his own accord brought a covered pitcher into which he had thrown a frog, and said to Harisarman, "Brahman, if you can guess what there is in this pitcher, I will do you great honour to-day." When the Brahman Harisarman heard that, he thought that his last hour had come, and he called to mind the pet name of "Froggie" which his father had given him in his childhood in sport, and, impelled by luck, he called to himself by his pet name, lamenting his hard fate, and suddenly called out: "This is a fine pitcher for you, Froggie; it will soon become the swift destroyer of your helpless self." The people there, when they heard him say that, raised a shout of applause, because his speech chimed in so well with the object presented to him, and murmured, "Ah! a great sage, he knows even about the frog!" Then the king, thinking that this was all due to knowledge of divination, was highly delighted, and gave Harisarman the revenue of more villages, with gold, an umbrella, and state carriages of all kinds. So Harisarman prospered in the world.

The Charmed Ring

A MERCHANT started his son in life with three hundred rupees, and bade him go to another country and try his luck in trade. The son took the money and departed. He had not gone far before he came across some herdsmen quarrelling over a dog, that some of them wished to kill. " Please do not kill the dog," pleaded the young and tender-hearted fellow; " I will give you one hundred rupees for it." Then and there, of course, the bargain was concluded, and the foolish fellow took the dog, and continued his journey. He next met with some people fighting about a cat. Some of them wanted to kill it, but others not. " Oh! please do not kill it," said he; " I will give you one hundred rupees for it." Of course they at once gave him the cat and took the money. He went on till he reached a village, where some folk were quarrelling over a snake that had just been caught. Some of them wished to kill it, but others did not. " Please do not kill the snake," said he; " I will give you one hundred rupees." Of course the people agreed, and were highly delighted.

What a fool the fellow was! What would he do now that all his money was gone? What could he do except return to his father? Accordingly he went home.

"You fool! You scamp!" exclaimed his father when he had heard how his son had wasted all the money that had been given to him. "Go and live in the stables and repent of your folly. You shall never again enter my house."

So the young man went and lived in the stables His bed was the grass spread for the cattle, and his companions were the dog, the cat, and the snake, which he had purchased so dearly. These creatures got very fond of him, and would follow him about during the day, and sleep by him at night; the cat used to sleep at his feet, the dog at his head, and the snake over his body, with its head hanging on one side and its tail on the other.

One day the snake in course of conversation said to its master, "I am the son of Raja Indrasha. One day, when I had come out of the ground to drink the air, some people seized me, and would have slain me had you not most opportunely arrived to my rescue. I do not know how I shall ever be able to repay you for your great kindness to me. Would that you knew my father! How glad he would be to see his son's preserver!"

"Where does he live? I should like to see him, if possible," said the young man.

"Well said!" continued the snake. "Do you see yonder mountain? At the bottom of that mountain there is a sacred spring. If you will come with me and dive into that spring, we shall both reach my father's country. Oh! how glad he will be to see you! He will wish to reward you, too. But how can he do that? However, you may be pleased to accept something at his hand. If he asks you what you would like, you would, perhaps, do well to reply, 'The ring on your right hand, and the famous pot and spoon which you possess.' With these in your possession, you would never need anything, for the ring is such that a man has only to speak to it, and immediately a beautiful furnished mansion will be provided for him, while the pot and the spoon will supply him with all manner of the rarest and most delicious foods."

Attended by his three companions the man walked to the well and prepared to jump in, according to the snake's directions. "O master!" exclaimed the cat and dog, when they saw what he was going to do. "What shall we do? Where shall we go?"

"Wait for me here," he replied. "I am not going far. I shall not be long away." On saying this, he dived into the water and was lost to sight.

"Now what shall we do?" said the dog to the cat.

"We must remain here," replied the cat, "as our master ordered. Do not be anxious about food. I will go to the people's houses and get plenty of food for both of us." And so the cat did, and they both lived very comfortably till their master came again and joined them.

The young man and the snake reached their destination in safety; and information of their arrival was sent to the Raja. His highness commanded his son and the stranger to appear before him. But the snake refused, saying that it could not go to its father till it was released from this stranger, who had saved it from a most terrible death, and whose slave it therefore was. Then the Raja went and embraced his son, and saluting the stranger welcomed him to his dominions. The young man stayed there a few days, during which he received the Raja's right-hand ring, and the pot and spoon, in recognition of His Highness's gratitude to him for having delivered his son. He then returned. On reaching the top of the spring he found his friends, the dog and the cat, waiting for him. They told one another all they had experienced since they had last seen each other, and were all very glad. Afterwards they walked together to the river side, where it was decided to try the powers of the charmed ring and pot and spoon.

The merchant's son spoke to the ring, and immediately a beautiful house and a lovely princess with golden hair appeared. He spoke to the pot and spoon, also, and the most delicious dishes of food were provided for them. So he married the princess, and they lived very happily for several years, until one morning the princess, while arranging her toilet, put the loose hairs into a hollow bit of reed and threw them into the river that flowed along under the window. The reed floated on the water for many miles, and was at last picked up by the prince of that country, who curiously opened it and saw the golden hair. On finding it the prince rushed off to the palace, locked himself up in his room, and would not leave it. He had fallen desperately in love with the woman whose hair he had picked up, and refused to eat, or drink, or sleep, or move, till she was brought to him. The king, his father, was in great distress about the matter, and did not know what to do. He feared lest his son should die and leave him without an heir. At last he determined to seek the counsel of his aunt, who was an ogress. The old woman consented to help him, and bade him not to be anxious, as she felt certain that she would succeed in getting the beautiful woman for his son's wife.

She assumed the shape of a bee and went along buzzing, and buzzing, and buzzing. Her keen sense of smell soon brought her to the beautiful princess, to whom she appeared as an old hag, holding in one hand a stick by way of support. She introduced herself to the beautiful princess and said, "I am your aunt, whom you have never seen before, because I left the country just after your birth." She also embraced and kissed the princess by way of adding force to her words. The beautiful princess was thoroughly deceived. She returned the ogress's embrace, and invited her to come and stay in the house as long as she could, and treated her with such honour and attention, that the ogress thought to herself, "I shall soon accomplish my errand." When she had been in the house three days, she began to talk of the charmed ring, and advised her to keep it instead of her husband, because the latter was constantly out shooting and on other such-like expeditions, and might lose it. Accordingly the beautiful princess asked her husband for the ring, and he readily gave it to her.

The ogress waited another day before she asked to see the precious thing. Doubting nothing, the beautiful princess complied, when the ogress seized the ring, and reassuming the form of a bee flew away with it to the palace, where the prince was lying nearly on the point of death. "Rise up. Be glad. Mourn no more," she said to him. "The woman for whom you yearn will appear at your summons. See, here is the charm, whereby you may bring her before you." The prince was almost mad with joy when he heard these words, and was so desirous of seeing the beautiful princess, that he immediately spoke to the ring, and the house with its fair occupant descended in the midst of the palace garden. He at once entered the building, and telling the beautiful princess of his intense love, entreated her to be his wife. Seeing no escape from the difficulty, she consented on the condition that he would wait one month for her.

Meanwhile the merchant's son had returned from hunting and was terribly distressed not to find his house and wife. There was the place only, just as he knew it before he had tried the charmed ring which Raja Indrasha had given him. He sat down and determined to put an end to himself. Presently the cat and dog came up. They had gone away and hidden themselves, when they saw the house and everything disappear. "O master!" they said, "stay your hand. Your trial is great, but it can be remedied. Give us one month, and we will go and try to recover your wife and house."

"Go," said he, "and may the great God aid your efforts. Bring back my wife, and I shall live."

So the cat and dog started off at a run, and did not stop till they reached the place whither their mistress and the house had been taken. "We may have some difficulty here," said the cat. "Look, the king has taken our master's wife and house for himself. You stay here. I will go to the house and try to see her." So the dog sat down, and the cat climbed up to the window of the room, wherein the beautiful princess was sitting, and entered. The princess recognised the cat, and informed it of all that had happened to her since she had left them.

"But is there no way of escape from the hands of these people?" she asked.

"Yes," replied the cat, "if you can tell me where the charmed ring is."

"The ring is in the stomach of the ogress," she said.

"All right," said the cat, "I will recover it. If we once get it, everything is ours." Then the cat descended the wall of the house, and went and laid down by a rat's hole and pretended she was dead. Now at that time a great wedding chanced to be going on among the rat community of that place, and all the rats of the neighbourhood were assembled in that one particular mine by which the cat had lain down. The eldest son of the king of the rats was about to be married. The cat got to know of this, and at once conceived the idea of seizing the bridegroom and making him render the necessary help. Consequently, when the procession poured forth from the hole squealing and jumping in honour of the occasion, it immediately spotted the bridegroom and pounced down on him. "Oh! let me go, let me go," cried the terrified rat. "Oh! let him go," squealed all the company. "It is his wedding day."

"No, no," replied the cat. "Not unless you do something for me. Listen. The ogress, who lives in that house with the prince and his wife, has swallowed a ring, which I very much want. If you will procure it for me, I will allow the rat to depart unharmed. If you do not, then your prince dies under my feet."

"Very well, we agree," said they all. "Nay, if we do not get the ring for you, devour us all."

This was rather a bold offer. However, they accom-

THE CHARMED RING

plished the thing. At midnight, when the ogress was sound asleep, one of the rats went to her bedside, climbed up on her face, and inserted its tail into her throat; whereupon the ogress coughed violently, and the ring came out and rolled on to the floor. The rat immediately seized the precious thing and ran off with it to its king, who was very glad, and went at once to the cat and released its son.

As soon as the cat received the ring, she started back with the dog to go and tell their master the good tidings. All seemed safe now. They had only to give the ring to him, and he would speak to it, and the house and beautiful princess would again be with them, and everything would go on as happily as before. "How glad master will be!" they thought, and ran as fast as their legs could carry them. Now, on the way they had to cross a stream. The dog swam, and the cat sat on its back. Now the dog was jealous of the cat, so he asked for the ring, and threatened to throw the cat into the water if it did not give it up; whereupon the cat gave up the ring. Sorry moment, for the dog at once dropped it, and a fish swallowed it.

"Oh! what shall I do? what shall I do?" said the dog.

"What is done is done," replied the cat. "We must try to recover it, and if we do not succeed we had better drown ourselves in this stream. I have a plan. You go and kill a small lamb, and bring it here to me."

"All right," said the dog, and at once ran off. He soon came back with a dead lamb, and gave it to the cat. The cat got inside the lamb and lay down, telling the dog to go away a little distance and keep quiet. Not long after this a nadhar, a bird whose look can break the bones of a fish, came and hovered over the lamb, and eventually pounced down on it to carry it away. On this the cat came out and jumped on to the bird, and threatened to kill it if it did not recover the lost ring. This was most readily promised by the nadhar, who immediately flew off to the king of the fishes, and ordered it to make inquiries and to restore the ring. The king of the fishes did so, and the ring was found and carried back to the cat.

"Come along now; I have got the ring," said the cat to the dog.

"No, I will not," said the dog, "unless you let me have the ring. I can carry it as well as you. Let me have it or I will kill you." So the cat was obliged to give up the ring. The careless dog very soon dropped it again. This time it was picked up and carried off by a kite.

"See, see, there it goes—away to that big tree," the cat exclaimed.

"Oh! oh! what have I done?" cried the dog.

"You foolish thing, I knew it would be so," said the cat. "But stop your barking, or you will frighten away the bird to some place where we shall not be able to trace it."

The cat waited till it was quite dark, and then climbed the tree, killed the kite, and recovered the ring. "Come along," it said to the dog when it reached the ground. "We must make haste now. We have been delayed. Our master will die from grief and suspense. Come on."

The dog, now thoroughly ashamed of itself, begged the cat's pardon for all the trouble it had given. It was afraid to ask for the ring the third time, so they both reached their sorrowing master in safety and gave him the precious charm. In a moment his sorrow was turned into joy. He spoke to the ring, and his beautiful wife and house reappeared, and he and everybody were as happy as ever they could be.

The Talkative Tortoise

THE future Buddha was once born in a minister's family, when Brahma-datta was reigning in Benares; and when he grew up, he became the king's adviser in things temporal and spiritual.

Now this king was very talkative; while he was speaking, others had no opportunity for a word. And the future Buddha, wanting to cure this talkativeness of his, was constantly seeking for some means of doing so.

At that time there was living, in a pond in the Himalaya mountains, a tortoise. Two young hamsas, or wild ducks, who came to feed there, made friends with him. And one day, when they had become very intimate with him, they said to the tortoise:

"Friend tortoise! the place where we live, at the Golden Cave on Mount Beautiful in the Himalaya country, is a delightful spot. Will you come there with us?"

"But how can I get there?"

"We can take you, if you can only hold your tongue, and will say nothing to anybody."

"Oh! that I can do. Take me with you."

"That's right," said they. And making the tortoise bite hold of a stick, they themselves took the two ends in their teeth, and flew up into the air.

Seeing him thus carried by the hamsas, some villagers called out, "Two wild ducks are carrying a tortoise along on a stick!" Whereupon the tortoise wanted to say, "If my friends choose to carry me, what is that to you, you wretched slaves!" So just as the swift flight of the wild ducks had brought him over the king's palace in the city

of Benares, he let go of the stick he was biting, and falling in the open courtyard, split in two! And there arose a universal cry, "A tortoise has fallen in the open courtyard, and has split in two!"

The king, taking the future Buddha, went to the place, surrounded by his courtiers; and looking at the tortoise, he asked the Bodisat, "Teacher! how comes he to be fallen here?"

The future Buddha thought to himself, "Long expecting, wishing to admonish the king, have I sought for some means of doing so. This tortoise must have made friends with the wild ducks; and they must have made him bite hold of the stick, and have flown up into the air to take him to the hills. But he, being unable to hold his tongue when he hears any one else talk, must have wanted to say something, and let go the stick; and so must have fallen down from the sky, and thus lost his life." And saying, "Truly, O king! those who are called chatter-boxes—people whose words have no end—come to grief like this," he uttered these Verses:

> "Verily the tortoise killed himself
> Whilst uttering his voice;
> Though he was holding tight the stick,
> By a word himself he slew.
>
> "Behold him then, O excellent by strength!
> And speak wise words, not out of season.
> You see how, by his talking overmuch,
> The tortoise fell into this wretched plight!"

The king saw that he was himself referred to, and said "O Teacher! are you speaking of us?"

And the Bodisat spake openly, and said, "O great king! be it thou, or be it any other, whoever talks beyond measure meets with some mishap like this."

And the king henceforth refrained himself, and became a man of few words.

A Lac of Rupees for a Bit of Advice

A POOR blind Brahman and his wife were dependent on their son for their subsistence. Every day the young fellow used to go out and get what he could by begging. This continued for some time, till at last he became quite tired of such a wretched life, and determined to go and try his luck in another country He informed his wife of his intention, and ordered her to manage somehow or other for the old people during the few months that he would be absent. He begged her to be industrious, lest his parents should be angry and curse him.

One morning he started with some food in a bundle,

and walked on day after day, till he reached the chief city of the neighbouring country. Here he went and sat down by a merchant's shop and asked alms. The merchant inquired whence he had come, why he had come, and what was his caste; to which he replied that he was a Brahman, and was wandering hither and thither begging a livelihood for himself and wife and parents. Moved with pity for the man, the merchant advised him to visit the kind and generous king of that country, and offered to accompany him to the court. Now, at that time it happened that the king was seeking for a Brahman to look after a golden temple which he had just had built. His Majesty was very glad, therefore, when he saw the Brahman and heard that he was good and honest. He at once deputed him to the charge of this temple, and ordered fifty kharwars of rice and one hundred rupees to be paid to him every year as wages.

Two months after this, the Brahman's wife, not having heard any news of her husband, left the house and went in quest of him. By a happy fate she arrived at the very place that he had reached, where she heard that every morning at the golden temple a golden rupee was given in the king's name to any beggar who chose to go for it. Accordingly, on the following morning she went to the place and met her husband.

"Why have you come here?" he asked. "Why have you left my parents? Care you not whether they curse me and I die? Go back immediately, and await my return."

"No, no," said the woman. "I cannot go back to starve and see your old father and mother die. There is not a grain of rice left in the house."

"O Bhagawant!" exclaimed the Brahman. "Here,

take this," he continued, scribbling a few lines on some paper, and then handing it to her, " and give it to the king. You will see that he will give you a lac of rupees for it." Thus saying he dismissed her, and the woman left.

On this scrap of paper were written three pieces of advice —First, If a person is travelling and reaches any strange place at night, let him be careful where he puts up, and not close his eyes in sleep, lest he close them in death. Secondly, If a man has a married sister, and visits her in great pomp, she will receive him for the sake of what she can obtain from him; but if he comes to her in poverty, she will frown on him and disown him. Thirdly, If a man has to do any work, he must do it himself, and do it with might and without fear.

On reaching her home the Brahmani told her parents of her meeting with her husband, and what a valuable piece of paper he had given her; but not liking to go before the king herself, she sent one of her relations. The king read the paper, and ordering the man to be flogged, dismissed him. The next morning the Brahmani took the paper, and while she was going along the road to the darbar reading it, the king's son met her, and asked what she was reading, whereupon she replied that she held in her hands a paper containing certain bits of advice, for which she wanted a lac of rupees. The prince asked her to show it to him, and when he had read it gave her a parwana for the amount, and rode on. The poor Brahmani was very thankful. That day she laid in a great store of provisions, sufficient to last them all for a long time.

In the evening the prince related to his father the meeting with the woman, and the purchase of the piece of paper.

He thought his father would applaud the act. But it was not so. The king was more angry than before, and banished his son from the country.

So the prince bade adieu to his mother and relations and friends, and rode off on his horse, whither he did not know. At nightfall he arrived at some place, where a man met him, and invited him to lodge at his house. The prince accepted the invitation, and was treated like a prince. Matting was spread for him to squat on, and the best provisions set before him.

"Ah!" thought he, as he lay down to rest, "here is a case for the first piece of advice that the Brahmani gave me. I will not sleep to-night."

It was well that he thus resolved, for in the middle of the night the man rose up, and taking a sword in his hand, rushed to the prince with the intention of killing him. But he rose up and spoke.

"Do not slay me," he said. "What profit would you get from my death? If you killed me you would be sorry afterwards, like that man who killed his dog."

"What man? What dog?" he asked.

"I will tell you," said the prince, "if you will give me that sword."

So he gave him the sword, and the prince began his story:

"Once upon a time there lived a wealthy merchant who had a pet dog. He was suddenly reduced to poverty, and had to part with his dog. He got a loan of five thousand rupees from a brother merchant, leaving the dog as a pledge, and with the money began business again. Not long after this the other merchant's shop was broken into by thieves and completely sacked. There was hardly ten rupees' worth left in the place. The faithful dog, however, knew what was going on, and went and followed the thieves, and saw where they deposited the things, and then returned.

"In the morning there was great weeping and lamentation in the merchant's house when it was known what had happened. The merchant himself nearly went mad. Meanwhile the dog kept on running to the door, and pulling at his master's shirt and paijamas, as though wishing him to go outside. At last a friend suggested that, perhaps, the dog knew something of the whereabouts of the things, and advised the merchant to follow its leadings. The merchant consented, and went after the dog right up to the very place where the thieves had hidden the goods. Here the animal scraped and barked, and showed in various ways that the things were underneath. So the merchant and his friends dug about the place, and soon came upon all the stolen property. Nothing was missing. There was everything just as the thieves had taken them.

"The merchant was very glad. On returning to his house, he at once sent the dog back to its old master with a letter rolled under the collar, wherein he had written about the sagacity of the beast, and begged his friend to forget the loan and to accept another five thousand rupees as a present. When this merchant saw his dog coming back again, he thought, 'Alas! my friend is wanting the money. How can I pay him? I have not had sufficient time to recover myself from my recent losses. I will slay the dog ere he reaches the threshold, and say that another must have slain it. Thus there will be an end of my debt. No dog, no loan.' Accordingly he ran out and killed the poor dog, when the letter fell out of its collar. The merchant picked it up and read it. How great was his grief and disappointment when he knew the facts of the case!

"Beware," continued the prince, 'lest you do that which afterwards you would give your life not to have done."

By the time the prince had concluded this story it was nearly morning, and he went away, after rewarding the man.

The prince then visited the country belonging to his brother-in-law. He disguised himself as a jogi, and sitting down by a tree near the palace, pretended to be absorbed in worship. News of the man and of his wonderful piety reached the ears of the king. He felt interested in him, as his wife was very ill; and he had sought for hakims to cure her, but in vain. He thought that, perhaps, this holy man could do something for her. So he sent to him. But the jogi refused to tread the halls of a king, saying that his dwelling was the open air, and that if his Majesty wished to see him he must come himself and bring his wife to the place. Then the king took his wife and brought her to the jogi. The holy man bade her prostrate herself before him, and when she had remained in this position for about three hours, he told her to rise and go, for she was cured.

In the evening there was great consternation in the palace, because the queen had lost her pearl rosary, and nobody knew anything about it. At length some one went to the jogi, and found it on the ground by the place where the queen had prostrated herself. When the king heard this he was very angry, and ordered the jogi to be executed. This stern order, however, was not carried out, as the prince bribed the men and escaped from the country. But he knew that the second bit of advice was true.

Clad in his own clothes, the prince was walking along one day when he saw a potter crying and laughing alternately with his wife and children. "O fool," said he, "what is the matter? If you laugh, why do you weep? If you weep, why do you laugh?"

"Do not bother me," said the potter. "What does it matter to you?"

"Pardon me," said the prince, "but I should like to know the reason."

"The reason is this, then," said the potter. "The king of this country has a daughter whom he is obliged to marry every day, because all her husbands die the first night of their stay with her. Nearly all the young men of the place have thus perished, and our son will be called on soon. We laugh at the absurdity of the thing—a potter's son marrying a princess, and we cry at the terrible consequence of the marriage. What can we do?"

"Truly a matter for laughing and weeping. But weep no more," said the prince. "I will exchange places with your son, and will be married to the princess instead of him. Only give me suitable garments, and prepare me for the occasion."

So the potter gave him beautiful raiment and ornaments, and the prince went to the palace. At night he was conducted to the apartment of the princess. "Dread hour!" thought he; "am I to die like the scores of young men before me?" He clenched his sword with firm grip, and lay down on his bed, intending to keep awake all the night and see what would happen. In the middle of the night he saw two Shahmars come out from the nostrils of the princess. They stole over towards him, intending to kill him, like the others who had been before him: but he was ready for them. He laid hold of his sword, and when the snakes reached his bed he struck at them and killed them. In the morning the king came as usual to inquire, and was surprised to hear his daughter and the prince talking gaily together. "Surely," said he, "this man must be her husband, as he only can live with her."

"Where do you come from? Who are you?" asked the king, entering the room.

"O king!" replied the prince, "I am the son of a king who rules over such-and-such a country."

When he heard this the king was very glad, and bade the prince to abide in his palace, and appointed him his successor to the throne. The prince remained at the palace for more than a year, and then asked permission to visit his own country, which was granted. The king gave him elephants, horses, jewels, and abundance of money for the expenses of the way and as presents for his father, and the prince started.

On the way he had to pass through the country belonging to his brother-in-law, whom we have already mentioned. Report of his arrival reached the ears of the king, who came with rope-tied hands and haltered neck to do him homage. He most humbly begged him to stay at his palace, and to accept what little hospitality could be provided. While the prince was staying at the palace he saw his sister, who greeted him with smiles and kisses. On leaving he told her how she and her husband had treated him at his first visit, and how he escaped; and then gave them two elephants, two beautiful horses, fifteen soldiers, and ten lacs rupees' worth of jewels.

Afterwards he went to his own home, and informed his mother and father of his arrival. Alas! his parents had both become blind from weeping about the loss of their son. "Let him come in," said the king, "and put his hands upon our eyes, and we shall see again." So the prince entered, and was most affectionately greeted by his old parents; and he laid his hands on their eyes, and they saw again.

Then the prince told his father all that had happened to him, and how he had been saved several times by attending to the advice that he had purchased from the Brahmani. Whereupon the king expressed his sorrow for having sent him away, and ali was joy and peace again.

The Gold-giving Serpent

NOW in a certain place there lived a Brahman named Haridatta. He was a farmer, but poor was the return his labour brought him. One day, at the end of the hot hours, the Brahman, overcome by the heat, lay down under the shadow of a tree to have a doze. Suddenly he saw a great-hooded snake creeping out of an ant-hill near at hand. So he thought to himself, " Sure this is the guardian deity of the field, and I have not ever worshipped it. That's why my farming is in vain. I will at once go and pay my respects to it."

When he had made up his mind, he got some milk, poured it into a bowl, and went to the ant-hill, and said aloud : " O Guardian of this Field ! all this while I did not know that you dwelt here. That is why I have not yet paid my respects to you ; pray forgive me." And he laid the milk down and went to his house. Next morning he came and looked, and he saw a gold denar in the bowl, and from that time onward every day the same thing occurred : he gave milk to the serpent and found a gold denar.

One day the Brahman had to go to the village, and so he ordered his son to take the milk to the ant-hill. The son brought the milk, put it down, and went back home. Next day he went again and found a denar, so he thought to himself: "This ant-hill is surely full of golden denars; I'll kill the serpent, and take them all for myself." So next day, while he was giving the milk to the serpent, the Brahman's son struck it on the head with a cudgel. But the serpent escaped death by the will of fate, and in a rage bit the Brahman's son with its sharp fangs, and he fell down dead at once. His people raised him a funeral pyre not far from the field and burnt him to ashes.

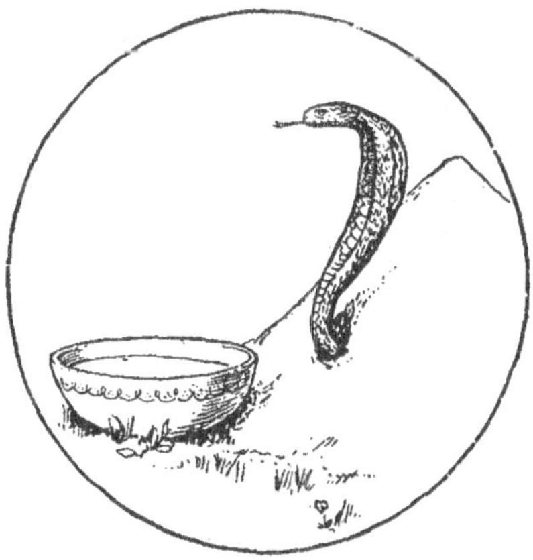

Two days afterwards his father came back, and when he learnt his son's fate he grieved and mourned. But after a time, he took the bowl of milk, went to the ant-hill, and praised the serpent with a loud voice. After a long, long time the serpent appeared, but only with its head out of the opening of the ant-hill, and spoke to the Brahman: "'Tis greed that brings you here, and makes you even forget the loss of your son. From this time forward friendship between us is impossible. Your son struck me in youthful ignorance, and I have bitten him to death. How can I forget the blow with the cudgel? And how can you forget the pain and grief at the loss of your son?" So speaking, it gave the Brahman a costly pearl and disappeared. But before it went away it said: "Come back no more." The Brahman took the pearl, and went back home, cursing the folly of his son.

The Son of Seven Queens

ONCE upon a time there lived a king who had seven Queens, but no children. This was a great grief to him, especially when he remembered that on his death there would be no heir to inherit the kingdom.

Now it happened one day that a poor old fakir came to the King, and said, "Your prayers are heard, your desire shall be accomplished, and one of your seven Queens shall bear a son."

The King's delight at this promise knew no bounds, and he gave orders for appropriate festivities to be prepared against the coming event throughout the length and breadth of the land.

Meanwhile the seven Queens lived luxuriously in a splendid palace, attended by hundreds of female slaves, and fed to their hearts' content on sweetmeats and confectionery.

Now the King was very fond of hunting, and one day, before he started, the seven Queens sent him a message saying, "May it please our dearest lord not to hunt towards the north to-day, for we have dreamt bad dreams, and fear lest evil should befall you."

The King, to allay their anxiety, promised regard for their wishes, and set out towards the south; but as luck would have it, although he hunted diligently, he found no game. Nor had he more success to the east or west, so that, being a keen sportsman, and determined not to go

home empty-handed, he forgot all about his promise, and turned to the north. Here also he was at first unsuccessful, but just as he had made up his mind to give up for that day, a white hind with golden horns and silver hoofs flashed past him into a thicket. So quickly did it pass that he scarcely saw it; nevertheless a burning desire to capture and possess the beautiful strange creature filled his breast.

He instantly ordered his attendants to form a ring round the thicket, and so encircle the hind; then, gradually narrowing the circle, he pressed forward till he could distinctly see the white hind panting in the midst. Nearer and nearer he advanced, till, just as he thought to lay hold of the beautiful strange creature, it gave one mighty bound, leapt clean over the King's head, and fled towards the mountains. Forgetful of all else, the King, setting spurs to his horse, followed at full speed. On, on he galloped, leaving his retinue far behind, keeping the white hind in view, never drawing bridle, until, finding himself in a narrrow ravine with no outlet, he reined in his steed. Before him stood a miserable hovel, into which, being tired after his long, unsuccessful chase, he entered to ask for a drink of water. An old woman, seated in the hut at a spinning-wheel, answered his request by calling to her daughter, and immediately from an inner room came a maiden so lovely and charming, so white-skinned and golden-haired, that the King was transfixed by astonishment at seeing so beautiful a sight in the wretched hovel.

She held the vessel of water to the King's lips, and as he drank he looked into her eyes, and then it became clear to him that the girl was no other than the white hind with the golden horns and silver feet he had chased so far.

Her beauty bewitched him, so he fell on his knees, begging her to return with him as his bride; but she only laughed, saying seven Queens were quite enough even for a King to manage. However, when he would take no refusal, but implored her to have pity on him, promising her everything she could desire, she replied, "Give me the eyes of your seven Queens, and then perhaps I may believe you mean what you say."

The King was so carried away by the glamour of the white hind's magical beauty, that he went home at once, had the eyes of his seven Queens taken out, and, after throwing the poor blind creatures into a noisome dungeon whence they could not escape, set off once more for the hovel in the ravine, bearing with him his horrible offering. But the white hind only laughed cruelly when she saw the fourteen eyes, and threading them as a necklace, flung it round her mother's neck, saying, " Wear that, little mother, as a keepsake, whilst I am away in the King's palace."

Then she went back with the bewitched monarch, as his bride, and he gave her the seven Queens' rich clothes and jewels to wear, the seven Queens' palace to live in, and the seven Queens' slaves to wait upon her; so that she really had everything even a witch could desire.

Now, very soon after the seven wretched hapless Queens had their eyes torn out, and were cast into prison, a baby was born to the youngest of the Queens. It was a handsome boy, but the other Queens were very jealous that the youngest amongst them should be so fortunate. But though at first they disliked the handsome little boy, he soon proved so useful to them, that ere long they all looked on him as their son. Almost as soon as he could walk about he began scraping at the mud wall of their dungeon, and in an incredibly short space of time had made a hole big enough for him to crawl through. Through this he disappeared, returning in an hour or so laden with sweetmeats, which he divided equally amongst the seven blind Queens.

As he grew older he enlarged the hole, and slipped out two or three times every day to play with the little nobles in the town. No one knew who the tiny boy was, but everybody liked him, and he was so full of funny tricks and antics, so merry and bright, that he was sure to be rewarded by some girdle-cakes, a handful of parched grain, or some sweetmeats. All these things he brought home to his seven mothers, as he loved to call the seven blind Queens, who by his help lived on in their dungeon when all the world thought they had starved to death ages before.

At last, when he was quite a big lad, he one day took his bow and arrow, and went out to seek for game. Coming by chance past the palace where the white hind lived in wicked splendour and magnificence, he saw some pigeons fluttering round the white marble turrets, and, taking good aim, shot one dead. It came tumbling past the very window where the white Queen was sitting; she rose to see what was the matter, and looked out. At the first glance of the handsome young lad standing there bow in hand, she knew by witchcraft that it was the King's son.

She nearly died of envy and spite, determining to destroy the lad without delay; therefore, sending a servant to bring him to her presence, she asked him if he would sell her the pigeon he had just shot.

"No," replied the sturdy lad, "the pigeon is for my seven blind mothers, who live in the noisome dungeon, and who would die if I did not bring them food."

"Poor souls!" cried the cunning white witch; "would you not like to bring them their eyes again? Give me the pigeon, my dear, and I faithfully promise to show you where to find them."

Hearing this, the lad was delighted beyond measure, and gave up the pigeon at once. Whereupon the white Queen told him to seek her mother without delay, and ask for the eyes which she wore as a necklace.

"She will not fail to give them," said the cruel Queen, "if you show her this token on which I have written what I want done."

So saying, she gave the lad a piece of broken potsherd, with these words inscribed on it—"Kill the bearer at once, and sprinkle his blood like water!"

Now, as the son of seven Queens could not read, he took the fatal message cheerfully, and set off to find the white Queen's mother.

Whilst he was journeying he passed through a town, where every one of the inhabitants looked so sad, that he could not help asking what was the matter. They told him it was because the King's only daughter refused to marry; so when her father died there would be no heir to the throne. They greatly feared she must be out of her mind, for though every good-looking young man in the kingdom had been shown to her, she declared she would only marry one who was the son of seven mothers, and who ever heard of such a thing? The King, in despair, had ordered every man who entered the city gates to be led before the Princess; so, much to the lad's impatience, for he was in an immense hurry to find his mothers' eyes, he was dragged into the presence-chamber.

No sooner did the Princess catch sight of him than she blushed, and, turning to the King, said, "Dear father, this is my choice!"

Never were such rejoicings as these few words produced.

THE SON OF SEVEN MOTHERS

The inhabitants nearly went wild with joy, but the son of seven Queens said he would not marry the Princess unless they first let him recover his mothers' eyes. When the beautiful bride heard his story, she asked to see the potsherd, for she was very learned and clever. Seeing the treacherous words, she said nothing, but taking another similar-shaped bit of potsherd, she wrote on it these words—" Take care of this lad, giving him all he desires," and returned it to the son of seven Queens, who, none the wiser, set off on his quest.

Ere long he arrived at the hovel in the ravine where the white witch's mother, a hideous old creature, grumbled dreadfully on reading the message, especially when the lad asked for the necklace of eyes. Nevertheless she took it off, and gave it him, saying, " There are only thirteen of 'em now, for I lost one last week."

The lad, however, was only too glad to get any at all, so he hurried home as fast as he could to his seven mothers, and gave two eyes apiece to the six elder Queens; but to the youngest he gave one, saying, " Dearest little mother!—I will be your other eye always!"

After this he set off to marry the Princess, as he had promised, but when passing by the white Queen's palace he saw some pigeons on the roof. Drawing his bow, he shot one, and it came fluttering past the window. The white hind looked out, and lo! there was the King's son alive and well.

She cried with hatred and disgust, but sending for the lad, asked him how he had returned so soon, and when she heard how he had brought home the thirteen eyes, and given them to the seven blind Queens, she could hardly restrain her rage. Nevertheless she pretended to be charmed with his success, and told him that if he would give her this pigeon also, she would reward him with the Jogi's wonderful cow, whose milk flows all day long, and makes a pond as big as a kingdom. The lad, nothing loth, gave her the pigeon · whereupon, as before, she bade him go ask her mother for the cow, and gave him a potsherd whereon was written —" Kill this lad without fail, and sprinkle his blood like water ! "

But on the way the son of seven Queens looked in on the Princess, just to tell her how he came to be delayed, and she, after reading the message on the potsherd, gave him another in its stead ; so that when the lad reached the old hag's hut and asked her for the Jogi's cow, she could not refuse, but told the boy how to find it ; and bidding him of all things not to be afraid of the eighteen thousand demons who kept watch and ward over the treasure, told him to be off before she became too angry at her daughter's foolishness in thus giving away so many good things.

Then the lad did as he had been told bravely. He journeyed on and on till he came to a milk-white pond, guarded by the eighteen thousand demons. They were really frightful to behold, but, plucking up courage, he whistled a tune as he walked through them, looking neither to the right nor the left. By-and-by he came upon the Jogi's cow, tall, white, and beautiful, while the Jogi himself, who was king of all the demons, sat milking her day and night, and the milk streamed from her udder, filling the milk-white tank.

The Jogi, seeing the lad, called out fiercely, " What do you want here ? "

Then the lad answered, according to the old hag's bidding,

"I want your skin, for King Indra is making a new kettle-drum, and says your skin is nice and tough."

Upon this the Jogi began to shiver and shake (for no Jinn or Jogi dares disobey King Indra's command), and, falling at the lad's feet, cried, "If you will spare me I will give you anything I possess, even my beautiful white cow!"

To this the son of seven Queens, after a little pretended hesitation, agreed, saying that after all it would not be difficult to find a nice tough skin like the Jogi's elsewhere; so, driving the wonderful cow before him, he set off homewards. The seven Queens were delighted to possess so marvellous an animal, and though they toiled from morning till night making curds and whey, besides selling milk to the confectioners, they could not use half the cow gave, and became richer and richer day by day.

Seeing them so comfortably off, the son of seven Queens started with a light heart to marry the Princess; but when passing the white hind's palace he could not resist sending a bolt at some pigeons which were cooing on the parapet. One fell dead just beneath the window where the white Queen was sitting. Looking out, she saw the lad hale and hearty standing before her, and grew whiter than ever with rage and spite.

She sent for him to ask how he had returned so soon, and when she heard how kindly her mother had received him, the very nearly had a fit; however, she dissembled her feelings as well as she could, and, smiling sweetly, said she was glad to have been able to fulfil her promise, and that if he would give her this third pigeon, she would do yet more for him than she had done before, by giving him the million-fold rice, which ripens in one night.

The lad was of course delighted at the very idea, and, giving up the pigeon, set off on his quest, armed as before with a potsherd, on which was written, "Do not fail this time. Kill the lad, and sprinkle his blood like water!"

But when he looked in on his Princess, just to prevent her becoming anxious about him, she asked to see the potsherd as usual, and substituted another, on which was written, "Yet again give this lad all he requires, for his blood shall be as your blood!"

Now when the old hag saw this, and heard how the lad wanted the million-fold rice which ripens in a single night, she fell into the most furious rage, but being terribly afraid of her daughter, she controlled herself, and bade the boy go and find the field guarded by eighteen millions of demons, warning him on no account to look back after having plucked the tallest spike of rice, which grew in the centre.

So the son of seven Queens set off, and soon came to the field where, guarded by eighteen millions of demons, the million-fold rice grew. He walked on bravely, looking neither to the right or left, till he reached the centre and plucked the tallest ear, but as he turned homewards a thousand sweet voices rose behind him, crying in tenderest accents, "Pluck me too! oh, please pluck me too!" He looked back, and lo! there was nothing left of him but a little heap of ashes!

Now as time passed by and the lad did not return, the old hag grew uneasy, remembering the message "his blood shall be as your blood;" so she set off to see what had happened.

Soon she came to the heap of ashes, and knowing by her arts what it was, she took a little water, and kneading the ashes into a paste, formed it into the likeness of a man; then, putting a drop of blood from her little finger into its mouth, she blew on it, and instantly the son of seven Queens started up as well as ever.

"Don't you disobey orders again!" grumbled the old hag, "or next time I'll leave you alone. Now be off, before I repent of my kindness!"

So the son of seven Queens returned joyfully to his seven mothers, who, by the aid of the million-fold rice, soon became the richest people in the kingdom. Then they celebrated their son's marriage to the clever Princess with all imaginable pomp; but the bride was so clever, she would not rest until she had made known her husband to his father, and punished the wicked white witch. So she made her husband build a palace exactly like the one in which the seven Queens had lived, and in which the white witch now dwelt in splendour. Then, when all was prepared, she bade her husband give a grand feast to the King. Now the King had heard much of the mysterious son of seven Queens, and his marvellous wealth, so he gladly accepted the invitation; but what was his astonishment when on entering the palace he found it was a facsimile of his own in every particular! And when his host, richly attired, led him straight to the private hall, where on royal thrones sat the seven Queens, dressed as he had last seen them, he was speechless with surprise, until the Princess, coming forward, threw herself at his feet, and told him the whole story. Then the King awoke from his enchantment, and his anger rose against the wicked white hind who had bewitched him so long, until he could not contain himself. So she was put to death and her grave ploughed over, and after that the seven Queens returned to their own splendid palace, and everybody lived happily.

A Lesson for Kings

ONCE upon a time, when Brahma-datta was reigning in Benares, the future Buddha returned to life as his son and heir. And when the day came for choosing a name, they called him Prince Brahma-datta. He grew up in due course; and when he was sixteen years old, went to Takkasila, and became accomplished in all arts. And after his father died he ascended the throne, and ruled the kingdom with righteousness and equity. He gave judgments without partiality, hatred, ignorance, or fear. Since he thus reigned with justice, with justice also his ministers administered the law. Law-suits being thus decided with justice, there were none who brought false cases. And as these ceased, the noise and tumult of litigation ceased in the king's court. Though the judges sat all day in the court, they had to leave without any one coming for justice. It came to this, that the Hall of Justice would have to be closed!

Then the future Buddha thought, "It cannot be from my reigning with righteousness that none come for judgments; the bustle has ceased, and the Hall of Justice will have to be closed. I must, therefore, now examine into my own faults; and if I find that anything is wrong in me, put that away, and practise only virtue."

Thenceforth he sought for some one to tell him his faults; but among those around him he found no one who would tell him of any fault, but heard only his own praise.

Then he thought, "It is from fear of me that these men speak only good things, and not evil things," and he sought among those people who lived outside the palace. And finding no fault-finder there, he sought among those who lived outside the city, in the suburbs, at the four gates. And there too finding no one to find fault, and hearing only his own praise, he determined to search the country places.

So he made over the kingdom to his ministers, and mounted his chariot; and taking only his charioteer, left the city in disguise. And searching the country through, up to the very boundary, he found no fault-finder, and heard only of his own virtue; and so he turned back from the outermost boundary, and returned by the high road towards the city.

Now at that time the king of Kosala, Mallika by name, was also ruling his kingdom with righteousness; and when seeking for some fault in himself, he also found no fault-finder in the palace, but only heard of his own virtue! So seeking in country places, he too came to that very spot. And these two came face to face in a low cart-track with precipitous sides, where there was no space for a chariot to get out of the way!

Then the charioteer of Mallika the king said to the charioteer of the king of Benares, "Take thy chariot out of the way!"

But he said, "Take thy chariot out of the way, O charioteer! In this chariot sitteth the lord over the kingdom of Benares, the great king Brahma-datta."

Yet the other replied, "In this chariot, O charioteer, sitteth the lord over the kingdom of Kosala, the great king Mallika. Take thy carriage out of the way, and make room for the chariot of our king!"

Then the charioteer of the king of Benares thought, "They say then that he too is a king! What *is* now to be done?" After some consideration, he said to himself, "I know a way. I'll find out how old he is, and then I'll let the chariot of the younger be got out of the way, and so make room for the elder."

And when he had arrived at that conclusion, he asked that charioteer what the age of the king of Kosala was. But on inquiry he found that the ages of both were equal. Then he inquired about the extent of his kingdom, and about his army, and his wealth, and his renown, and about the country he lived in, and his caste and tribe and family. And he found that both were lords of a kingdom three hundred leagues in extent; and that in respect of army and wealth and renown, and the countries in which they lived, and their caste and their tribe and their family, they were just on a par!

Then he thought, "I will make way for the most righteous." And he asked, "What kind of righteousness has this king of yours."

Then the charioteer of the king of Kosala, proclaiming his king's wickedness as goodness, uttered the First Stanza:

> "The strong he overthrows by strength,
> The mild by mildness, does Mallika;
> The good he conquers by goodness,
> And the wicked by wickedness too.
> Such is the nature of *this* king!
> Move out of the way, O charioteer"

But the charioteer of the king of Benares asked him, "Well, have you told all the virtues of your king?"

"Yes," said the other.

"If these are his *virtues*, where are then his faults?" replied he.

The other said, "Well, for the nonce they shall be faults if you like! But pray, then, what is the kind of goodness your king has?"

And then the charioteer of the king of Benares called unto him to hearken, and uttered the Second Stanza:

> "Anger he conquers by calmness,
> And by goodness the wicked;
> The stingy he conquers by gifts,
> And by truth the speaker of lies.
> Such is the nature of *this* king!
> Move out of the way, O charioteer!"

And when he had thus spoken, both Mallika the king and his charioteer alighted from their chariot. And they took out the horses, and removed their chariot, and made way for the king of Benares!

Pride goeth before a Fall

IN a certain village there lived ten cloth merchants, who always went about together. Once upon a time they had travelled far afield, and were returning home with a great deal of money which they had obtained by selling their wares. Now there happened to be a dense forest near their village, and this they reached early one morning. In it there lived three notorious robbers, of whose existence the traders had never heard, and while they were still in the middle of it the robbers stood before them, with swords and cudgels in their hands, and ordered them to lay down all they had. The traders had no weapons with them, and so, though they were many more in number, they had to submit themselves to the robbers, who took away everything from them, even the very clothes they wore, and gave to each only a small loin-cloth a span in breadth and a cubit in length.

The idea that they had conquered ten men and plundered all their property, now took possession of the robbers' minds. They seated themselves like three monarches before the men they had plundered, and ordered them to dance to them before returning home. The merchants now mourned their fate. They had lost all they had, except their loin-cloth, and still the robbers were not satisfied, but ordered them to dance

There was, among the ten merchants, one who was very clever. He pondered over the calamity that had come upon him and his friends, the dance they would have to perform, and the magnificent manner in which the three robbers had seated themselves on the grass. At the same time he observed that these last had placed their weapons on the ground, in the assurance of having thoroughly cowed the traders, who were now commencing to dance. So he took the lead in the dance, and, as a song is always sung by the leader on such occasions, to which the rest keep time with hands and feet, he thus began to sing:

> "We are enty men,
> They are erith men:
> If each erith man,
> Surround eno men
> Eno man remains.
> *Tâ, tai, tôm, tadingana.*"

The robbers were all uneducated, and thought that the leader was merely singing a song as usual. So it was in one sense; for the leader commenced from a distance, and had sung the song over twice before he and his companions commenced to approach the robbers. They had understood his meaning, because they had been trained in trade.

When two traders discuss the price of an article in

the presence of a purchaser, they use a riddling sort of language.

"What is the price of this cloth?" one trader will ask another.

"Enty rupees," another will reply, meaning "ten rupees."

Thus, there is no possibility of the purchaser knowing what is meant unless he be acquainted with trade language. By the rules of this secret language erith means "three" enty means "ten," and eno means "one." So the leader by his song meant to hint to his fellow-traders that they were ten men, the robbers only three, that if three pounced upon each of the robbers, nine of them could hold them down, while the remaining one bound the robbers' hands and feet.

The three thieves, glorying in their victory, and little understanding the meaning of the song and the intentions of the dancers, were proudly seated chewing betel and tobacco. Meanwhile the song was sung a third time. *Tâ tai tôm* had left the lips of the singer; and, before *tadingana* was out of them, the traders separated into parties of three, and each party pounced upon a thief. The remaining one—

the leader himself—tore up into long narrow strips a large piece of cloth, six cubits long, and tied the hands and feet of the robbers. These were entirely humbled now, and rolled on the ground like three bags of rice!

The ten traders now took back all their property, and armed themselves with the swords and cudgels of their enemies; and when they reached their village, they often amused their friends and relatives by relating their adventure.

Raja Rasalu

ONCE there lived a great Raja, whose name was Salabhan, and he had a Queen, by name Lona, who, though she wept and prayed at many a shrine, had never a child to gladden her eyes. After a long time, however, a son was promised to her.

Queen Lona returned to the palace, and when the time for the birth of the promised son drew nigh, she inquired of three Jogis who came begging to her gate, what the child's fate would be, and the youngest of them answered and said, "Oh, Queen! the child will be a boy, and he will live to be a great man. But for twelve years you must not look upon his face, for if either you or his father see it before the twelve years are past, you will surely die! This is what you must do; as soon as the child is born you must send him away to a cellar underneath the ground, and never let him see the light of day for twelve years. After they are over, he may come forth, bathe in the river, put on new clothes, and visit you. His name shall be Raja Rasalu, and he shall be known far and wide."

So, when a fair young Prince was in due time born into

the world, his parents hid him away in an underground palace, with nurses, and servants, and everything else a King's son might desire. And with him they sent a young colt, born the same day, and sword, spear, and shield, against the day when Raja Rasalu should go forth into the world.

So there the child lived, playing with his colt, and talking to his parrot, while the nurses taught him all things needful for a King's son to know.

Young Rasalu lived on; far from the light of day, for eleven long years, growing tall and strong, yet contented to remain playing with his colt, and talking to his parrot; but when the twelfth year began, the lad's heart leapt up with desire for change, and he loved to listen to the sounds of life which came to him in his palace-prison from the outside world.

"I must go and see where the voices come from!" he said; and when his nurses told him he must not go for one year more, he only laughed aloud, saying, "Nay! I stay no longer here for any man!"

Then he saddled his Arab horse Bhaunr, put on his shining armour, and rode forth into the world; but, mindful of what his nurses had oft told him, when he came to the river, he dismounted, and, going into the water, washed himself and his clothes.

Then, clean of raiment, fair of face, and brave of heart, he rode on his way until he reached his father's city. There he sat down to rest awhile by a well, where the women were drawing water in earthen pitchers. Now, as they passed him, their full pitchers poised upon their heads, the gay young prince flung stones at the earthen vessels, and broke them all. Then the women, drenched with water, went weeping and wailing to the palace, complaining to the King that a mighty young Prince in shining armour, with a parrot on his wrist and a gallant steed beside him, sat by the well, and broke their pitchers.

Now, as soon as Raja Salabhan heard this, he guessed at once that it was Prince Rasalu come forth before the time, and, mindful of the Jogis' words that he would die if he looked on his son's face before twelve years were past, he did not dare to send his guards to seize the offender and bring him to be judged. So he bade the women be comforted, and take pitchers of iron and brass, giving new ones from the treasury to those who did not possess any of their own.

But when Prince Rasalu saw the women returning to the well with pitchers of iron and brass, he laughed to himself, and drew his mighty bow till the sharp-pointed arrows pierced the metal vessels as though they had been clay.

Yet still the King did not send for him, so he mounted his steed and set off in the pride of his youth and strength to the palace. He strode into the audience hall, where his father sat trembling, and saluted him with all reverence; but Raja Salabhan, in fear of his life, turned his back hastily and said never a word in reply.

Then Prince Rasalu called scornfully to him across the hall:

"I came to greet thee, King, and not to harm thee!
  What have I done that thou shouldst turn away?
Sceptre and empire have no power to charm me—
  I go to seek a worthier prize than they!"

Then he strode away, full of bitterness and anger; but

as he passed under the palace windows, he heard his mother weeping, and the sound softened his heart, so that his wrath died down, and a great loneliness fell upon him, because he was spurned by both father and mother. So he cried sorrowfully,

"“Oh heart crown'd with grief, hast thou nought
But tears for thy son?
Art mother of mine? Give one thought
To my life just begun!”

And Queen Lona answered through her tears:

“Yea! mother am I, though I weep,
So hold this word sure,—
Go, reign king of all men, but keep
Thy heart good and pure!”

So Raja Rasalu was comforted, and began to make ready for fortune. He took with him his horse Bhaunr and his parrot, both of whom had lived with him since he was born.

So they made a goodly company, and Queen Lona, when she saw them going, watched them from her window till she saw nothing but a cloud of dust on the horizon; then she bowed her head on her hands and wept, saying:

“Oh! son who ne'er gladdened mine eyes,
Let the cloud of thy going arise,
Dim the sunlight and darken the day;
For the mother whose son is away
Is as dust!”

Rasalu had started off to play chaupur with King Sarkap. And as he journeyed there came a fierce storm of thunder and lightning, so that he sought shelter, and found none save an old graveyard, where a headless corpse lay upon the ground. So lonesome was it that even the corpse seemed company, and Rasalu, sitting down beside it, said:

"There is no one here, nor far nor near,
Save this breathless corpse so cold and grim;
Would God he might come to life again,
'Twould be less lonely to talk to him."

And immediately the headless corpse arose and sat beside Raja Rasalu. And he, nothing astonished, said to it:

"The storm beats fierce and loud,
The clouds rise thick in the west;
What ails thy grave and shroud,
Oh corpse! that thou canst not rest?"

Then the headless corpse replied:

"On earth I was even as thou,
My turban awry like a king,
My head with the highest, I trow,
Having my fun and my fling,
Fighting my foes like a brave,
Living my life with a swing.
And, now I am dead,
Sins, heavy as lead,
Will give me no rest in my grave!"

So the night passed on, dark and dreary, while Rasalu sat in the graveyard and talked to the headless corpse. Now when morning broke and Rasalu said he must continue his journey, the headless corpse asked him whither he was going, and when he said "to play chaupur with King Sarkap," the corpse begged him to give up the idea saying, "I am King Sarkap's brother, and I know his ways. Every day, before breakfast, he cuts off the heads of two or three men just to amuse himself. One day no one else was at hand, so he cut off mine, and he will surely cut off yours on some pretence or another. However, if you are determined to go and play chaupur with him, take some of the bones from this graveyard, and make your dice out of them, and then the enchanted dice with which my brother plays will lose their virtue. Otherwise he will always win."

So Rasalu took some of the bones lying about, and fashioned them into dice, and these he put into his pocket. Then, bidding adieu to the headless corpse, he went on his way to play chaupur with the King.

Now, as Raja Rasalu, tender-hearted and strong, journeyed along to play chaupur with the King, he came to a burning forest, and a voice rose from the fire saying, "Oh, traveller! for God's sake save me from the fire!"

Then the Prince turned towards the burning forest, and, lo! the voice was the voice of a tiny cricket. Nevertheless, Rasalu, tender-hearted and strong, snatched it from the fire and set it at liberty. Then the little creature, full of gratitude, pulled out one of its feelers, and giving it to its preserver, said, "Keep this, and should you ever be in trouble, put it into the fire, and instantly I will come to your aid."

The Prince smiled, saying, "What help could *you* give *me?*" Nevertheless, he kept the hair and went on his way.

Now, when he reached the city of King Sarkap, seventy maidens, daughters of the King, came out to meet him—seventy fair maidens, merry and careless, full of smiles and laughter; but one, the youngest of them all, when she saw the gallant young Prince riding on Bhaunr Iraqi, going gaily to his doom, was filled with pity, and called to him saying:

"Fair Prince, on the charger so gray,
Turn thee back! turn thee back!
Or lower thy lance for the fray;
Thy head will be forfeit to-day!
Dost love life? then, stranger, I pray,
Turn thee back! turn thee back!"

But he, smiling at the maiden, answered lightly:

"Fair maiden, I come from afar
Sworn conqueror in love and in war!
King Sarkap my coming will rue,
His head in four pieces I'll hew;
Then forth as a bridegroom I'll ride,
With you, little maid, as my bride!"

Now when Rasalu replied so gallantly, the maiden looked in his face, and seeing how fair he was, and how brave and strong, she straightway fell in love with him, and would gladly have followed him through the world.

But the other sixty-nine maidens, being jealous, laughed scornfully at her, saying, "Not so fast, oh gallant warrior! If you would marry our sister you must first do our bidding, for you will be our younger brother."

"Fair sisters!" quoth Rasalu gaily, "give me my task and I will perform it."

So the sixty-nine maidens mixed a hundredweight of millet seed with a hundredweight of sand, and giving it to Rasalu, bade him separate the seed from the sand.

Then he bethought him of the cricket, and drawing the feeler from his pocket, thrust it into the fire. And immediately there was a whirring noise in the air, and a great flight of crickets alighted beside him, and amongst them the cricket whose life he had saved.

Then Rasalu said, "Separate the millet seed from the sand."

"Is that all?" quoth the cricket; "had I known how small a job you wanted me to do, I would not have assembled so many of my brethren."

With that the flight of crickets set to work, and in one night they separated the seed from the sand.

Now when the sixty-nine fair maidens, daughters of the king, saw that Rasalu had performed his task, they set him another, bidding him swing them all, one by one, in their swings, until they were tired.

Whereupon he laughed, saying, "There are seventy of you, counting my little bride yonder, and I am not going to spend my life swinging girls! Why, by the time I have given each of you a swing, the first will be wanting another! No! if you want a swing, get in, all seventy of you, into one swing, and then I'll see what can be done."

So the seventy maidens climbed into one swing, and Raja Rasalu, standing in his shining armour, fastened the ropes to his mighty bow, and drew it up to its fullest bent. Then he let go, and like an arrow the swing shot into the air, with its burden of seventy fair maidens, merry and careless, full of smiles and laughter.

But as it swung back again, Rasalu, standing there in his shining armour, drew his sharp sword and severed the ropes. Then the seventy fair maidens fell to the ground headlong; and some were bruised and some broken, but the only one who escaped unhurt was the maiden who loved Rasalu for she fell out last, on the top of the others, and so came to no harm.

After this, Rasalu strode on fifteen paces, till he came to the seventy drums, that every one who came to play chaupur with the King had to beat in turn; and he beat them so loudly that he broke them all. Then he came to the seventy gongs, all in a row, and he hammered them so hard that they cracked to pieces.

Seeing this, the youngest Princess, who was the only one who could run, fled to her father the King in a great fright, saying:

"A mighty Prince, Sarkap! making havoc, rides along,
He swung us, seventy maidens fair, and threw us out headlong;
He broke the drums you placed there and the gongs too in his pride,
Sure, he will kill thee, father mine, and take me for his bride!"

But King Sarkap replied scornfully:

"Silly maiden, thy words make a lot
Of a very small matter;
For fear of my valour, I wot,
His armour will clatter.
As soon as I've eaten my bread
I'll go forth and cut off his head!"

Notwithstanding these brave and boastful words, he was in reality very much afraid, having heard of Rasalu's renown. And learning that he was stopping at the house of an old woman in the city, till the hour for playing chaupur arrived, Sarkap sent slaves to him with trays of sweetmeats and fruit, as to an honoured guest. But the food was poisoned.

Now when the slaves brought the trays to Raja Rasalu, he rose up haughtily, saying, "Go, tell your master I have nought to do with him in friendship. I am his sworn enemy, and I eat not of his salt!"

So saying, he threw the sweetmeats to Raja Sarkap's dog, which had followed the slave, and lo! the dog died.

Then Rasalu was very wroth, and said bitterly, "Go back to Sarkap, slaves! and tell him that Rasalu deems it no act of bravery to kill even an enemy by treachery."

Now, when evening came, Raja Rasalu went forth to play chaupur with King Sarkap, and as he passed some potters' kilns he saw a cat wandering about restlessly; so he asked what ailed her, that she never stood still, and she replied, "My kittens are in an unbaked pot in the kiln yonder. It has just been set alight, and my children will be baked alive; therefore I cannot rest!"

Her words moved the heart of Raja Rasalu, and, going to the potter, he asked him to sell the kiln as it was; but the potter replied that he could not settle a fair price till the pots were burnt, as he could not tell how many would come out whole. Nevertheless, after some bargaining, he consented at last to sell the kiln, and Rasalu, having searched all the pots, restored the kittens to their mother, and she, in gratitude for his mercy, gave him one of them, saying, "Put it in your pocket, for it will help you when you are in difficulties." So Raja Rasalu put the kitten in his pocket, and went to play chaupur with the King.

Now, before they sat down to play, Raja Sarkap fixed his stakes,—on the first game, his kingdom; on the second, the wealth of the whole world; and, on the third, his own head. So, likewise, Raja Rasalu fixed his stakes,—on the first game, his arms; on the second, his horse; and, on the third, his own head.

Then they began to play, and it fell to Rasalu's lot to make the first move. Now he, forgetful of the dead man's warning, played with the dice given him by Raja Sarkap, besides which, Sarkap let loose his famous rat, Dhol Raja, and it ran about the board, upsetting the chaupur pieces on the sly, so that Rasalu lost the first game, and gave up his shining armour.

Then the second game began, and once more Dhol Raja, the rat, upset the pieces; and Rasalu, losing the game, gave up his faithful steed. Then Bhaunr, the Arab steed, who stood by, found voice, and cried to his master,

"Sea-born am I, bought with much gold;
Dear Prince! trust me now as of old.
I'll carry you far from these wiles—
My flight, all unspurr'd, will be swift as a bird,
For thousands and thousands of miles!
Or if needs you must stay; ere the next game you play,
Place hand in your pocket, I pray!"

Hearing this, Raja Sarkap frowned, and bade his slaves remove Bhaunr, the Arab steed, since he gave his master advice in the game. Now, when the slaves came to lead the faithful steed away, Rasalu could not refrain from tears,

Raja Rasalu plays chaupur with Raja Sarkap.

thinking over the long years during which Bhaunr, the Arab steed, had been his companion. But the horse cried out agian,

"Weep not, dear Prince! I shall not eat my bread
Of stranger hands, nor to strange stall be led.
Take thy right hand, and place it as I said."

These words roused some recollection in Rasalu's mind, and when, just at this moment, the kitten in his pocket began to struggle, he remembered all about the warning, and the dice made from dead men's bones. Then his heart rose up once more, and he called boldly to Raja Sarkap, "Leave my horse and arms here for the present. Time enough to take them away when you have won my head!"

Now, Raja Sarkap, seeing Rasalu's confident bearing, began to be afraid, and ordered all the women of his palace to come forth in their gayest attire and stand before Rasalu, so as to distract his attention from the game. But he never even looked at them, and drawing the dice from his pocket, said to Sarkap, "We have played with your dice all this time; now we will play with mine."

Then the kitten went and sat at the window through which the rat Dhol Raja used to come, and the game began.

After a while, Sarkap, seeing Raja Rasalu was winning, called to his rat, but when Dhol Raja saw the kitten he was afraid, and would not go further. So Rasalu won, and took back his arms. Next he played for his horse, and once more Raja Sarkap called for his rat; but Dhol Raja, seeing the kitten keeping watch, was afraid. So Rasalu won the second stake, and took back Bhaunr, the Arab steed.

Then Sarkap brought all his skill to bear on the third and last game, saying,

"Oh moulded pieces! favour me to-day!
For sooth this is a man with whom I play.
No paltry risk—but life and death at stake;
As Sarkap does, so do, for Sarkap's sake!"

But Rasalu answered back,

"Oh moulded pieces! favour me to-day!
For sooth it is a man with whom I play.
No paltry risk—but life and death at stake;
As Heaven does, so do, for Heaven's sake!"

So they began to play, whilst the women stood round in a circle, and the kitten watched Dhol Raja from the window. Then Sarkap lost, first his kingdom, then the wealth of the whole world, and lastly his head.

Just then, a servant came in to announce the birth of a daughter to Raja Sarkap, and he, overcome by misfortunes, said, "Kill her at once! for she has been born in an evil moment, and has brought her father ill luck!"

But Rasalu rose up in his shining armour, tender-hearted and strong, saying, "Not so, oh king! She has done no evil. Give me this child to wife; and if you will vow, by all you hold sacred, never again to play chaupur for another's head, I will spare yours now!"

Then Sarkap vowed a solemn vow never to play for another's head; and after that he took a fresh mango branch, and the new-born babe, and placing them on a golden dish gave them to Rasalu.

Now, as he left the palace, carrying with him the new-born babe and the mango branch, he met a band of prisoners, and they called out to him,

> "A royal hawk art thou, oh King. the rest
> But timid wild-fowl. Grant us our request,—
> Unloose these chains, and live for ever blest!"

And Raja Rasalu hearkened to them, and bade King Sarkap set them at liberty.

Then he went to the Murti Hills, and placed the new-born babe, Kokilan, in an underground palace, and planted the mango branch at the door, saying, "In twelve years the mango tree will blossom; then will I return and marry Kokilan."

And after twelve years, the mango tree began to flower, and Raja Rasalu married the Princess Kokilan, whom he won from Sarkap when he played chaupur with the King.

The Ass in the Lion's Skin

AT the same time, when Brahma-datta was reigning in Benares, the future Buddha was born one of a peasant family; and when he grew up, he gained his living by tilling the ground.

At that time a hawker used to go from place to place, trafficking in goods carried by an ass. Now at each place he came to, when he took the pack down from the ass's back, he used to clothe him in a lion's skin, and turn him loose in the rice and barley fields. And when the watchmen in the fields saw the ass, they dared not go near him, taking him for a lion.

So one day the hawker stopped in a village; and whilst he was getting his own breakfast cooked, he dressed the ass in a lion's skin, and turned him loose in a barley-field. The watchmen in the field dared not go up to him; but going home, they published the news. Then all the villagers came out with weapons in their hands; and blowing chanks, and beating drums, they went near the field and shouted. Terrified with the fear of death, the ass uttered a cry—the bray of an ass!

And when he knew him then to be an ass, the future Buddha pronounced the First Verse:

> "This is not a lion's roaring,
> Nor a tiger's, nor a panther's;
> Dressed in a lion's skin,
> 'Tis a wretched ass that roars!"

But when the villagers knew the creature to be an ass, they beat him till his bones broke; and, carrying off the lion's skin, went away. Then the hawker came; and seeing the ass fallen into so bad a plight, pronounced the Second Verse:

> "Long might the ass,
> Clad in a lion's skin,
> Have fed on the barley green.
> But he brayed!
> And that moment he came to ruin."

And even whilst he was yet speaking the ass died on the spot!

The Farmer and the Money-lender

THERE was once a farmer who suffered much at the hands of a money-lender. Good harvests, or bad, the farmer was always poor, the money-lender rich. At the last, when he hadn't a farthing left, the farmer went to the money-lender's house, and said, "You can't squeeze water from a stone, and as you have nothing to get by me now, you might tell me the secret of becoming rich."

"My friend," returned the money-lender, piously, "riches come from Ram—ask *him*."

"Thank you, I will!" replied the simple farmer; so he prepared three girdle-cakes to last him on the journey, and set out to find Ram.

First he met a Brahman, and to him he gave a cake asking him to point out the road to Ram; but the Brahman only took the cake and went on his way without a word. Next the farmer met a Jogi or devotee, and to him he gave a cake, without receiving any help in return. At last, he came upon a poor man sitting under a tree, and finding out he was hungry, the kindly farmer gave him his last cake, and sitting down to rest beside him, entered into conversation.

"And where are you going?" asked the poor man, at length.

"Oh, I have a long journey before me, for I am going to find Ram!" replied the farmer. "I don't suppose you could tell me which way to go?"

"Perhaps I can," said the poor man, smiling, "for *I* am Ram! What do you want of me?"

Then the farmer told the whole story, and Ram, taking pity on him, gave him a conch shell, and showed him how to blow it in a particular way, saying, "Remember! whatever you wish for, you have only to blow the conch that way, and your wish will be fulfilled. Only have a care of that money-lender, for even magic is not proof against their wiles!"

The farmer went back to his village rejoicing. In fact the money-lender noticed his high spirits at once, and said to himself, "Some good fortune must have befallen the stupid fellow, to make him hold his head so jauntily." Therefore he went over to the simple farmer's house, and congratulated him on his good fortune, in such cunning words, pretending to have heard all about it, that before long the farmer found himself telling the whole story—all except the secret of blowing the conch, for, with all his simplicity, the farmer was not quite such a fool as to tell that.

Nevertheless, the money-lender determined to have the conch by hook or by crook, and as he was villain enough not to stick at trifles, he waited for a favourable opportunity and stole the conch.

But, after nearly bursting himself with blowing the conch in every conceivable way, he was obliged to give up the secret as a bad job. However, being determined to succeed he went back to the farmer, and said, coolly, "Look here; I've got your conch, but I can't use it; you haven't got it, so it's clear you can't use it either. Business is at a stand still unless we make a bargain. Now, I promise to give you back your conch, and never to interfere with your using it, on one condition, which is this,—whatever you get from it, I am to get double."

"Never!" cried the farmer; "that would be the old business all over again!"

"Not at all!" replied the wily money-lender; "you will have your share! Now, don't be a dog in the manger, for if *you* get all you want, what can it matter to you if *I* am rich or poor?"

At last, though it went sorely against the grain to be of any benefit to a money-lender, the farmer was forced to yield, and from that time, no matter what he gained by the power of the conch, the money-lender gained double. And the knowledge that this was so preyed upon the farmer's mind day and night, so that he had no satisfaction out of anything.

At last, there came a very dry season,—so dry that the farmer's crops withered for want of rain. Then he blew his conch, and wished for a well to water them, and lo! there was the well, *but the money-lender had two!*—two beautiful new wells! This was too much for any farmer to stand; and our friend brooded over it, and brooded over it, till at last a bright idea came into his head. He seized the conch, blew it loudly, and cried out, "Oh, Ram! I wish to be blind of one eye!" And so he was, in a twinkling, but the money-lender of course was blind of both, and in trying to steer his way between the two new wells, he fell into one, and was drowned.

Now this true story shows that a farmer once got the better of a money-lender—but only by losing one of his eyes.

The Boy who had a Moon on his Forehead and a Star on his Chin

In a country were seven daughters of poor parents, who used to come daily to play under the shady trees in the King's garden with the gardener's daughter; and daily she used to say to them, "When I am married I shall have a son. Such a beautiful boy as he will be has never been seen. He will have a moon on his forehead and a star on his chin." Then her playfellows used to laugh at her and mock her.

But one day the King heard her telling them about the beautiful boy she would have when she was married, and he said to himself he should like very much to have such a son; the more so that though he had already four Queens he had no child. He went, therefore, to the gardener and told him he wished to marry his daughter. This delighted the gardener and his wife, who thought it would indeed be grand for their daughter to become a princess. So they said "Yes" to the King, and invited all their friends to the wedding. The

King invited all his, and he gave the gardener as much money as he wanted. Then the wedding was held with great feasting and rejoicing.

A year later the day drew near on which the gardener's daughter was to have her son; and the King's four other Queens came constantly to see her. One day they said to her, "The King hunts every day; and the time is soon coming when you will have your child. Suppose you fell ill whilst he was out hunting and could therefore know nothing of your illness, what would you do then?"

When the King came home that evening, the gardener's daughter said to him, "Every day you go out hunting. Should I ever be in trouble or sick while you are away, how could I send for you?" The King gave her a kettle-drum which he placed near the door for her, and he said to her, "Whenever you want me, beat this kettle-drum. No matter how far away I may be, I shall hear it, and will come at once to you."

Next morning when the King had gone out to hunt, his four other Queens came to see the gardener's daughter. She told them all about her kettle-drum. "Oh," they said, "do drum on it just to see if the King really will come to you."

"No, I will not," she said; "for why should I call him from his hunting when I do not want him?"

"Don't mind interrupting his hunting," they answered. "Do try if he really will come to you when you beat your kettle-drum." So at last, just to please them, she beat it, and the King stood before her.

"Why have you called me?" he said. "See, I have left my hunting to come to you."

"I want nothing," she answered; "I only wished to

know if you really would come to me when I beat my drum."

"Very well," answered the King; "but do not call me again unless you really need me." Then he returned to his hunting.

The next day, when the King had gone out hunting as usual, the four Queens again came to see the gardener's daughter. They begged and begged her to beat her drum once more, "just to see if the King will really come to see you this time." At first she refused, but at last she consented. So she beat her drum, and the King came to her. But when he found she was neither ill nor in trouble, he was angry, and said to her, "Twice I have left my hunting and lost my game to come to you when you did not need me. Now you may call me as much as you like, but I will not come to you," and then he went away in a rage.

The third day the gardener's daughter fell ill, and she beat and beat her kettle-drum; but the King never came. He heard her kettle-drum, but he thought, "She does not really want me; she is only trying to see if I will go to her."

Meanwhile the four other Queens came to her, and they said, "Here it is the custom before a child is born to bind its mother's eyes with a handkerchief that she may not see it just at first. So let us bind your eyes." She answered, "Very well, bind my eyes." The four wives then tied a handkerchief over them.

Soon after, the gardener's daughter had a beautiful little son, with a moon on his forehead and a star on his chin, and before the poor mother had seen him, the four wicked Queens took the boy to the nurse and said to her, "Now you must not let this child make the least sound for fear his mother should hear him ; and in the night you must either kill him, or else take him away, so that his mother may never see him. If you obey our orders, we will give you a great many rupees." All this they did out of spite. The nurse took the little child and put him into a box, and the four Queens went back to the gardener's daughter.

First they put a stone into her boy's little bed, and then they took the handkerchief off her eyes and showed it her, saying, "Look! this is your son!" The poor girl cried bitterly, and thought, "What will the King say when he finds no child?" But she could do nothing.

When the King came home, he was furious at hearing his youngest wife, the gardener's daughter, had given him a stone instead of the beautiful little son she had promised him. He made her one of the palace servants, and never spoke to her.

In the middle of the night the nurse took the box in which was the beautiful little prince, and went out to a broad plain in the jungle. There she dug a hole, made the fastenings of the box sure, and put the box into the hole, although the child in it was still alive. The King's dog, whose name was Shankar, had followed her to see what she did with the box. As soon as she had gone back to the four Queens (who gave her a great many rupees), the dog went to the hole in which she had put the box, took the box out, and opened it. When he saw the beautiful little boy, he was very much delighted and said, "If it pleases Khuda that this child should live, I will not hurt him; I will not eat him, but I will swallow him whole and hide him in my stomach." This he did.

After six months had passed, the dog went by night to the

jungle, and thought, " I wonder whether the boy is alive or dead." Then he brought the child out of his stomach and rejoiced over his beauty. The boy was now six months old. When Shankar had caressed and loved him, he swallowed him again for another six months. At the end of that time he went once more by night to the broad jungle-plain. There he brought up the child out of his stomach (the child was now a year old), and caressed and petted him a great deal, and was made very happy by his great beauty.

But this time the dog's keeper had followed and watched the dog; and he saw all that Shankar did, and the beautiful little child, so he ran to the four Queens and said to them, " Inside the King's dog there is a child! the loveliest child! He has a moon on his forehead and a star on his chin. Such a child has never been seen!" At this the four wives were very much frightened, and as soon as the King came home from hunting they said to him, " While you were away your dog came to our rooms, and tore our clothes and knocked about all our things. We are afraid he will kill us." " Do not be afraid," said the King. Eat your dinner and be happy. I will have the dog shot to-morrow morning."

Then he ordered his servants to shoot the dog at dawn, but the dog heard him, and said to himself, " What shall I do? The King intends to kill me. I don't care about that, but what will become of the child if I am killed? He will die. But I will see if I cannot save him."

So when it was night, the dog ran to the King's cow, who was called Suri, and said to her, " Suri, I want to give you something, for the King has ordered me to be shot to-morrow. Will you take great care of whatever I give you?"

" Let me see what it is," said Suri, " I will take care of it if

I can." Then they both went together to the wide plain, and there the dog brought up the boy. Suri was enchanted with him. "I never saw such a beautiful child in this country," she said. "See, he has a moon on his forehead and a star on his chin. I will take the greatest care of him." So saying she swallowed the little prince. The dog made her a great many salaams, and said, "To-morrow I shall die;" and the cow then went back to her stable.

Next morning at dawn the dog was taken to the jungle and shot.

The child now lived in Suri's stomach; and when one whole year had passed, and he was two years old, the cow went out to the plain, and said to herself, "I do not know whether the child is alive or dead. But I have never hurt it, so I will see." Then she brought up the boy; and he played about, and Suri was delighted; she loved him and caressed him, and talked to him. Then she swallowed him, and returned to her stable.

At the end of another year she went again to the plain and brought up the child. He played and ran about for an hour to her great delight, and she talked to him and caressed him. His great beauty made her very happy. Then she swallowed him once more and returned to her stable. The child was now three years old.

But this time the cowherd had followed Suri, and had seen the wonderful child and all she did to it. So he ran and told the four Queens, "The King's cow has a beautiful boy inside her. He has a moon on his forehead and a star on his chin. Such a child has never been seen before!"

At this the Queens were terrified. They tore their clothes and their hair and cried. When the King came home at evening, he asked them why they were so agitated. "Oh," they said, "your cow came and tried to kill us; but we ran away. She tore our hair and our clothes." "Never mind," said the King. "Eat your dinner and be happy. The cow shall be killed to-morrow morning."

Now Suri heard the King give this order to the servants, so she said to herself, "What shall I do to save the child?" When it was midnight, she went to the King's horse called Katar, who was very wicked, and quite untamable. No one had ever been able to ride him; indeed no one could go near him with safety, he was so savage. Suri said to this horse, "Katar, will you take care of something that I want to give you, because the King has ordered me to be killed to-morrow?"

"Good," said Katar; "show me what it is." Then Suri brought up the child, and the horse was delighted with him. "Yes," he said, "I will take the greatest care of him. Till now no one has been able to ride me, but this child shall ride me." Then he swallowed the boy, and when he had done so, the cow made him many salaams, saying, "It is for this boy's sake that I am to die." The next morning she was taken to the jungle and there killed.

The beautiful boy now lived in the horse's stomach, and he stayed in it for one whole year. At the end of that time the horse thought, "I will see if this child is alive or dead." So he brought him up; and then he loved him, and petted him, and the little prince played all about the stable, out of which the horse was never allowed to go. Katar was very glad to see the child, who was now four years old. After he had played for some time, the horse swallowed him again. At the end of another year, when the boy was five years old.

Katar brought him up again, caressed him, loved him, and let him play about the stable as he had done a year before. Then the horse swallowed him again.

But this time the groom had seen all that happened, and when it was morning, and the King had gone away to his hunting, he went to the four wicked Queens, and told them all he had seen, and all about the wonderful, beautiful child that lived inside the King's horse Katar. On hearing the groom's story the four Queens cried, and tore their hair and clothes, and refused to eat. When the King returned at evening and asked them why they were so miserable, they said, "Your horse Katar came and tore our clothes, and upset all our things, and we ran away for fear he should kill us."

"Never mind," said the King. "Only eat your dinner and be happy. I will have Katar shot to-morrow." Then he thought that two men unaided could not kill such a wicked horse, so he ordered his servants to bid his troop of sepoys shoot him.

So the next day the King placed his sepoys all round the stable, and he took up his stand with them; and he said he would himself shoot any one who let his horse escape.

Meanwhile the horse had overheard all these orders. So he brought up the child and said to him, "Go into that little room that leads out of the stable, and you will find in it a saddle and bridle which you must put on me. Then you will find in the room some beautiful clothes such as princes wear; these must you put on yourself; and you must take the sword and gun you will find there too. Then you must mount on my back." Now Katar was a fairy-horse, and came from the fairies' country, so he could get anything he wanted; but neither the King nor any of his people knew this. When all was ready, Katar burst out of his stable, with the prince on his back, rushed past the King himself before the King had time to shoot him, galloped away to the great jungle-plain, and galloped about all over it. The King saw his horse had a boy on his back, though he could not see the boy distinctly. The sepoys tried in vain to shoot the horse; he

galloped much too fast; and at last they were all scattered over the plain. Then the King had to give it up and go home; and the sepoys went to their homes. The King could not shoot any of his sepoys for letting his horse escape, for he himself had let him do so.

Then Katar galloped away, on, and on, and on; and when night came they stayed under a tree, he and the King's son. The horse ate grass, and the boy wild fruits which he found in the jungle. Next morning they started afresh, and went far, and far, till they came to a jungle in another country, which did not belong to the little prince's father, but to another king. Here Katar said to the boy, " Now get off my back." Off jumped the prince. " Unsaddle me and take off my bridle ; take off your beautiful clothes and tie them all up in a bundle with your sword and gun." This the boy did. Then the horse gave him some poor, common clothes, which he told him to put on. As soon as he was dressed in them the horse said, " Hide your bundle in this grass, and I will take care of it for you. I will always stay in this jungle-plain, so that when you want me you will always find me. You must now go away and find service with some one in this country."

This made the boy very sad. I know nothing about anything," he said. " What shall I do all alone in this country ? "

" Do not be afraid," answered Katar. " You will find service, and I will always stay here to help you when you want me. So go, only before you go, twist my right ear." The boy did so, and his horse instantly became a donkey. " Now twist your right ear," said Katar. And when the boy had twisted it, he was no longer a handsome prince, but a poor, common-looking, ugly man ; and his moon and star were hidden.

Then he went away further into the country, until he came to a grain merchant of the country, who asked him who he was. " I am a poor man," answered the boy, " and I want service." " Good," said the grain merchant, " you shall be my servant."

Now the grain merchant lived near the King's palace, and

one night at twelve o'clock the boy was very hot; so he went out into the King's cool garden, and began to sing a lovely song. The seventh and youngest daughter of the King heard him, and she wondered who it was who could sing so deliciously. Then she put on her clothes, rolled up her hair, and came down to where the seemingly poor common man was lying singing. "Who are you? where do you come from?" she asked.

But he answered nothing.

"Who is this man who does not answer when I speak to him?" thought the little princess, and she went away. On the second night the same thing happened, and on the third night too. But on the third night, when she found she could not make him answer her, she said to him, "What a strange man you are not to answer me when I speak to you." But still he remained silent, so she went away.

The next day, when he had finished his work, the young prince went to the jungle to see his horse, who asked him, "Are you quite well and happy?" "Yes, I am," answered the boy. "I am servant to a grain merchant. The last three nights I have gone into the King's garden and sung a song, and each night the youngest princess has come to me and asked me who I am, and whence I came, and I have answered nothing. What shall I do now?" The horse said, "Next time she asks you who you are, tell her you are a very poor man, and came from your own country to find service here."

The boy then went home to the grain merchant, and at night, when every one had gone to bed, he went to the King's garden and sang his sweet song again. The youngest princess heard him, got up, dressed, and came to him. "Who are you? Whence do you come?" she asked.

THE BOY WITH THE MOON ON HIS FOREHEAD

"I am a very poor man," he answered. "I came from my own country to seek service here, and I am now one of the grain merchant's servants." Then she went away. For three more nights the boy sang in the King's garden, and each night the princess came and asked him the same questions as before, and the boy gave her the same answers.

Then she went to her father, and said to him, "Father, I wish to be married; but I must choose my husband myself." Her father consented to this, and he wrote and invited all the Kings and Rajas in the land, saying, "My youngest daughter wishes to be married, but she insists on choosing her husband herself. As I do not know who it is she wishes to marry, I beg you will all come on a certain day, for her to see you and make her choice."

A great many Kings, Rajas, and their sons accepted this invitation and came. When they had all arrived, the little princess's father said to them, "To-morrow morning you must all sit together in my garden" (the King's garden was very large), "for then my youngest daughter will come and see you all, and choose her husband. I do not know whom she will choose."

The youngest princess ordered a grand elephant to be ready for her the next morning, and when the morning came, and all was ready, she dressed herself in the most lovely clothes, and put on her beautiful jewels; then she mounted her elephant, which was painted blue. In her hand she took a gold necklace.

Then she went into the garden where the Kings, Rajas, and their sons were seated. The boy, the grain merchant's servant, was also in the garden: not as a suitor, but looking on with the other servants.

The princess rode all round the garden, and looked at all the Kings and Rajas and princes, and then she hung the gold necklace round the neck of the boy, the grain merchant's servant. At this everybody laughed, and the Kings were greatly astonished. But then they and the Rajas said, "What fooling is this?" and they pushed the pretended poor man away, and took the necklace off his neck, and said to him, "Get out of the way, you poor, dirty man. Your clothes are far too dirty for you to come near us!" The boy went far away from them, and stood a long way off to see what would happen.

Then the King's youngest daughter went all round the garden again, holding her gold necklace in her hand, and once more she hung it round the boy's neck. Every one laughed at her and said, "How can the King's daughter think of marrying this poor, common man!" and the Kings and the Rajas, who had come as suitors, all wanted to turn him out of the garden. But the princess said, "Take care! take care! You must not turn him out. Leave him alone." Then she put him on her elephant, and took him to the palace.

The Kings and Rajas and their sons were very much astonished, and said, "What does this mean? The princess does not care to marry one of us, but chooses that very poor man!" Her father then stood up, and said to them all, "I promised my daughter she should marry any one she pleased, and as she has twice chosen that poor, common man, she shall marry him." And so the princess and the boy were married with great pomp and splendour: her father and mother were quite content with her choice; and the Kings, the Rajas and their sons, all returned to their homes.

Now the princess's six sisters had all married rich princes, and they laughed at her for choosing such a poor ugly husband as hers seemed to be, and said to each other, mockingly, "See! our sister has married this poor, common man!" Their six husbands used to go out hunting every day, and every evening they brought home quantities of all kinds of game to their wives, and the game was cooked for their dinner and for the King's; but the husband of the youngest princess always stayed at home in the palace, and never went out hunting at all. This made her very sad, and she said to herself, "My sisters' husbands hunt every day, but my husband never hunts at all."

At last she said to him, "Why do you never go out hunting as my sisters' husbands do every day, and every day they bring home quantities of all kinds of game? Why do you always stay at home, instead of doing as they do?"

One day he said to her, "I am going out to-day to eat the air."

"Very good," she answered; "go, and take one of the horses."

"No," said the young prince, "I will not ride, I will walk." Then he went to the jungle-plain where he had left Katar, who all this time had seemed to be a donkey, and he told Katar everything. "Listen," he said; "I have married the youngest princess; and when we were married everybody laughed at her for choosing me, and said, 'What a very poor, common man our princess has chosen for her husband!' Besides, my wife is very sad, for her six sisters' husbands all hunt every day, and bring home quantities of game, and their wives therefore are very proud of them. But I stay at home all day, and never hunt. To-day I should like to hunt very much."

"Well," said Katar, "then twist my left ear;" and as soon as the boy had twisted it, Katar was a horse again, and not a donkey any longer. "Now," said Katar, "twist your left ear, and you will see what a beautiful young prince you will become." So the boy twisted his own left ear, and there he stood no longer a poor, common, ugly man, but a grand young prince with a moon on his forehead and a star on his chin. Then he put on his splendid clothes, saddled and bridled Katar, got on his back with his sword and gun, and rode off to hunt.

He rode very far, and shot a great many birds and a quantity of deer. That day his six brothers-in-law could find no game, for the beautiful young prince had shot it all. Nearly all the day long these six princes wandered about looking in vain for game; till at last they grew hungry and thirsty, and could find no water, and they had no food with them. Meanwhile the beautiful young prince had sat down under a tree, to dine and rest, and there his six brothers-in-law found him. By his side was some delicious water, and also some roast meat.

When they saw him the six princes said to each other, "Look at that handsome prince. He has a moon on his forehead and a star on his chin. We have never seen such a prince in this jungle before; he must come from another country." Then they came up to him, and made him many salaams, and begged him to give them some food and water. "Who are you?" said the young prince. "We are the husbands of the six elder daughters of the King of this country," they answered; "and we have hunted all day, and are very hungry and thirsty." They did not recognise their brother-in-law in the least.

"Well," said the young prince, "I will give you something to eat and drink if you will do as I bid you." "We will do all you tell us to do," they answered, "for if we do not get water to drink, we shall die." "Very good," said the young prince. "Now you must let me put a red-hot pice on the back of each of you, and then I will give you food and water. Do you agree to this?" The six princes consented, for they thought, "No one will ever see the mark of the pice, as it will be covered by our clothes; and we shall die if we have no water to drink." Then the young prince took six pice, and made them red-hot in the fire; he laid one on the back of each of the six princes, and gave them good food and water. They ate and drank; and when they had finished they made him many salaams and went home.

The young prince stayed under the tree till it was evening; then he mounted his horse and rode off to the King's palace. All the people looked at him as he came riding along, saying, "What a splendid young prince that is! He has a moon on his forehead and a star on his chin." But no one recognised him. When he came near the King's palace, all the King's servants asked him who he was; and as none of them knew him, the gate-keepers would not let him pass in. They all wondered who he could be, and all thought him the most beautiful prince that had ever been seen.

At last they asked him who he was. "I am the husband of your youngest princess," he answered.

"No, no, indeed you are not," they said; "for he is a poor, common-looking, and ugly man."

"But I am he," answered the prince; only no one would believe him.

"Tell us the truth," said the servants; "who are you?"

"Perhaps you cannot recognise me," said the young prince, "but call the youngest princess here. I wish to speak to her." The servants called her, and she came. "That man is not my husband," she said at once. "My husband is not nearly as handsome as that man. This must be a prince from another country."

Then she said to him, "Who are you? Why do you say you are my husband?"

"Because I am your husband. I am telling you the truth," answered the young prince.

"No, you are not, you are not telling me the truth," said the little princess. "My husband is not a handsome man like you. I married a very poor, common-looking man."

"That is true," he answered, "but nevertheless I am your husband. I was the grain merchant's servant; and one hot night I went into your father's garden and sang, and you heard me, and came and asked me who I was and where I came from, and I would not answer you. And the same thing happened the next night, and the next, and on the fourth I told you I was a very poor man, and had come from my country to seek service in yours, and that I was the grain merchant's servant. Then you told your father you wished to marry, but must choose your own husband; and when all the Kings and Rajas were seated in your father's garden, you sat on an elephant and went round and looked at them all; and then twice hung your gold necklace round my neck, and chose me. See, here is your necklace, and here are the ring and the handkerchief you gave me on our wedding day."

Then she believed him, and was very glad that her husband was such a beautiful young prince. "What a strange man you are !" she said to him. "Till now you have been poor, and ugly, and common-looking. Now you are beautiful and look like a prince; I never saw such a handsome man as you are before; and yet I know you must be my husband" Then she worshipped God and thanked him for letting her have such a husband. "I have," she said, "a beautiful husband. There is no one like him in this country. He has a moon on his forehead and a star on his chin." Then she took him into the palace, and showed him to her father and mother and to every one. They all said they had never seen any one like him, and were all very happy. And the young prince lived as before in the King's palace with his wife, and Katar lived in the King's stables,

One day, when the King and his seven sons-in-law were in his court-house, and it was full of people, the young prince said to him, "There are six thieves here in your court-house." "Six thieves!" said the King. "Where are they? Show them to me." "There they are," said the young prince, pointing to his six brothers-in-law. The King and every one else in the court-house were very much astonished, and would not believe the young prince. "Take off their coats," he said, "and then you will see for yourselves that each of them has the mark of a thief on his back." So their coats were taken off the six princes, and the King and everybody in the court-house saw the mark of the red-hot pice. The six princes were very much ashamed, but the young prince was very glad. He had not forgotten how his brothers-in-law had laughed at him and mocked him when he seemed a poor, common man.

Now, when Katar was still in the jungle, before the prince was married, he had told the boy the whole story of his birth, and all that had happened to him and his mother. "When you are married," he said to him, "I will take you back to your father's country." So two months after the young prince had revenged himself on his brothers-in-law, Katar said to him, "It is time for you to return to your father. Get the King to let you go to your own country, and I will tell you what to do when we get there."

The prince always did what his horse told him to do; so he went to his wife and said to her, "I wish very much to go to my own country to see my father and mother." "Very well," said his wife; "I will tell my father and mother, and ask them to let us go." Then she went to them, and told them, and they consented to let her and her husband leave them. The King gave his daughter and the young prince a great many horses, and elephants, and all sorts of presents, and also a great many sepoys to guard them. In this grand state they travelled to the prince's country, which was not a great many miles off. When they reached it they pitched their tents on the same plain in which the prince had been left in his box by the nurse, where Shankar and Suri had swallowed him so often.

When the King, his father, the gardener's daughter's husband, saw the prince's camp, he was very much alarmed, and thought a great King had come to make war on him. He sent one of his servants, therefore, to ask whose camp it was. The young prince then wrote him a letter, in which he said, "You are a great King. Do not fear me. I am not come to make war on you. I am as if I were your son. I am a prince who has come to see your country and to speak with you. I wish to give you a grand feast, to which every one in your country must come—men and women, old and young, rich and poor, of all castes; all the children, fakirs, and sepoys. You must bring them all here to me for a week, and I will feast them all."

The King was delighted with this letter, and ordered all the men, women, and children of all castes, fakirs, and sepoys, in his country to go to the prince's camp to a grand feast the prince would give them. So they all came, and the King brought his four wives too. All came, at least all but the gardener's daughter. No one had told her to go to the feast, for no one had thought of her.

When all the people were assembled, the prince saw his mother was not there, and he asked the King, "Has every one in your country come to my feast?"

"Yes, every one," said the King.

"Are you sure of that?" asked the prince.

"Quite sure," answered the King.

"I am sure one woman has not come," said the prince. "She is your gardener's daughter, who was once your wife and is now a servant in your palace."

"True," said the King, "I had forgotten her." Then the prince told his servants to take his finest palanquin and to fetch the gardener's daughter. They were to bathe her, dress her in beautiful clothes and handsome jewels, and then bring her to him in the palanquin.

While the servants were bringing the gardener's daughter, the King thought how handsome the young prince was; and he noticed particularly the moon on his forehead and the star on his chin, and he wondered in what country the young prince was born.

And now the palanquin arrived bringing the gardener's daughter, and the young prince went himself and took her out of it, and brought her into the tent. He made her a great many salaams. The four wicked wives looked on and were very much surprised and very angry. They remembered that, when they arrived, the prince had made them no salaams, and since then had not taken the least notice of them; whereas he could not do enough for the gardener's daughter, and seemed very glad to see her.

When they were all at dinner, the prince again made the gardener's daughter a great many salaams, and gave her food from all the nicest dishes. She wondered at his kindness to her, and thought, "Who is this handsome prince, with a moon on his forehead and a star on his chin? I never saw any one so beautiful. What country does he come from?"

Two or three days were thus passed in feasting, and all that time the King and his people were talking about the prince's beauty, and wondering who he was.

One day the prince asked the King if he had any children. "None," he answered.

"Do you know who I am?" asked the prince.

"No," said the King. "Tell me who you are."

"I am your son," answered the prince, "and the gardener's daughter is my mother."

The King shook his head sadly. "How can you be my son," he said, "when I have never had any children?"

"But I am your son," answered the prince. "Your four wicked Queens told you the gardener's daughter had given you a stone and not a son; but it was they who put the stone in my little bed, and then they tried to kill me."

The King did not believe him. "I wish you were my

son," he said; "but as I never had a child, you cannot be my son." "Do you remember your dog Shankar, and how you had him killed? And do you remember your cow Suri, and how you had her killed too? Your wives made you kill them because of me. And," he said, taking the King to Katar, "do you know whose horse that is?"

The King looked at Katar, and then said, "That is my horse Katar." "Yes," said the prince. "Do you not remember how he rushed past you out of his stable with me on his back?" Then Katar told the King the prince was really his son, and told him all the story of his birth, and of his life up to that moment; and when the King found the beautiful prince was indeed his son, he was so glad, so glad. He put his arms round him and kissed him and cried for joy.

"Now," said the King, "you must come with me to my palace, and live with me always."

"No," said the prince, "that I cannot do. I cannot go to your palace. I only came here to fetch my mother; and now that I have found her. I will take her with me to my father-in-law's palace. I have married a King's daughter, and we live with her father."

"But now that I have found you, I cannot let you go," said his father. "You and your wife must come and live with your mother and me in my palace."

"That we will never do," said the prince, "unless you will kill your four wicked Queens with your own hand. If you will do that, we will come and live with you."

So the King killed his Queens, and then he and his wife, the gardener's daughter, and the prince and his wife, all went to live in the King's palace, and lived there happily together for ever after ; and the King thanked God for giving him such a beautiful son, and for ridding him of his four wicked wives.

Katar did not return to the fairies' country, but stayed always with the young prince, and never left him.

The Prince and the Fakir

THERE was once upon a time a King who had no children. Now this King went and laid him down to rest at a place where four roads met, so that every one who passed had to step over him.

At last a Fakir came along, and he said to the King, "Man, why are you lying here ?'

He replied, " Fakir, a thousand men have come and passed by; you pass on too."

But the Fakir said, " Who are you, man ? "

The King replied, " I am a King, Fakir. Of goods and gold I have no lack, but I have lived long and have no children. So I have come here, and have laid me down at the cross-roads. My sins and offences have been very many, so I have come and am lying here that men may pass over me, and perchance my sins may be forgiven me, and God may be merciful, and I may have a son."

The Fakir answered him, "O King! If you have children, what will you give me?"

"Whatever you ask, Fakir," answered the King.

The Fakir said, "Of goods and gold I have no lack, but I will say a prayer for you, and you will have two sons; one of those sons will be mine."

Then he took out two sweetmeats and handed them to the King, and said, "King! take these two sweetmeats and give them to your wives; give them to the wives you love best."

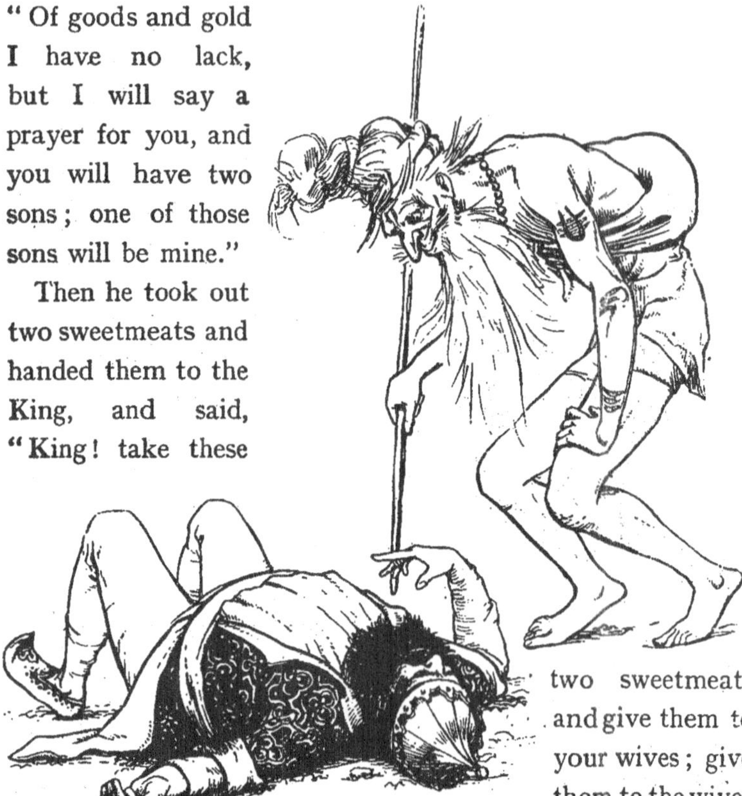

The King took the sweetmeats and put them in his bosom.

Then the Fakir said, "King! in a year I will return, and of the two sons who will be born to you one is mine and one yours."

The King said, "Well, I agree."

Then the Fakir went on his way, and the King came home and gave one sweetmeat to each of his two wives. After some time two sons were born to the King. Then what did the King do but place those two sons in an underground room, which he had built in the earth.

Some time passed, and one day the Fakir appeared, and said, "King! bring me that son of yours!"

What did the King do but bring two slave-girls' sons and present them to the Fakir. While the Fakir was sitting there the King's sons were sitting down below in their cellar eating their food. Just then a hungry ant had carried away a grain of rice from their food, and was going along with it to her children. Another stronger ant came up and attacked her in order to get this grain of rice. The first ant said "O ant, why do you drag this away from me? I have long been lame in my feet, and I have got just one grain, and am carrying it to my children. The King's sons are sitting in the cellar eating their food; you go and fetch a grain from there; why should you take mine from me?" On this the second ant let go and did not rob the first, but went off to where the King's sons were eating their food.

On hearing this the Fakir said, "King! these are not your sons; go and bring those children who are eating their food in the cellar."

Then the King went and brought his own sons. The Fakir chose the eldest son and took him away, and set off with him on his journey. When he got home he told the King's son to go out to gather fuel.

So the King's son went out to gather cow-dung, and when he had collected some he brought it in.

Then the Fakir looked at the King's son and put on a great pot, and said, "Come round here, my pupil."

But the King's son said, "Master first, and pupil after."

The Fakir told him to come once, he told him twice, he told him three times, and each time the King's son answered, "Master first, and pupil after."

Then the Fakir made a dash at the King's son, thinking to catch him and throw him into the caldron. There were about a hundred gallons of oil in this caldron, and the fire was burning beneath it. Then the King's son, lifting the Fakir, gave him a jerk and threw him into the caldron, and he was burnt, and became roast meat. He then saw a key of the Fakir's lying there; he took this key and opened the door of the Fakir's house. Now many men were locked up in this house; two horses were standing there in a hut of the Fakir's; two greyhounds were tied up there; two simurgs were imprisoned, and two tigers also stood there. So the King's son let all the creatures go, and took them out of the house, and they all returned thanks to God. Next he let out all the men who were in prison. He took away with him the two horses, and he took away the two tigers, and he took away the two hounds, and he took away the two simurgs, and with them he set out for another country.

As he went along the road he saw above him a bald man, grazing a herd of calves, and this bald man called out to him, "Fellow! can you fight at all?"

The King's son replied, "When I was little I could fight a bit, and now, if any one wants to fight, I am not so unmanly as to turn my back. Come, I will fight you."

The bald man said, "If I throw you, you shall be my slave; and if you throw me, I will be your slave." So they got ready and began to fight, and the King's son threw him.

On this the King's son said, "I will leave my beasts here my simurgs, tigers, and dogs, and horses; they will all stay here while I go to the city to see the sights. I appoint the tiger as guard over my property. And you are my slave; you, too, must stay here with my belongings." So the King's son started off to the city to see the sights, and arrived at a pool.

He saw that it was a pleasant pool, and thought he would stop and bathe there, and therewith he began to strip off his clothes.

Now the King's daughter, who was sitting on the roof of the palace, saw his royal marks, and she said, "This man is a king; when I marry, I will marry him and no other." So she said to her father, "My father; I wish to marry."

"Good," said her father.

Then the King made a proclamation: "Let all men, great and small, attend to-day in the hall of audience, for the King's daughter will to-day take a husband."

All the men of the land assembled, and the traveller Prince also came, dressed in the Fakir's clothes, saying to himself, "I must see this ceremony to-day." He went in and sat down.

The King's daughter came out and sat in the balcony, and cast her glance round all the assembly. She noticed that the traveller Prince was sitting in the assembly in Fakir's attire.

The Princess said to her handmaiden, "Take this dish of henna, go to that traveller dressed like a Fakir, and sprinkle scent on him from the dish."

The handmaiden obeyed the Princess's order, went to him, and sprinkled the scent over him.

Then the people said, "The slave-girl has made a mistake."

But she replied, "The slave-girl has made no mistake, 'tis her mistress has made the mistake."

On this the King married his daughter to the Fakir, who was really no Fakir, but a Prince.

What fate had decreed came to pass in that country, and they were married. But the King of that city became very sad in his heart, because when so many chiefs and nobles were sitting there his daughter had chosen none of them, but had chosen that Fakir; but he kept these thoughts concealed in his heart.

One day the traveller Prince said, "Let all the King's sons-in-law come out with me to-day to hunt."

People said, "What is this Fakir that he should go a-hunting?"

However, they all set out for the hunt, and fixed their meeting-place at a certain pool.

The newly-married Prince went to his tigers, and told his tigers and hounds to kill and bring in a great number of gazelles and hog-deer and markhor. Instantly they killed and brought in a great number. Then taking with him these spoils of the chase, the Prince came to the pool settled on as a meeting-place. The other Princes, sons-in-law of the King of that city, also assembled there; but they had brought in no game, and the new Prince had brought a great deal. Thence they returned home to the town, and went to the King, their father-in-law, to present their game.

Now that King had no son. Then the new Prince told him that in fact he, too, was a Prince. At this the King, his father-in-law, was greatly delighted and took him by the hand and embraced him. He seated him by himself, saying, "O Prince, I return thanks that you have come here and become my son-in-law; I am very happy at this, and I make over my kingdom to you."

Why the Fish Laughed

AS a certain fisherwoman passed by a palace crying her fish, the Queen appeared at one of the windows and beckoned her to come near and show what she had. At that moment a very big fish jumped about in the bottom of the basket.

"Is it a he or a she?" inquired the Queen. "I wish to purchase a she-fish."

On hearing this the fish laughed aloud.

"It's a he," replied the fisherwoman, and proceeded on her rounds.

The Queen returned to her room in a great rage; and on coming to see her in the evening, the King noticed that something had disturbed her.

"Are you indisposed?" he said.

"No; but I am very much annoyed at the strange behaviour of a fish. A woman brought me one to-day, and on my inquiring whether it was a male or female, the fish laughed most rudely."

"A fish laugh! Impossible! You must be dreaming."

"I am not a fool. I speak of what I have seen with my own eyes and have heard with my own ears."

"Passing strange! Be it so. I will inquire concerning it."

On the morrow the King repeated to his vizier what his wife had told him, and bade him investigate the matter, and be ready with a satisfactory answer within six months, on pain of death. The vizier promised to do his best, though he felt almost certain of failure. For five months he laboured indefatigably to find a reason for the laughter of the fish. He sought everywhere and from every one. The wise and learned, and they who were skilled in magic and in all manner of trickery, were consulted. Nobody, however, could explain the matter; and so he returned broken-hearted to his house, and began to arrange his affairs in prospect of certain death, for he had had sufficient experience of the King to know that his Majesty would not go back from his threat. Amongst other things, he advised his son to travel for a time, until the King's anger should have somewhat cooled.

The young fellow, who was both clever and handsome, started off whithersoever Kismat might lead him. He had been gone some days, when he fell in with an old farmer, who also was on a journey to a certain village. Finding the old man very pleasant, he asked him if he might accompany him, professing to be on a visit to the same place. The old farmer agreed, and they walked along together. The day was hot, and the way was long and weary.

"Don't you think it would be pleasanter if you and I sometimes gave one another a lift?" said the youth.

"What a fool the man is!" thought the old farmer.

Presently they passed through a field of corn ready for the sickle, and looking like a sea of gold as it waved to and fro in the breeze.

"Is this eaten or not?" said the young man.

Not understanding his meaning, the old man replied, "I don't know."

After a little while the two travellers arrived at a big village, where the young man gave his companion a clasp-knife, and said, "Take this, friend, and get two horses with it; but mind and bring it back, for it is very precious."

The old man, looking half amused and half angry, pushed back the knife, muttering something to the effect that his friend was either a fool himself or else trying to play the fool with him. The young man pretended not to notice his reply, and remained almost silent till they reached the city, a short distance outside which was the old farmer's house. They walked about the bazar and went to the mosque, but nobody saluted them or invited them to come in and rest.

"What a large cemetery!" exclaimed the young man.

"What does the man mean," thought the old farmer, "calling this largely populated city a cemetery?"

On leaving the city their way led through a cemetery where a few people were praying beside a grave and distributing chapatis and kulchas to passers-by, in the name of their beloved dead. They beckoned to the two travellers and gave them as much as they would.

"What a splendid city this is!" said the young man.

"Now, the man must surely be demented!" thought the old farmer. "I wonder what he will do next? He will be calling the land water, and the water land; and be speaking of light where there is darkness, and of darkness when it is light." However, he kept his thoughts to himself.

Presently they had to wade through a stream that ran along the edge of the cemetery. The water was rather deep, so the old farmer took off his shoes and paijamas and crossed over; but the young man waded through it with his shoes and paijamas on.

"Well! I never did see such a perfect fool, both in word and in deed," said the old man to himself.

However, he liked the fellow; and thinking that he would amuse his wife and daughter, he invited him to come and stay at his house as long as he had occasion to remain in the village.

"Thank you very much," the young man replied; "but let me first inquire, if you please, whether the beam of your house is strong."

The old farmer left him in despair, and entered his house laughing.

"There is a man in yonder field," he said, after returning their greetings. "He has come the greater part of the way with me, and I wanted him to put up here as long as he had to stay in this village. But the fellow is such a fool that I cannot make anything out of him. He wants to know if the beam of this house is all right. The man must be mad!" and saying this, he burst into a fit of laughter.

"Father," said the farmer's daughter, who was a very sharp and wise girl, "this man, whosoever he is, is no fool, as you deem him. He only wishes to know if you can afford to entertain him."

"Oh! of course," replied the farmer. "I see. Well, perhaps you can help me to solve some of his other mysteries. While we were walking together he asked whether he should carry me or I should carry him, as he thought that would be a pleasanter mode of proceeding."

"Most assuredly," said the girl. "He meant that one of you should tell a story to beguile the time."

"Oh yes. Well, we were passing through a corn-field, when he asked me whether it was eaten or not."

"And didn't you know the meaning of this, father? He simply wished to know if the man was in debt or not; because, if the owner of the field was in debt, then the produce of the field was as good as eaten to him; that is, it would have to go to his creditors."

"Yes, yes, yes, of course! Then, on entering a certain village, he bade me take his clasp-knife and get two horses with it, and bring back the knife again to him."

"Are not two stout sticks as good as two horses for helping one along on the road? He only asked you to cut a couple of sticks and be careful not to lose his knife."

"I see," said the farmer. "While we were walking over the city we did not see anybody that we knew, and not a soul gave us a scrap of anything to eat, till we were passing the cemetery; but there some people called to us and put into our hands some chapatis and kulchas; so my companion called the city a cemetery, and the cemetery a city."

"This also is to be understood, father, if one thinks of the city as the place where everything is to be obtained, and of inhospitable people as worse than the dead. The city, though crowded with people, was as if dead, as far as you were concerned; while, in the cemetery, which is crowded with the dead, you were saluted by kind friends and provided with bread."

"True, true!" said the astonished farmer. "Then, just now, when we were crossing the stream, he waded through it without taking off his shoes and paijamas."

"I admire his wisdom," replied the girl. "I have often thought how stupid people were to venture into that swiftly flowing stream and over those sharp stones with bare feet. The slightest stumble and they would fall, and be wetted from head to foot. This friend of yours is a most wise man. I should like to see him and speak to him."

"Very well," said the farmer; "I will go and find him, and bring him in."

"Tell him, father, that our beams are strong enough, and then he will come in. I'll send on ahead a present to the man, to show him that we can afford to have him for our guest."

Accordingly she called a servant and sent him to the young man with a present of a basin of ghee, twelve chapatis, and a jar of milk, and the following message:—"O friend, the moon is full; twelve months make a year, and the sea is overflowing with water."

Half-way the bearer of this present and message met his little son, who, seeing what was in the basket, begged his father to give him some of the food. His father foolishly complied. Presently he saw the young man, and gave him the rest of the present and the message.

"Give your mistress my salaam," he replied, "and tell her that the moon is new, and that I can only find eleven months in the year, and the sea is by no means full."

Not understanding the meaning of these words, the servant repeated them word for word, as he had heard them, to his mistress; and thus his theft was discovered, and he was severely punished. After a little while the young man appeared with the old farmer. Great attention was shown to him and he was treated in every way as if he were the son of a great man, although his humble host knew nothing of his origin. At length he told them everything—about the laughing of the fish, his father's threatened execution, and his own banishment—and asked their advice as to what he should do.

"The laughing of the fish," said the girl, "which seems to have been the cause of all this trouble, indicates that there is a man in the palace who is plotting against the King's life."

"Joy, joy!" exclaimed the vizier's son. "There is yet time for me to return and save my father from an ignominious and unjust death, and the King from danger."

The following day he hastened back to his own country, taking with him the farmer's daughter. Immediately on arrival he ran to the palace and informed his father of what he had heard. The poor vizier, now almost dead from the expectation of death, was at once carried to the King, to whom he repeated the news that his son had just brought.

"Never!" said the King.

"But it must be so, your Majesty," replied the vizier; "and in order to prove the truth of what I have heard, I pray you to call together all the maids in your palace, and order them to jump over a pit, which must be dug. We'll soon find out whether there is any man there."

The King had the pit dug, and commanded all the maids

belonging to the palace to try to jump it. All of them tried, but only one succeeded. That one was found to be a man!!

Thus was the Queen satisfied, and the faithful old vizier saved.

Afterwards, as soon as could be, the vizier's son married the old farmer's daughter; and a most happy marriage it was.

The Demon with the Matted Hair

THIS story the Teacher told in Jetavana about a Brother who had ceased striving after righteousness. Said the Teacher to him: "Is it really true that you have ceased all striving?"—"Yes, Blessed One," he replied. Then the Teacher said: "O Brother, in former days wise men made effort in the place where effort should be made, and so attained unto royal power." And he told a story of long ago.

Once upon a time, when Brahmadatta was King of Benares, the Bodhisatta was born as son of his chief queen. On his name-day they asked 800 Brahmans, having satisfied them with all their desires, about his lucky marks. The Brahmans who had skill in divining from such marks beheld the excellence of his, and made answer:

"Full of goodness, great King, is your son, and when you die he will become king; he shall be famous and renowned for his skill with the five weapons, and shall be the chief man in all India. On hearing what the Brahmans had to say, they gave him the name of the Prince of the Five Weapons, sword, spear, bow, battle-axe, and shield.

When he came to years of discretion, and had attained the measure of sixteen years, the King said to him:

"My son, go and complete your education."

"Who shall be my teacher?" the lad asked.

"Go, my son; in the kingdom of Candahar, in the city of Takkasila, is a far-famed teacher from whom I wish you to learn. Take this, and give it him for a fee." With that he gave him a thousand pieces of money, and dismissed him.

The lad departed. and was educated by this teacher; he received the Five Weapons from him as a gift, bade him farewell, and leaving Takkasila, he began his journey to Benares, armed with the Five Weapons.

On his way he came to a forest inhabited by the Demon with the Matted Hair. At the entering of the forest some men saw him, and cried out:

"Hullo, young sir, keep clear of that wood! There's a Demon in it called he of the Matted Hair: he kills every man he sees!" And they tried to stop him. But the Bodhisatta, having confidence in himself, went straight on, fearless as a maned lion.

When he reached mid-forest the Demon showed himself. He made himself as tall as a palm-tree; his head was the size of a pagoda, his eyes as big as saucers, and he had two tusks all over knobs and bulbs; he had the face of a hawk, a variegated belly, and blue hands and feet.

"Where are you going?" he shouted. "Stop! You'll make a meal for me!"

Said the Bodhisatta: "Demon, I came here trusting in myself. I advise you to be careful how you come near me. Here's a poisoned arrow, which I'll shoot at you and knock you down!" With this menace, he fitted to his bow an arrow dipped in deadly poison, and let fly. The arrow stuck fast in the Demon's hair. Then he shot and shot, till he had shot away fifty arrows; and they all stuck in the Demon's hair. The Demon snapped them all off short, and threw them down at his feet; then came up to the Bodhisatta, who drew his sword and struck the Demon, threatening him the while. His sword—it was three-and-thirty inches long—stuck in the Demon's hair! The Bodhisatta struck him with his spear—that stuck too! He struck him with his club—and that stuck too!

When the Bodhisatta saw that this had stuck fast, he addressed the Demon. "You, Demon!" said he, "did you never hear of me before—the Prince of the Five Weapons? When I came into the forest which you live in I did not trust to my bow and other weapons. This day will I pound you and grind you to powder!" Thus did he declare his resolve, and with a shout he hit at the Demon with his right hand. It stuck fast in his hair! He hit him with his left hand—that stuck too! With his right foot he kicked him—that stuck too; then with his left—and that stuck too! Then he butted at him with his head, crying, "I'll pound you to powder!" and his head stuck fast like the rest.

Thus the Bodhisatta was five times snared, caught fast in five places, hanging suspended: yet he felt no fear—was not even nervous.

Thought the Demon to himself: "Here's a lion of a man! A noble man! More than man is he! Here he is, caught by

THE DEMON WITH THE MATTED HAIR

a Demon like me; yet he will not fear a bit. Since I have ravaged this road, I never saw such a man. Now, why is it that he does not fear?" He was powerless to eat the man, but asked him: "Why is it, young sir, that you are not frightened to death?"

"Why should I fear, Demon?" replied he. "In one life a man can die but once. Besides, in my belly is a thunderbolt; if you eat me, you will never be able to digest it; this will tear your inwards into little bits, and kill you: so we shall both perish. That is why I fear nothing." (By this, the Bodhisatta meant the weapon of knowledge which he had within him.)

When he heard this, the Demon thought: "This young man speaks the truth. A piece of the flesh of such a lion-man as he would be too much for me to digest, if it were no bigger than a kidney-bean. I'll let him go!" So, being frightened to death, he let go the Bodhisatta, saying:

"Young sir, you are a lion of a man! I will not eat you up. I set you free from my hands, as the moon is disgorged from the jaws of Rāhu after the eclipse. Go back to the company of your friends and relations!"

And the Bodhisatta said: "Demon, I will go, as you say. You were born a Demon, cruel, blood-bibbing, devourer of the flesh and gore of others, because you did wickedly in former lives. If you still go on doing wickedly, you will go from darkness to darkness. But now that you have seen me you will find it impossible to do wickedly. Taking the life of living creatures causes birth, as an animal, in the world of Petas, or in the body of an Asura, or, if one is reborn as a man, it makes his life short." With this and the like monition he told him the disadvantage of the five kinds of wickedness, and the profit of the five kinds of virtue, and frightened the Demon in various ways, discoursing to him until he subdued him and made him self-denying, and established him in the five kinds of virtue; he made him worship the deity to whom offerings were made in that wood; and having carefully admonished him, departed out of it.

At the entrance of the forest he told all to the people thereabout; and went on to Benares, armed with his five weapons. Afterwards he became king, and ruled righteously; and after giving alms and doing good he passed away according to his deeds.

And the Teacher, when this tale was ended, became perfectly enlightened, and repeated this verse:

Whose mind and heart from all desire is free,
Who seeks for peace by living virtuously,
He in due time will sever all the bonds
That bind him fast to life, and cease to be.

Thus the Teacher reached the summit, through sainthood and the teaching of the law, and thereupon he declared the Four Truths. At the end of the declaring of the Truths, this Brother also attained to sainthood. Then the Teacher made the connexion, and gave the key to the birth-tale, saying: "At that time Angulimala was the Demon, but the Prince of the Five Weapons was I myself."

The Ivory City and its Fairy Princess

ONE day a young prince was out practising archery with the son of his father's chief vizier, when one of the arrows accidentally struck the wife of a merchant, who was walking about in an upper room of a house close by. The prince aimed at a bird that was perched on the window-sill of that room, and had not the slightest idea that anybody was at hand, or he would not have shot in that direction. Consequently, not knowing what had happened, he and the vizier's son walked away, the vizier's son chaffing him because he had missed the bird.

Presently the merchant went to ask his wife about something, and found her lying, to all appearance, dead in the middle of the room, and an arrow fixed in the ground within half a yard of her head. Supposing that she was dead, he rushed to the window and shrieked, "Thieves, thieves! They have killed my wife." The neighbours quickly gathered, and the servants came running upstairs to see what was the matter. It happened that the woman had fainted, and that there was only a very slight wound in her breast where the arrow had grazed.

As soon as the woman recovered her senses she told them that two young men had passed by the place with their bows and arrows, and that one of them had most deliberately aimed at her as she stood by the window.

On hearing this the merchant went to the King, and told him what had taken place. His Majesty was much enraged at such audacious wickedness, and swore that most terrible punishment should be visited on the offender if he could be discovered. He ordered the merchant to go back and ascertain whether his wife could recognise the young men if she saw them again.

" Oh yes," replied the woman, ' I should know them again among all the people in the city."

"Then," said the King, when the merchant brought back this reply, " to-morrow I will cause all the male inhabitants of this city to pass before your house, and your wife will stand at the window and watch for the man who did this wanton deed."

A royal proclamation was issued to this effect. So the next day all the men and boys of the city, from the age of ten years upwards, assembled and marched by the house of the merchant. By chance (for they both had been excused from obeying this order) the King's son and the vizier's son were also in the company, and passed by in the crowd. They came to see the tamasha.

As soon as these two appeared in front of the merchant's window they were recognised by the merchant's wife, and at once reported to the King.

"My own son and the son of my chief vizier!" exclaimed the King, who had been present from the commencement. "What examples for the people! Let them both be executed."

"Not so, your Majesty," said the vizier, "I beseech you. Let the facts of the case be thoroughly investigated. How is it?" he continued, turning to the two young men. "Why have you done this cruel thing?"

"I shot an arrow at a bird that was sitting on the sill of an open window in yonder house, and missed," answered the prince. "I suppose the arrow struck the merchant's wife. Had I known that she or anybody had been near I should not have shot in that direction."

"We will speak of this later on," said the King, on hearing this answer. "Dismiss the people. Their presence is no longer needed."

In the evening his Majesty and the vizier had a long and earnest talk about their two sons. The King wished both of them to be executed, but the vizier suggested that the prince should be banished from the country. This was finally agreed to.

Accordingly, on the following morning, a little company of soldiers escorted the prince out of the city. When they reached the last custom-house the vizier's son overtook them. He had come with all haste, bringing with him four bags of muhrs on four horses. "I am come," he said, throwing his arms round the prince's neck, "because I cannot let you go alone. We have lived together, we will be exiled together, and we will die together. Turn me not back, if you love me."

"Consider," the prince answered, "what you are doing, All kinds of trial may be before me. Why should you leave your home and country to be with me?"

"Because I love you," he said, "and shall never be happy without you."

So the two friends walked along hand in hand as fast as they could to get out of the country, and behind them marched the soldiers and the horses with their valuable burdens. On reaching a place on the borders of the King's dominions the prince gave the soldiers some gold, and ordered them to return. The soldiers took the money and left; they did not, however, go very far, but hid themselves behind rocks and stones, and waited till they were quite sure that the prince did not intend to come back.

On and on the exiles walked, till they arrived at a certain village, where they determined to spend the night under one of the big trees of the place. The prince made preparations for a fire, and arranged the few articles of bedding that they had with them, while the vizier's son went to the baniya and the baker and the butcher to get something for their dinner. For some reason he was delayed; perhaps the tsut was not quite ready, or the baniya had not got all the spices prepared. After waiting half an hour the prince became impatient, and rose up and walked about.

He saw a pretty, clear little brook running along not far

from their resting-place, and hearing that its source was not far distant, he started off to find it. The source was a beautiful lake, which at that time was covered with the magnificent lotus flower and other water plants. The prince sat down on the bank, and being thirsty took up some of the water in his hand. Fortunately he looked into his hand before drinking, and there, to his great astonishment, he saw reflected whole and clear the image of a beautiful fairy. He looked round, hoping to see the reality; but seeing no person, he drank the water, and put out his hand to take some more. Again he saw the reflection in the water which was in his palm. He looked around as before, and this time discovered a fairy sitting by the bank on the opposite side of the lake. On seeing her he fell so madly in love with her that he dropped down in a swoon.

When the vizier's son returned, and found the fire lighted, the horses securely fastened, and the bags of muhrs lying altogether in a heap, but no prince, he did not know what to think. He waited a little while, and then shouted; but not getting any reply, he got up and went to the brook. There he came across the footmarks of his friend. Seeing these, he went back at once for the money and the horses, and bringing them with him, he tracked the prince to the lake, where he found him lying to all appearance dead.

"Alas! alas!" he cried, and lifting up the prince, he poured some water over his head and face. "Alas! my brother, what is this? Oh! do not die and leave me thus. Speak, speak! I cannot bear this!"

In a few minutes the prince, revived by the water, opened his eyes, and looked about wildly.

"Thank God!" exclaimed the vizier's son. "But what is the matter, brother?"

"Go away," replied the prince. "I don't want to say anything to you, or to see you. Go away."

"Come, come; let us leave this place. Look, I have brought some food for you, and horses, and everything. Let us eat and depart."

"Go alone," replied the prince.

"Never," said the vizier's son. "What has happened to suddenly estrange you from me? A little while ago we were brethren, but now you detest the sight of me."

"I have looked upon a fairy," the prince said. "But a moment I saw her face; for when she noticed that I was looking at her she covered her face with lotus petals. Oh, how beautiful she was! And while I gazed she took out of her bosom an ivory box, and held it up to me. Then I fainted. Oh! if you can get me that fairy for my wife, I will go anywhere with you."

"Oh, brother," said the vizier's son, "you have indeed seen a fairy. She is a fairy of the fairies. This is none other than Gulizar of the Ivory City. I know this from the signs that she gave you. From her covering her face with lotus petals I learn her name, and from her showing you the ivory box I learn where she lives. Be patient, and rest assured that I will arrange your marriage with her."

When the prince heard these encouraging words he felt much comforted, rose up, and ate, and then went away gladly with his friend.

On the way they met two men. These two men belonged to a family of robbers. There were eleven of them altogether. One, an elder sister, stayed at home and cooked the food, and the other ten—all brothers—went out, two and two, and walked about the four different ways that ran through that part of the country, robbing those travellers who could not resist them, and inviting others, who were too powerful for two of them to manage, to come and rest at their house, where the whole family attacked them and stole their goods. These thieves lived in a kind of tower, which had several strong-rooms in it, and under it was a great pit, wherein they threw the corpses of the poor unfortunates who chanced to fall into their power.

The two men came forward, and, politely accosting them, begged them to come and stay at their house for the night. "It is late," they said, "and there is not another village within several miles."

"Shall we accept this good man's invitation, brother?" asked the prince.

The vizier's son frowned slightly in token of disapproval; but the prince was tired, and thinking that it was only a whim of his friend's, he said to the men, "Very well. It is very kind of you to ask us."

So they all four went to the robbers' tower.

Seated in a room, with the door fastened on the outside, the two travellers bemoaned their fate.

"It is no good groaning," said the vizier's son. "I will climb to the window, and see whether there are any means of escape. Yes! yes!" he whispered, when he had reached the window-hole. "Below there is a ditch surrounded by a high wall. I will jump down and reconnoitre. You stay here, and wait till I return."

Presently he came back and told the prince that he had seen a most ugly woman, whom he supposed was the robbers' housekeeper. She had agreed to release them on the promise of her marriage with the prince.

So the woman led the way out of the enclosure by a secret door.

"But where are the horses and the goods?" the vizier's son inquired.

"You cannot bring them," the woman said. "To go out by any other way would be to thrust oneself into the grave."

"All right, then; they also shall go out by this door. I have a charm, whereby I can make them thin or fat." So the vizier's son fetched the horses without any person knowing it, and repeating the charm, he made them pass through the narrow doorway like pieces of cloth, and when they were all outside restored them to their former condition. He at once mounted his horse and laid hold of the halter of one of the other horses, and then beckoning to the prince to do likewise, he rode off. The prince saw his opportunity, and in a moment was riding after him, having the woman behind him.

Now the robbers heard the galloping of the horses, and ran out and shot their arrows at the prince and his companions. And one of the arrows killed the woman, so they had to leave her behind.

On, on they rode, until they reached a village where they stayed the night. The following morning they were off again, and asked for Ivory City from every passer-by. At length they came to this famous city, and put up at a little hut that belonged to an old woman, from whom they feared no harm, and with whom, therefore, they could abide in peace and comfort. At first the old woman did not like the idea of these travellers staying in her house, but the sight of a muhr, which the prince dropped in the bottom of a cup in which she had given him water, and a present of another muhr from the vizier's son, quickly made her change her mind. She agreed to let them stay there for a few days.

As soon as her work was over the old woman came and sat down with her lodgers. The vizier's son pretended to be utterly ignorant of the place and people. "Has this city a name?" he asked the old woman.

"Of course it has, you stupid. Every little village, much more a city, and such a city as this, has a name."

"What is the name of this city?"

"Ivory City. Don't you know that? I thought the name was known all over the world."

On the mention of the name Ivory City the prince gave a deep sigh. The vizier's son looked as much as to say, "Keep quiet, or you'll discover the secret."

"Is there a king of this country?" continued the vizier's son.

"Of course there is, and a queen, and a princess."

"What are their names?"

"The name of the princess is Gulizar, and the name of the queen——"

The vizier's son interrupted the old woman by turning to look at the prince, who was staring like a madman. "Yes," he said to him afterwards, "we are in the right country We shall see the beautiful princess."

One morning the two travellers noticed the old woman's most careful toilette: how careful she was in the arrangement of her hair and the set of her kasabah and puts.

"Who is coming?" said the vizier's son.

"Nobody," the old woman replied.

"Then where are you going?"

"I am going to see my daughter, who is a servant of the Princess Gulizar. I see her and the princess every day. I should have gone yesterday, if you had not been here and taken up all my time."

"Ah-h-h! Be careful not to say anything about us in the hearing of the princess." The vizier's son asked her not to speak about them at the palace, hoping that, because she had been told not to do so, she would mention their arrival, and thus the princess would be informed of their coming.

On seeing her mother the girl pretended to be very angry. "Why have you not been for two days?" she asked.

"Because, my dear," the old woman answered, "two young travellers, a prince and the son of some great vizier, have taken up their abode in my hut, and demand so much of my attention. It is nothing but cooking and cleaning, and cleaning and cooking, all day long. I can't understand the men," she added; "one of them especially appears very stupid. He asked me the name of this country and the name of the King. Now where can these men have come from, that they do not know these things? However, they are very great and very rich. They each give me a muhr every morning and every evening."

After this the old woman went and repeated almost the

same words to the princess, on the hearing of which the princess beat her severely, and threatened her with a severer punishment if she ever again spoke of the strangers before her.

In the evening, when the old woman had returned to her hut, she told the vizier's son how sorry she was that she could not help breaking her promise, and how the princess had struck her because she mentioned their coming and all about them.

"Alas! alas!" said the prince, who had eagerly listened to every word. "What, then, will be her anger at the sight of a man?"

"Anger?" said the vizier's son, with an astonished air. "She would be exceedingly glad to see one man. I know this. In this treatment of the old woman I see her request that you will go and see her during the coming dark fortnight."

"Heaven be praised!" the prince exclaimed.

The next time the old woman went to the palace Gulizar called one of her servants and ordered her to rush into the room while she was conversing with the old woman; and if the old woman asked what was the matter, she was to say that the King's elephants had gone mad, and were rushing about the city and bazaar in every direction, and destroying everything in their way.

The servant obeyed, and the old woman, fearing lest the elephants should go and push down her hut and kill the prince and his friend, begged the princess to let her depart. Now Gulizar had obtained a charmed swing, that landed whoever sat on it at the place wherever they wished to be. "Get the swing," she said to one of the servants standing.

by. When it was brought she bade the old woman step into it and desire to be at home.

The old woman did so, and was at once carried through the air quickly and safely to her hut, where she found her two lodgers safe and sound. "Oh!" she cried, "I thought that both of you would be killed by this time. The royal elephants have got loose and are running about wildly. When I heard this I was anxious about you. So the princess gave me this charmed swing to return in. But come, let us get outside before the elephants arrive and batter down the place."

"Don't believe this," said the vizier's son. "It is a mere hoax. They have been playing tricks with you."

"You will soon have your heart's desire," he whispered aside to the prince. "These things are signs."

Two days of the dark fortnight had elapsed, when the prince and the vizier's son seated themselves in the swing, and wished themselves within the grounds of the palace. In a moment they were there, and there too was the object of their search standing by one of the palace gates, and longing to see the prince quite as much as he was longing to see her.

Oh, what a happy meeting it was!

"At last," said Gulizar, "I have seen my beloved, my husband."

"A thousand thanks to Heaven for bringing me to you," said the prince.

Then the prince and Gulizar betrothed themselves to one another and parted, the one for the hut and the other for the palace, both of them feeling happier than they had ever been before.

Henceforth the prince visited Gulizar every day and returned to the hut every night. One morning Gulizar begged him to stay with her always. She was constantly afraid of some evil happening to him—perhaps robbers would slay him, or sickness attack him, and then she would be deprived of him. She could not live without seeing him. The prince showed her that there was no real cause for fear, and said that he felt he ought to return to his friend at night, because he had left his home and country and risked his life for him; and, moreover, if it had not been for his friend's help he would never have met with her.

Gulizar for the time assented, but she determined in her heart to get rid of the vizier's son as soon as possible. A few days after this conversation she ordered one of her maids to make a pilaw. She gave special directions that a certain poison was to be mixed into it while cooking, and as soon as it was ready the cover was to be placed on the saucepan, so that the poisonous steam might not escape. When the pilaw was ready she sent it at once by the hand of a servant to the vizier's son with this message: "Gulizar, the princess, sends you an offering in the name of her dead uncle."

On receiving the present the vizier's son thought that the prince had spoken gratefully of him to the princess, and therefore she had thus remembered him. Accordingly he sent back his salaam and expressions of thankfulness.

When it was dinner-time he took the saucepan of pilaw and went out to eat it by the stream. Taking off the lid, he threw it aside on the grass and then washed his hands. During the minute or so that he was performing these ablutions, the green grass under the cover of the saucepan turned quite yellow. He was astonished, and suspecting that there was poison in the pilaw, he took a little and threw it to some crows that were hopping about. The moment the crows ate what was thrown to them they fell down dead.

"Heaven be praised," exclaimed the vizier's son, "who has preserved me from death at this time!"

On the return of the prince that evening the vizier's son was very reticent and depressed. The prince noticed this change in him, and asked what was the reason. "Is it because I am away so much at the palace?" The vizier's son saw that the prince had nothing to do with the sending of the pilaw, and therefore told him everything.

"Look here," he said, "in this handkerchief is some pilaw that the princess sent me this morning in the name of her deceased uncle. It is saturated with poison. Thank Heaven, I discovered it in time!"

"Oh, brother! who could have done this thing? Who is there that entertains enmity against you?"

"The Princess Gulizar. Listen. The next time you go to see her, I entreat you to take some snow with you; and just before seeing the princess put a little of it into both your eyes. It will provoke tears, and Gulizar will ask you why you are crying. Tell her that you weep for the loss of your friend, who died suddenly this morning. Look! take, too, this wine and this shovel, and when you have feigned intense grief at the death of your friend, bid the princess to drink a little of the wine. It is strong, and will immediately send her into a deep sleep. Then, while she is asleep, heat the shovel and mark her back with it. Remember to bring back the shovel again, and also to take her pearl necklace. This done, return. Now fear not to execute these instructions, because on the fulfilment of them depends your fortune and happiness. I will arrange that your marriage with the princess shall be accepted by the King, her father, and all the court."

The prince promised that he would do everything as the vizier's son had advised him; and he kept his promise.

The following night, on the return of the prince from his visit to Gulizar, he and the vizier's son, taking the horses and bags of muhrs, went to a graveyard about a mile or so distant. It was arranged that the vizier's son should act the part of a fakir and the prince the part of the fakir's disciple and servant.

In the morning, when Gulizar had returned to her senses, she felt a smarting pain in her back, and noticed that her pearl necklace was gone. She went at once and informed the King of the loss of her necklace, but said nothing to him about the pain in her back.

The King was very angry when he heard of the theft, and caused proclamation concerning it to be made throughout all the city and surrounding country.

"It is well," said the vizier's son, when he heard of this proclamation. "Fear not, my brother, but go and take this necklace, and try to sell it in the bazaar."

The prince took it to a goldsmith and asked him to buy it.

"How much do you want for it?" asked the man.

"Fifty thousand rupees," the prince replied.

"All right," said the man; "wait here while I go and fetch the money."

The prince waited and waited, till at last the goldsmith

returned, and with him the kotwal, who at once took the prince into custody on the charge of stealing the princess's necklace.

"How did you get the necklace?" the kotwal asked.

"A fakir, whose servant I am, gave it to me to sell in the bazaar," the prince replied. "Permit me, and I will show you where he is."

The prince directed the kotwal and the policeman to the place where he had left the vizier's son, and there they found the fakir with his eyes shut and engaged in prayer. Presently, when he had finished his devotions, the kotwal asked him to explain how he had obtained possession of the princess's necklace.

"Call the King hither," he replied, "and then I will tell his Majesty face to face."

On this some men went to the King and told him what the fakir had said. His Majesty came, and seeing the fakir so solemn and earnest in his devotions, he was afraid to rouse his anger, lest peradventure the displeasure of Heaven should descend on him, and so he placed his hands together in the attitude of a supplicant, and asked, "How did you get my daughter's necklace?"

"Last night," replied the fakir, "we were sitting here by this tomb worshipping Khuda, when a ghoul, dressed as a princess, came and exhumed a body that had been buried a few days ago, and began to eat it. On seeing this I was filled with anger, and beat her back with a shovel, which lay on the fire at the time. While running away from me her necklace got loose and dropped. You wonder at these words, but they are not difficult to prove. Examine your daughter, and you will find the marks of the burn on her back. Go, and if it is as I say, send the princess to me, and I will punish her."

The King went back to the palace, and at once ordered the princess's back to be examined.

"It is so," said the maid-servant; "the burn is there."

"Then let the girl be slain immediately," the King shouted.

"No, no, your Majesty," they replied. "Let us send her to the fakir who discovered this thing, that he may do whatever he wishes with her."

The King agreed, and so the princess was taken to the graveyard.

"Let her be shut up in a cage, and be kept near the grave whence she, took out the corpse," said the fakir.

This was done, and in a little while the fakir and his disciple and the princess were left alone in the graveyard. Night had not long cast its dark mantle over the scene when the fakir and his disciple threw off their disguise, and taking their horses and luggage, appeared before the cage. They released the princess, rubbed some ointment over the scars on her back, and then sat her upon one of their horses behind the prince. Away they rode fast and far, and by the morning were able to rest and talk over their plans in safety. The vizier's son showed the princess some of the poisoned pilaw that she had sent him, and asked whether she had repented of her ingratitude. The princess wept, and acknowledged that he was her greatest helper and friend.

A letter was sent to the chief vizier telling him of all that had happened to the prince and the vizier's son since they had left their country. When the vizier read the letter he went and informed the King. The King caused a reply to be sent to the two exiles, in which he ordered them not to return, but to send a letter to Gulizar's father, and inform him of everything. Accordingly they did this; the prince wrote the letter at the vizier's son's dictation.

On reading the letter Gulizar's father was much enraged with his viziers and other officials for not discovering the presence in his country of these illustrious visitors, as he was especially anxious to ingratiate himself in the favour of the prince and the vizier's son. He ordered the execution of some of the viziers on a certain date.

"Come," he wrote back to the vizier's son, "and stay at the palace. And if the prince desires it, I will arrange for his marriage with Gulizar as soon as possible."

The prince and the vizier's son most gladly accepted the invitation, and received a right noble welcome from the King. The marriage soon took place, and then after a few weeks the King gave them presents of horses and elephants, and jewels and rich cloths, and bade them start for their own land; for he was sure that the King would now receive them. The night before they left, the viziers and others, whom the King intended to have executed as soon as his visitors had left, came and besought the vizier's son to plead for them, and promised that they each would give him a daughter in marriage. He agreed to do so, and succeeded in obtaining their pardon.

Then the prince, with his beautiful bride Gulizar, and the vizier's son, attended by a troop of soldiers, and a large number of camels and horses bearing very much treasure, left for their own land. In the midst of the way they passed the tower of the robbers, and with the help of the soldiers they razed it to the ground, slew all its inmates, and seized the treasure which they had been amassing there for several years.

At length they reached their own country, and when the King saw his son's beautiful wife and his magnificent retinue he was at once reconciled, and ordered him to enter the city and take up his abode there.

Henceforth all was sunshine on the path of the prince. He became a great favourite, and in due time succeeded to the throne, and ruled the country for many, many years in peace and happiness.

How Sun, Moon, and Wind went out to Dinner

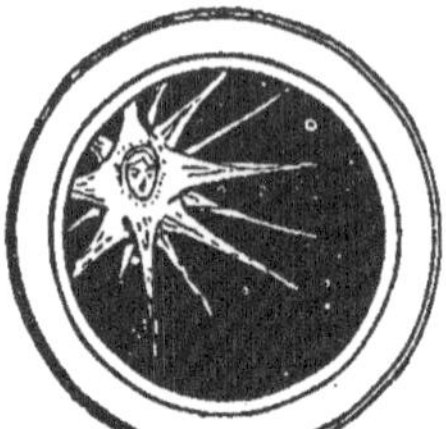

ONE day Sun, Moon, and Wind went out to dine with their uncle and aunts Thunder and Lightning. Their mother (one of the most distant Stars you see far up in the sky) waited alone for her children's return.

Now both Sun and Wind were greedy and selfish. They enjoyed the great feast that had been prepared for them, without a thought of saving any of it to take home to their mother—but the gentle Moon did not forget her. Of every dainty dish that was brought round, she placed a small portion under one of her beautiful long finger-nails, that Star might also have a share in the treat.

On their return, their mother, who had kept watch for them all night long with her little bright eye, said, "Well, children, what have you brought home for me?" Then Sun (who was eldest) said, "I have brought nothing home for you. I went out to enjoy myself with my friends—not to fetch a dinner for my mother!" And Wind said, "Neither have I brought anything home for you, mother. You could hardly expect me to bring a collection of good things for you, when I merely went out for my own pleasure." But Moon said, "Mother, fetch a plate, see what I have brought you." And shaking her hands she showered down such a choice dinner as never was seen before.

Then Star turned to Sun and spoke thus, "Because you went out to amuse yourself with your friends, and feasted and enjoyed yourself, without any thought of your mother at home—you shall be cursed. Henceforth, your rays shall ever be hot and scorching, and shall burn all that they touch. And men shall hate you, and cover their heads when you appear."

(And that is why the Sun is so hot to this day.)

Then she turned to Wind and said, "You also who forgot your mother in the midst of your selfish pleasures—hear your doom. You shall always blow in the hot dry weather, and shall parch and shrivel all living things. And men shall detest and avoid you from this very time."

(And that is why the Wind in the hot weather is still so disagreeable.)

But to Moon she said, "Daughter, because you remembered your mother, and kept for her a share in your own enjoyment, from henceforth you shall be ever cool, and calm, and bright. No noxious glare shall accompany your pure rays, and men shall always call you 'blessed.'"

(And that is why the Moon's light is so soft, and cool, and beautiful even to this day.)

How the Wicked Sons were Duped

A VERY wealthy old man, imagining that he was on the point of death, sent for his sons and divided his property among them. However, he did not die for several years afterwards; and miserable years many of them were. Besides the weariness of old age, the old fellow had to bear with much abuse and cruelty from his sons. Wretched, selfish ingrates! Previously they vied with one another in trying to please their father, hoping thus to receive more money, but now they had received their patrimony, they cared not how soon he left them—nay, the sooner the better, because he was only a needless trouble and expense. And they let the poor old man know what they felt.

One day he met a friend and related to him all his troubles. The friend sympathised very much with him, and promised to think over the matter, and call in a little while and tell him what to do. He did so; in a few days he visited the old man and put down four bags full of stones and gravel before him.

"Look here, friend," said he. "Your sons will get to know of my coming here to-day, and will inquire about it. You must pretend that I came to discharge a long-standing debt with you, and that you are several thousands of rupees richer than you thought you were. Keep these bags in your own hands, and on no account let your sons get to them as long as you are alive. You will soon find them change their conduct towards you. Salaam. I will come again soon to see how you are getting on."

When the young men got to hear of this further increase of wealth they began to be more attentive and pleasing to their father than ever before. And thus they continued to the day of the old man's demise, when the bags were greedily opened, and found to contain only stones and gravel!

The Pigeon and the Crow

ONCE upon a time the Bodhisatta was a Pigeon, and lived in a nest-basket which a rich man's cook had hung up in the kitchen, in order to earn merit by it. A greedy Crow, flying near, saw all sorts of delicate food lying about in the kitchen, and fell a-hungering after it. "How in the world can I get some?" thought he. At last he hit upon a plan.

When the Pigeon went to search for food, behind him, following, following, came the Crow.

"What do you want, Mr. Crow? You and I don't feed alike."

"Ah, but I like you and your ways! Let me be your chum, and let us feed together."

The Pigeon agreed, and they went on in company. The Crow pretended to feed along with the Pigeon, but ever and anon he would turn back, peck to bits some heap of cow-dung, and eat a fat worm. When he had got a bellyful of them, up he flies, as pert as you like:

"Hullo, Mr. Pigeon, what a time you take over your meal! One ought to draw the line somewhere. Let's be going home before it is too late." And so they did.

The cook saw that his Pigeon had brought a friend, and hung up another basket for him.

A few days afterwards there was a great purchase of fish which came to the rich man's kitchen. How the Crow longed for some! So there he lay, from early morn, groaning and making a great noise. Says the Pigeon to the Crow:

"Come, Sir Crow, and get your breakfast!"

"Oh dear! oh dear! I have such a fit of indigestion!" says he.

"Nonsense! Crows never have indigestion," said the Pigeon. "If you eat a lamp-wick, that stays in your stomach a little while; but anything else is digested in a trice, as soon as you eat it. Now do what I tell you; don't behave in this way just for seeing a little fish."

"Why do you say that, master? I have indigestion."

"Well, be careful," said the Pigeon, and flew away.

The cook prepared all the dishes, and then stood at the kitchen door, wiping the sweat off his body. "Now's my time!" thought Mr. Crow, and alighted on a dish containing some dainty food. Click! The cook heard it, and looked round. Ah! he caught the Crow, and plucked all the feathers out of his head, all but one tuft; he powdered ginger and cummin, mixed it up with butter-milk, and rubbed it well all over the bird's body.

"That's for spoiling my master's dinner and making me throw it away!" said he, and threw him into his basket. Oh, how it hurt!

By-and-by the Pigeon came in, and saw the Crow lying there, making a great noise. He made great game of him, and repeated a verse of poetry:

"Who is this tufted crane I see
Lying where he's no right to be?
Come out! my friend, the crow is near,
And he may do you harm, I fear!"

To this the Crow answered with another:

"No tufted crane am I—no, no!
I'm nothing but a greedy crow.
I would not do as I was told,
So now I'm plucked, as you behold."

And the Pigeon rejoined with a third verse:

"You'll come to grief again, I know—
It is your nature to do so;
If people make a dish of meat,
'Tis not for little birds to eat."

Then the Pigeon flew away, saying: "I can't live with this creature any longer." And the Crow lay there groaning till he died.

Notes and References

THE story literature of India is in a large measure the outcome of the moral revolution of the peninsula connected with the name of Gautama Buddha. As the influence of his life and doctrines grew, a tendency arose to connect all the popular stories of India round the great teacher. This could be easily effected owing to the wide spread of the belief in metempsychosis. All that was told of the sages of the past could be interpreted of the Buddha by representing them as pre-incarnations of him. Even with Fables, or beast-tales, this could be done, for the Hindus were Darwinists long before Darwin, and regarded beasts as cousins of men and stages of development in the progress of the soul through the ages. Thus, by identifying the Buddha with the heroes of all folk-tales and the chief characters in the beast-drolls, the Buddhists were enabled to incorporate the whole of the story-store of Hindustan in their sacred books, and enlist on their side the tale-telling instincts of men.

In making Buddha the centre figure of the popular literature of India, his followers also invented the Frame as a method of literary art. The idea of connecting a number of disconnected stories familiar to us from *The Arabian Nights*, Boccaccio's *Decamerone*, Chaucer's *Canterbury Tales*, or even *Pickwick*, is directly traceable to the plan of making Buddha the central figure of India folk-literature. Curiously enough, the earliest instance of this in Buddhist literature was intended to be a Decameron, ten tales of Buddha's previous births, told of each of the ten Perfections. Asvagosha, the early Boccaccio, died when he had completed thirty-four of the Birth-Tales. But other collections were made, and at last a corpus of the ATAKAS, or Birth-Tales of the Buddha, was carried over to Ceylon, possibly as early as the first introduction of Buddhism, 241 B.C. There they have remained till the present day, and have at last been made accessible in a complete edition in the original Pali by Prof. Fausböll.

These JĀTAKAS, as we now have them, are enshrined in a commentary on the *gathas*, or moral verses, written in Ceylon by one of Buddhaghosa's school in the fifth century A.D. They invariably begin with a "Story of the Present," an incident in Buddha's life which calls up to him a "Story of the Past," a folk-tale in which he had played a part during one of his former incarnations. Thus the fable of the Lion and the Crane, which opens the present collection, is introduced by a "Story of the Present" in the following words:—

"A service have we done thee" [the opening words of the *gatha* or moral verse]. "This the Master told while living at Jetavana concerning Devadatta's treachery. Not only now, O Bhickkus, but in a former existence was Devadatta ungrateful. And having said this he told a tale." Then follows the tale as given above (pp. 1, 2), and the commentary concludes: "The Master having given the lesson, summed up the Jātaka thus: 'At that time, the Lion was Devadatta, and the Crane was I myself.'" Similarly, with each story of the past the Buddha identifies himself, or is mentioned as identical with, the virtuous hero of the folk-tale. These Jātakas are 550 in number, and have been reckoned to include some 2000 tales. Some of these had been translated by Mr. Rhys-Davids (*Buddhist Birth Stories*, *I.*, Trübner's Oriental Library, 1880), Prof. Fausböll (*Five Jātakas*, Copenhagen), and Dr. R. Morris (*Folk-lore Journal*, vols. ii.-v.). A few exist sculptured on the earliest Buddhist Stupas. Thus several of the circular figure designs on the reliefs from Amaravati, now on the grand staircase of the British Museum, represent Jātakas, or previous births of the Buddha.

Some of the Jātakas bear a remarkable resemblance to some of the most familiar FABLES OF ÆSOP. So close is the resemblance, indeed, that it is impossible not to surmise an historical relation between the two. What this relation is I have discussed at considerable length in the "History of the Æsopic Fable," which forms the introductory volume to my edition of Caxton's *Esope* (London, D. Nutt, "Bibliothèque de Carabas," 1889). In this place I can only roughly summarise my results. I conjecture that a collection of fables existed in India before Buddha and independently of the Jātakas, and connected with the name of Kasyapa, who was afterwards made by the Buddhists into the latest of the twenty-seven pre-incarnations of the Buddha. This collection of the Fables of Kasyapa was brought to Europe with a deputation from the Cingalese King Chandra Muka Siwa (obiit 52 A.D.) to the Emperor Claudius about 50 A.D, and was done into Greek as the Λόγοι Λυβικοί of "Kybises." These were utilised by Babrius (from whom the Greek Æsop is derived) and Avian, and so came into the European Æsop. I have discussed all those that are to be found in the Jātakas in the "History" before mentioned, i. pp. 54–72 (see Notes i. xv. xx.). In these Notes henceforth I refer to the "History" as my *Æsop*.

There were probably other Buddhist collections of a similar nature to the Jātakas with a framework. When the Hindu reaction against Buddhism came, the Brahmins adapted these, with the omission of Buddha as the central figure. There is scarcely any doubt that the so-called FABLES OF BIDPAI were thus derived from Buddhistic sources. In its Indian form this is now extant as a *Panchatantra* or Pentateuch, five books of tales connected by a Frame. This collection is of special interest to us in the present connection, as it has come to Europe in various forms and shapes. I have edited Sir Thomas North's English version of an Italian adaptation of a Spanish translation of a Latin version of a Hebrew translation of an Arabic adaptation of the Pehlevi version of the Indian original (*Fables of Bidpai*, London, D. Nutt, "Bibliothèque de Carabas," 1888). In this I give a genealogical table of the various versions, from which I calculate that the tales have been translated into thirty-eight languages in 112 different versions, twenty different ones in English alone. Their influence on European folk-tales has been very great: it is probable that nearly one-tenth of these can be traced to the Biddai literature. (See Notes v. ix. x. xiii. xv.)

Other collections of a similar character, arranged in a frame, and derived ultimately from Buddhistic sources, also reached Europe and formed popular reading in the Middle Ages. Among these may be mentioned THE TALES OF SINDIBAD, known to Europe as *The Seven Sages of Rome*: from this we get the Gellert story (*cf. Celtic Fairy Tales*), though it also occurs in the Bidpai. Another popular collection was that associated with the life of St. Buddha, who has been canonised as St. Josaphat: BARLAAM AND JOSAPHAT tells of his conversion and much else besides, including the tale of The Three Caskets, used by Shakespeare in the *Merchant of Venice*.

Some of the Indian tales reached Europe at the time of the Crusades, either orally or in collections no longer extant. The earliest selection of these was the *Disciplina Clericalis* of Petrus Alphonsi, a Spanish Jew converted about 1106; his tales were to be used as seasoning for sermons, and strong seasoning they must have proved. Another Spanish collection of considerably later date was entitled *El Conde Lucanor* (Eng. trans. by W. York): this contains the fable of *The Man, his Son, and their Ass*, which they ride or carry as the popular voice decides. But the most famous collection of this kind was that known as GESTA ROMANORUM, much of which was certainly derived from Oriental and ultimately Indian sources, and so might more appropriately be termed *Gesta Indorum*.

All these collections, which reached Europe in the twelfth and thirteenth centuries, became very popular, and were used by monks and friars to enliven their sermons as EXEMPLA. Prof. Crane has given a full account of this very curious phenomenon in his erudite edition of the *Exempla of Jacques de Vitry* (Folk Lore Society, 1890). The Indian stories were also used by the Italian *Novellieri*, much of Boccaccio and his school being derived from this source. As these again gave material for the Elizabethan Drama, chiefly in W. Painter's *Palace of Pleasure*, a collection of translated *Novelle* which I have edited (Lond., 3 vols. 1890), it is not surprising that we can at times trace portions of Shakespeare back to India. It should also be mentioned that one-half of La Fontaine's Fables (Bks. vii.–xii.) are derived from Indian sources. (*See* Note on No. v.)

In India itself the collection of stories in frames went on and still goes on. Besides those already mentioned there are the stories of *Vikram and the Vampire* (Vetala), translated among others by the late Sir Richard Burton, and the seventy stories of a parrot (*Suka Saptati*). The whole of this literature was summed up by Somadeva, C. 1200 A.D. in a huge compilation entitled *Katha Sarit Sagara* ("Ocean of the Stream of Stories"). Of this work, written in very florid style, Mr. Tawney has produced a translation in two volumes, in the *Bibliotheca Indica*. Unfortunately, there is a Divorce Court atmosphere about the whole book, and my selections from it have been accordingly restricted. (Notes, No. xi.)

So much for a short sketch of Indian folk-tales so far as they have been reduced to writing in the native literature.* The Jātakas are probably the oldest collection of such tales in literature, and the greater part of the rest are demonstrably more than a thousand years old. It is certain that much (perhaps one-fifth) of the popular literature of modern Europe is derived from those portions of this large bulk which came West with the Crusades through the medium of Arabs and Jews. In his elaborate *Einleitung* to the *Pantschatantra*, the Indian version of the Fables of Bidpai, Prof. Benfey contended with enormous erudition that the majority of folk-tale incidents were to be found in the Bidpai literature. His introduction consisted of over 200 mono-

---

* An admirable and full account of this literature was given by M. A. Barth in *Mélusine*, t. iv. No. 12, and t. v. No. 1. See also Table i. of Prof. Rhys-Davids' *Birth Stories*.

graphs on the spread of Indian tales to Europe. He wrote in 1859, before the great outburst of folk-tale collection in Europe, and he had not thus adequate materials to go about in determining the extent of Indian influence on the popular mind of Europe. But he made it clear that for beast-tales and for drolls, the majority of those current in the mouths of occidental people were derived from Eastern and mainly Indian sources. He was not successful, in my opinion, in tracing the serious fairy tale to India. Few of the tales in the Indian literary collections could be dignified by the name of fairy tales, and it was clear that, if these were to be traced to India, an examination of the contemporary folk-tales of the peninsula would have to be attempted.

The collection of current Indian folk-tales has been the work of the last quarter of a century, a work, even after what has been achieved, still in its initial stages. The credit of having begun the process is due to Miss Frere, who, while her father was Governor of the Bombay Presidency, took down from the lips of her *ayah*, Anna de Souza, one of a Lingaet family from Goa who had been Christian for three generations, the tales she afterwards published with Mr. Murray in 1868, under the title, "*Old Deccan Days, or, Indian Fairy Legends current in Southern India, collected from oral tradition by M. Frere, with an introduction and notes by Sir Bartle Frere.*" Her example was followed by Miss Stokes in her *Indian Fairy Tales* (London, Ellis & White, 1880), who took down her tales from two *ayahs* and a *Khitmatgar*, all of them Bengalese—the *ayahs* Hindus, and the man a Mohammedan. Mr. Ralston introduced the volume with some remarks which dealt too much with sun-myths for present-day taste. Another collection from Bengal was that of Lal Behari Day, a Hindu gentleman, in his *Folk-Tales of Bengal* (London, Macmillan, 1883). The Panjab and the Kashmir then had their turn: Mrs. Steel collected, and Captain (now Major) Temple edited and annotated, their *Wideawake Stories* (London, Trübner, 1884), stories capitally told and admirably annotated. Captain Temple increased the value of this collection by a remarkable analysis of all the incidents contained in the two hundred Indian folk-tales collected up to this date. It is not too much to say that this analysis marks an onward step in the scientific study of the folk-tale: there is such a thing, derided as it may be. I have throughout the Notes been able to draw attention to Indian parallels by a simple reference to Major Temple's Analysis.

Major Temple has not alone himself collected: he has been the cause that many others have collected. In the pages of the *Indian Antiquary*, edited by him, there have appeared from time to time folk-tales collected from all parts of India. Some of these have been issued separately. Sets of tales from Southern India, collected by the Pandit Natesa Sastri, have been issued under the title *Folk-Lore of Southern India*, three fascicules of which have been recently re-issued by Mrs. Kingscote under the title, *Tales of the Sun* (W. H. Allen, 1891): it would have been well if the identity of the two works had been clearly explained. The largest addition to our knowledge of the Indian folk-tale that has been made since *Wideawake Stories* is that contained in Mr. Knowles' *Folk-Tales of Kashmir* (Trübner's Oriental Library, 1887), sixty-three stories, some of great length. These, with Mr. Campbell's *Santal Tales* (1892); Ramaswami Raju's *Indian Fables* (London, Sonnenschein, n.d.); M. Thornhill, *Indian Fairy Tales* (London, 1889); and E. J. Robinson, *Tales of S. India* (1885), together with those contained in books of travel like Thornton's *Bannu* or Smeaton's *Karens of Burmah*, bring up the list of printed Indian folk-tales to over 350—a respectable total indeed, but a mere drop in the ocean of the stream of stories that must exist in such a huge population as that of India: the Central Provinces in particular are practically unexplored. There are doubtless many collections still unpublished. Col. Lewin has large numbers, besides the few published in his *Lushai Grammar;* and Mr. M. L. Dames has a number of Baluchi tales which I have been privileged to use. Altogether, India now ranks among the best represented countries for printed folk-tales, coming only after Russia (1500), Germany (1200), Italy and France (1000 each).* Counting the ancient with the modern, India has probably some 600 to 700 folk-tales printed and translated in accessible form. There should be enough material to determine the vexed question of the relations between the European and the Indian collections.

This question has taken a new departure with the researches of M. Emanuel Cosquin in his *Contes populaires de Lorraine* (Paris, 1886, 2e tirage, 1890), undoubtedly the most important contribution to the scientific study of the folk-tale since the Grimms. M. Cosquin gives in the annotations to the eighty-four tales which he has collected in Lorraine a mass of information as to the various forms which the tales take in other countries of Europe and in the East. In my opinion, the work he has done for the European folk-tale is even more valuable than the conclusions he draws from it as to the relations with India. He has taken up the work which Wilhelm Grimm dropped in 1859, and shown from the huge accumulations of folk-tales that have appeared during the last thirty years that there is a common fund of folk-tales which every country of Europe without exception possesses,

* Finland boasts of 12,000, but most of these lie unprinted among the archives of the Helsingfors Literary Society.

though this does not, of course, preclude them from possessing others that are not shared by the rest. M. Cosquin further contends that the whole of these have come from the East, ultimately from India, not by literary transmission, as Benfey contended, but by oral transmission. He has certainly shown that very many of the most striking incidents common to European folk-tales are also to be found in Eastern *mährchen*. What, however, he has failed to show is that some of these may not have been carried out to the Eastern world by Europeans. Borrowing tales is a mutual process, and when Indian meets European, European meets Indian; which borrowed from which, is a question which we have very few criteria to decide. It should be added that Mr. W. A. Clouston has in England collected with exemplary industry a large number of parallels between Indian and European folk-tale incidents in his *Popular Tales and Fictions* (Edinburgh, 2 vols., 1887) and *Book of Noodles* (London, 1888). Mr. Clouston has not openly expressed his conviction that all folk-tales are Indian in origin: he prefers to convince us *non vi sed sæpe cadendo*. He has certainly made out a good case for tracing all European drolls, or comic folk-tales, from the East.

With the fairy tale strictly so called—*i.e.*, the serious folk-tale of romantic adventure—I am more doubtful. It is mainly a modern product in India as in Europe, so far as literary evidence goes. The vast bulk of the Jātakas does not contain a single example worthy the name, nor does the Bidpai literature. Some of Somadeva's tales, however, approach the nature of fairy tales, but there are several Celtic tales which can be traced to an earlier date than his (1200 A.D.) and are equally near to fairy tales. Yet it is dangerous to trust to mere non-appearance in literature as proof of non-existence among the folk. To take our own tales here in England, there is not a single instance of a reference to *Jack and the Beanstalk* for the last three hundred years, yet it is undoubtedly a true folk-tale. And it is indeed remarkable how many of the *formulæ* of fairy tales have been found of recent years in India. Thus, the *Magic Fiddle*, found among the Santals by Mr. Campbell in two variants (see Notes on vi.), contains the germ idea of the widespread story represented in Great Britain by the ballad of *Binnorie* (see *English Fairy Tales*, No. ix.). Similarly, Mr. Knowles' collection has added considerably to the number of Indian variants of European "formulæ" beyond those noted by M. Cosquin.

It is still more striking as regards *incidents*. In a paper read before the Folk-Lore Congress of 1891, and reprinted in the *Transactions*, pp. 76 *seq.*, I have drawn up a list of some 630 incidents found in common among European folk-tales (including drolls). Of these, I reckon that about 250 have been already found among Indian folk-tales, and the number is increased by each new collection that is made or printed. The moral of this is, that India belongs to a group of peoples who have a common store of stories; India belongs to Europe for purposes of comparative folk-tales.

Can we go further and say that India is the source of all the incidents that are held in common by European children? I think we may answer "Yes" as regards droll incidents, the travels of many of which we can trace, and we have the curious result that European children owe their earliest laughter to Hindu wags. As regards the serious incidents, further inquiry is needed. Thus, we find the incident of an "external soul" (Life Index, Captain Temple very appropriately named it) in Asbjornsen's *Norse Tales* and in Miss Frere's *Old Deccan Days* (see Notes on *Punchkin*). Yet the latter is a very suspicious source, since Miss Frere derived her tales from a Christian *ayah* whose family had been in Portuguese Goa for a hundred years. May they not have got the story of the giant with his soul outside his body from some European sailor touching at Goa? This is to a certain extent negatived by the fact of the frequent occurrence of the incident in Indian folk-tales (Captain Temple gave a large number of instances in *Wideawake Stories*, pp. 404–5). On the other hand, Mr. Frazer in his *Golden Bough* has shown the wide spread of the idea among all savage or semi-savage tribes. (See Note on No. iv.)

In this particular case we may be doubtful; but in others, again—as the incident of the rat's tail up nose (see Notes on *The Charmed Ring*)—there can be little doubt of the Indian origin. And generally, so far as the incidents are marvellous and of true fairy-tale character, the presumption is in favour of India, because of the vitality of animism or metempsychosis in India throughout all historic time. No Hindu would doubt the fact of animals speaking or of men transformed into plants and animals. The European may once have had these beliefs, and may still hold them implicitly as "survivals"; but in the "survival" stage they cannot afford material for artistic creation, and the fact that the higher minds of Europe for the last thousand years have discountenanced these beliefs has not been entirely without influence. Of one thing there is practical certainty: the fairy tales that are common to the Indo-European world were invented once for all in a certain locality, and thence spread to all the countries in culture contact with the original source. The mere fact that contiguous countries have more similarities in their story store than distant ones is sufficient to prove this: indeed, the fact that any single country has spread throughout it a definite set of folk-tales as distinctive as its flora and fauna is sufficient to prove it. It is equally certain that not all folk-tales have come from one source, for each country has tales peculiar to itself. The question is as to the source of the tales that are common to all European children, and increasing evidence seems to show that this common nucleus is derived from India and India alone. The Hindus have been more successful than others, because of two facts: they have had the appropriate "atmosphere" of metempsychosis, and they have also had spread among the people sufficient literary training and mental grip to invent plots. The Hindu tales have ousted the native European, which undoubtedly existed independently; indeed, many still survive, especially in Celtic lands. Exactly in the same way, Perrault's tales have ousted the older English folk-tales, and it is with the utmost difficulty that one can get true English fairy tales because *Red Riding Hood*, *Cinderella*, *Blue Beard*, *Puss in Boots* and the rest, have survived in the struggle for existence among English folk-tales. So far as Europe has a common store of fairy tales, it owes this to India.

I do not wish to be misunderstood. I do not hold with Benfey that all European folk-tales are derived from the Bidpai literature and similar literary products, nor with M. Cosquin that they are all derived from India. The latter scholar has proved that there is a nucleus of stories in every European land which is common to all. I calculate that this includes from 30 to 50 per cent. of the whole, and it is this common stock of Europe that I regard as coming from India mainly at the time of the Crusades, and chiefly by oral transmission. It includes all the beast tales and most of the drolls, but evidence is still lacking about the more serious fairy tales, though it is increasing with every fresh collection of folk-tales in India, the great importance of which is obvious from the above considerations.

In the following Notes I give, as on the two previous occasions, the *source* whence I derived the tale, then *parallels*, and finally *remarks*. For Indian *parallels* I have been able to refer to Major Temple's remarkable Analysis of Indian Folk-tale incidents at the end of *Wide-awake Stories* (pp. 386–436), for European ones to my alphabetical List of Incidents, with bibliographical references, in *Transactions of Folk-Lore Congress*, 1892, pp. 87–98. My *remarks* have been mainly devoted to tracing the relation between the Indian and the European tales, with the object of showing that the latter have been derived from the former. I have, however, to some extent handicapped myself, as I have avoided giving again the Indian versions of stories already given in *English Fairy Tales* or *Celtic Fairy Tales*.

I. THE LION AND THE CRANE.

Source.—V. Fausböll, *Five Jātakas*, Copenhagen, 1861, pp. 35–8, text and translation of the *Jāvasakuna Jātaka*. I have ventured to English Prof. Fausböll's version, which was only intended as a "crib" to the Pali. For the omitted Introduction, see *supra*.

Parallels.—I have given a rather full collection of parallels, running to about a hundred numbers, in my *Æsop*, pp. 232–4. The chief of these are: (1) for the East, the Midrashic version ("Lion and Egyptian Partridge"), in the great Rabbinic commentary on Genesis (*Bereshith-rabba*, c. 64); (2) in classical antiquity, Phædrus, i. 8 ("Wolf and Crane"), and Babrius, 94 ("Wolf and Heron"), and the Greek proverb Suidas, ii. 248 ("Out of the Wolf's Mouth"); (3) in the Middle Ages, the so-called Greek *Æsop*. ed. Halm, 276 *b*, really prose versions of Babrius and "Romulus," or prose of Phædrus, i. 8, also the Romulus of Ademar (fl. 1030), 64; it occurs also on the Bayeux Tapestry, in Marie de France, 7, and in Benedict of Oxford's *Mishle Shualim* (Heb.), 8; (4) Stainhöwel took it from the "Romulus" into his German Æsop (1480), whence all the modern European Æsops are derived.

Remarks.—I have selected *The Wolf and the Crane* as my typical example in my "History of the Æsopic Fable," and can only give here a rough summary of the results I there arrived at concerning the fable, merely premising that these results are at present no more than hypotheses. The similarity of the Jātaka form with that familiar to us, and derived by us in the last resort from Phædrus, is so striking that few will deny some historical relation between them. I conjecture that the Fable originated in India, and came West by two different routes. First, it came by oral tradition to Egypt, as one of the Libyan Fables which the ancients themselves distinguished from the Æsopic Fables. It was, however, included by Demetrius Phalereus, tyrant of Athens, and founder of the Alexandrian library c. 300 B.C., in his *Assemblies of Æsopic Fables*, which I have shown to be the source of Phædrus' Fables c. 30 A.D. Besides this, it came from Ceylon in the Fables of Kybises—*i.e.*, Kasyapa the Buddha—c. 50 A.D., was adapted into Hebrew, and used for political purposes, by Rabbi Joshua ben Chananyah in a harangue to the Jews, c. 120 A.D., begging them to be patient while within the jaws of Rome. The Hebrew form uses the lion, not the wolf, as the ingrate, which enables us to decide on the Indian *provenance* of the Midrashic version. It may be remarked that the use of the lion in this and other Jātakas is indirectly a testimony to their great age, as the lion has become rarer and rarer in India during historic times, and is now confined to the Gir forest of Kathiáwar, where only a dozen specimens exist, and are strictly preserved.

The verses at the end are the earliest parts of the Jãtaka, being in more archaic Pali than the rest: the story is told by the commentator (c. 400 A.D.) to illustrate them It is probable that they were brought over on the first introduction of Buddhism into Ceylon, c. 241 B.C. This would give them an age of over two thousand years, nearly three hundred years earlier than Phædrus, from whom comes our *Wolf and Crane.*

II. PRINCESS LABAM.

Source.—Miss Stokes, *Indian Fairy Tales*, No. xxii. pp. 153–63, told by Muniyá, one of the ayahs. I have left it unaltered, except that I have replaced "God" by "Khuda," the word originally used (see Notes *l. c.*, p. 237).

Parallels.—The tabu, as to a particular direction, occurs in other Indian stories as well as in European folk-tales (see notes on Stokes, p. 286). The *grateful animals* theme occurs in "The Soothsayer's Son" (*infra*, No. x.), and frequently in Indian folk-tales (see Temple's Analysis, III. i. 5–7; *Wideawake Stories*, pp. 412–3). The thorn in the tiger's foot is especially common (Temple, *l. c.*, 6, 9), and recalls the story of Androclus, which occurs in the derivates of Phædrus, and may thus be Indian in origin (see Benfey, *Panschatantra*, i. 211, and the parallels given in my *Æsop*, Ro. iii. 1, p. 243). The theme is, however, equally frequent in European folk-tales: see my List of Incidents, *Proc. Folk-Lore Congress*, p. 91, s.v. "Grateful Animals" and "Gifts by Grateful Animals." Similarly, the "Bride Wager" incident at the end is common to a large number of Indian and European folk-tales (Temple, Analysis, p. 430; my List, *l.c. sub voce*). The tasks are also equally common (*c.f.* "Battle of the Birds" in *Celtic Fairy Tales*), though the exact forms as given in "Princess Labam" are not known in Europe.

Remarks.—We have here a concrete instance of the relation of Indian and European fairy-tales. The human mind may be the same everywhere, but it is not likely to hit upon the sequence of incidents, *Direction tabu—Grateful Animals—Bride-Wager—Tasks*, by accident or independently: Europe must have borrowed from India, or India from Europe. As this must have occurred within historic times, indeed within the last thousand years, when even European peasants are not likely to have *invented*, even if they believed, in the incident of the grateful animals, the probability is in favour of borrowing from India, possibly through the intermediation of Arabs at the time of the

Crusades. It is only a probability, but we cannot in any case reach more than probability in this matter, just at present.

III. LAMBIKIN.

Source.—Steel-Temple, *Wideawake Stories*, pp. 69-72, originally published in *Indian Antiquary*, xii. 175. The droll is common throughout the Panjab.

Parallels.—The similarity of the concluding episode with the finish of the "Three Little Pigs" (*Eng. Fairy Tales*, No. xiv.). In my notes on that droll I have pointed out that the pigs were once goats or kids with "hair on their chinny chin chin." This brings the tale a stage nearer to the Lambikin.

Remarks.—The similarity of Pig No. 3 rolling down hill in the churn and the Lambikin in the Drumikin can scarcely be accidental, though, it must be confessed, the tale has undergone considerable modification before it reached England.

IV. PUNCHKIN.

Source.—Miss Frere, *Old Deccan Days*, pp. 1-16, from her ayah, Anna de Souza, of a Lingaet family settled and Christianised at Goa for three generations. I should perhaps add that a Prudhan is a Prime Minister or Vizier; Punts are the same, and Sirdars, nobles.

Parallels.—The son of seven mothers is a characteristic Indian conception, for which see Notes on "The Son of Seven Queens" in this collection, No. xvi. The mother transformed, envious stepmother, ring recognition, are all incidents common to East and West; bibliographical references for parallels may be found under these titles in my List of Incidents. The external soul of the ogre has been studied by Mr. E. Clodd in *Folk-Lore Journal*, vol. ii., "The Philosophy of Punchkin," and still more elaborately in the section, "The External Soul in Folk-Tales," in Mr. Frazer's *Golden Bough*, ii. pp. 296-326. See also Major Temple's Analysis, II. iii., *Wideawake Stories*, pp. 404-5, who there gives the Indian parallels.

Remarks.—Both Mr. Clodd and Mr. Frazer regard the essence of the tale to consist in the conception of an external soul or "life-index," and they both trace in this a 'survival" of savage philosophy, which they consider occurs among all men at a certain stage of culture. But the most cursory examination of the sets of tales containing these incidents in Mr. Frazer's analyses shows that many, indeed the majority, of these tales cannot be independent of one another; for they contain not alone the incident of an external materialised soul, but the further point that this is contained in something else, which is enclosed in another thing, which is again surrounded by a wrapper. This Chinese ball arrangement is found in the Deccan ("Punchkin"); in Bengal (Day, *Folk-Tales of Bengal*); in Russia (Ralston, p. 103 *seq.*, "Koschkei the Deathless," also in Mr. Lang's *Red Fairy Book*); in Servia (Mijatovics, *Servian Folk-Lore*, p. 172); in South Slavonia (Wratislaw, p. 225); in Rome (Miss Busk, p. 164); in Albania (Dozon, p. 132 *seq.*); in Transylvania (Haltrich, No. 34); in Schleswig-Holstein (Müllenhoff, p. 404); in Norway (Asbjörnsen, No. 36, *ap.* Dasent, *Pop. Tales*, p. 55, "The Giant who had no Heart in his Body"); and finally, in the Hebrides (Campbell, *Pop. Tales*, p. 10, *cf. Celtic Fairy Tales*, No. xvii., "Sea Maiden"). Here we have the track of this remarkable idea of an external soul enclosed in a succession of wrappings, which we can trace from Hindostan to the Hebrides.

It is difficult to imagine that we have not here the actual migration of the tale from East to West. In Bengal we have the soul "in a necklace, in a box, in the heart of a *boal* fish, in a tank"; in Albania "it is in a pigeon, in a hare, in the silver tusk of a wild boar"; in Rome it is "in a stone, in the head of a bird, in the head of a leveret, in the middle head of a seven-headed hydra"; in Russia "it is in an egg, in a duck, in a hare, in a casket, in an oak"; in Servia it is "in a board, in the heart of a fox, in a mountain"; in Transylvania "it is in a light, in an egg, in a duck, in a pond, in a mountain;" in Norway it is "in an egg, in a duck, in a well, in a church, on an island, in a lake"; in the Hebrides it is "in an egg, in the belly of a duck, in the belly of a wether, under a flagstone on the threshold." It is impossible to imagine the human mind independently imagining such bizarre convolutions. They were borrowed from one nation to the other, and till we have reason shown to the contrary, the original lender was a Hindu. I should add that the mere conception of an external soul occurs in the oldest Egyptian tale of "The Two Brothers," but the wrappings are absent.

V. THE BROKEN POT.

Source.—Pantschatantra, V. ix., tr. Benfey, ii. 345–6.

Parallels.—Benfey, in § 209 of his *Einleitung*, gives bibliographical references to most of those which are given at length in Prof. M. Müller's brilliant essay on "The Migration of Fables" (*Selected Essays*, i. 500–76), which is entirely devoted to the travels of the fable from India to La Fontaine. See also Mr. Clouston, *Pop. Tales*, ii. 432 *seq.* I have translated the Hebrew version in my essay, "Jewish Influence on the Diffusion of Folk-Tales," pp. 6–7. Our proverb, "Do not count your chickens before they are hatched," is ultimately to be derived from India.

Remarks.—The stories of Alnaschar, the Barber's fifth brother in the *Arabian Nights*, and of La Perette, who counted her chickens before they were hatched, in La Fontaine, are demonstrably derived from the same Indian original from which our story was obtained. The travels of the "Fables of Bidpai" from India to Europe are well known and distinctly traceable. I have given a rough summary of the chief critical results in the introduction to my edition of the earliest English version of the *Fables of Bidpai*, by Sir Thomas North, of Plutarch fame (London, D. Nutt, "Bibliothèque de Carabas," 1888), where I have given an elaborate genealogical table of the multitudinous versions. La Fontaine's version, which has rendered the fable so familiar to us all, comes from Bonaventure des Periers, *Contes et Nouvelles*, who got it from the *Dialogus Creaturarum* of Nicholaus Pergamenus, who derived it from the *Sermones* of Jacques de Vitry (see Prof. Crane's edition, No. li.), who probably derived it from the *Directorium Humanæ Vitæ* of John of Capua, a converted Jew, who translated it from the Hebrew version of the Arabic *Kalilah wa Dimnah*, which was itself derived from the old Syriac version of a Pehlevi translation of the original Indian work, probably called after Karataka and Damanaka, the names of two jackals who figure in the earlier stories of the book. Prof. Rhys-Davids informs me that these names are more akin to Pali than to Sanskrit, which makes it still more probable that the whole literature is ultimately to be derived from a Buddhist source.

The theme of La Perette is of interest as showing the *literary* transmission of tales from Orient to Occident. It also shows the possibility of an influence of literary on oral tradition, as is shown by our proverb, and by the fact, which Benfey mentions, that La Fontaine's story has had influence on two of Grimm's tales, Nos. 164, 168.

VI. THE MAGIC FIDDLE.

Source.—A. Campbell, *Santal Folk Tales*, 1892, pp. 52–6, with some verbal alterations. A Bonga is the presiding spirit of a certain kind of rice land; Doms and Hadis are low-caste aborigines, whose touch is considered polluting. The Santals are a forest tribe, who live in the

Santal Parganas, 140 miles N.W. of Calcutta (Sir W. W. Hunter, *The Indian Empire*, 57–60).

Parallels.—Another version occurs in Campbell, p. 106 *seq.*, which shows that the story is popular among the Santals. It is obvious, however, that neither version contains the real finish of the story, which must have contained the denunciation of the magic fiddle of the murderous sisters. This would bring it under the formula of *The Singing Bone*, which M. Monseur has recently been studying with a remarkable collection of European variants in the Bulletin of the Wallon Folk-Lore Society of Liège (*cf. Eng. Fairy Tales*, No. ix.). There is a singing bone in Steel-Temple's *Wideawake Stories*, pp. 127 *seq.* ("Little Anklebone").

Remarks.—Here we have another theme of the common store of European folk-tales found in India. Unfortunately, the form in which it occurs is mutilated, and we cannot draw any definite conclusion from it.

VII. THE CRUEL CRANE OUTWITTED.

Source.—The Baka-Jātaka, Fausböll, No. 38, tr. Rhys-Davids, pp. 315–21. The Buddha this time is the Genius of the Tree.

Parallels.—This Jātaka got into the Bidpai literature, and occurs in

all its multitudinous offshoots (*see* Benfey, *Einleitung*, § 60) among others in the earliest English translation by North (my edition, pp. 118–22), where the crane becomes "a great Paragone of India (of those that liue a hundredth yeares and neuer mue their feathers)." The crab, on hearing the ill news "called to Parliament all the Fishes of the Lake," and before all are devoured destroys the Paragon, as in the Jātaka, and returned to the remaining fishes, who "all with one consent give hir many a thanke."

Remarks.—An interesting point, to which, I have drawn attention in my Introduction to North's Bidpai, is the probability that the illustrations of the tales as well as the tales themselves, were translated, so to speak, from one country to another. We can trace them in Latin, Hebrew, and Arabic MSS, and a few are extant on Buddhist Stupas. Under these circumstances, it may be of interest to compare with Mr. Batten's conception of the Crane and the Crab (*supra*, p. 50) that of the German artist who illustrated the first edition of the Latin Bidpai, probably following the traditional representations of the MS., which itself could probably trace back to India.

VIII. LOVING LAILI.

Source.—Miss Stokes, *Indian Fairy Tales*, pp. 73–84. Majnun and Laili are conventional names for lovers, the Romeo and Juliet of Hindostan.

Parallels.—Living in animals' bellies occurs elsewhere in Miss Stokes' book, pp. 66, 124; also in Miss Frere's, 188. The restoration of beauty by fire occurs as a frequent theme (Temple, Analysis, III. vi. f. p. 418). Readers will be reminded of the *dénouement* of Mr. Rider Haggard's *She.* Resuscitation from ashes has been used very effectively by Mr. Lang in his delightful *Prince Prigio.*

Remarks.—The white skin and blue eyes of Prince Majnun deserve attention. They are possibly a relic of the days of Aryan conquest, when the fair-skinned, fair-haired Aryan conquered the swarthier aboriginals. The name for caste in Sanskrit is *varna*, "colour"; and one Hindu cannot insult another more effectually than by calling him a black man. *Cf.* Stokes, pp. 238–9, who suggests that the red hair is something solar, and derived from myths of the solar hero.

IX. THE TIGER, THE BRAHMAN, AND THE JACKAL.

Source.—Steel-Temple, *Wideawake Stories*, pp. 116–20; first published in *Indian Antiquary*, xii. p. 170 *seq.*

Parallels.—No less than 94 parallels are given by Prof. K. Krohn in his elaborate discussion of this fable in his dissertation, *Mann und Fuchs* (Helsingfors, 1891), pp. 38–60; to which may be added three Indian variants, omitted by him, but mentioned by Capt. Temple, *l. c.*, p. 324

in the *Bhâgavata Purâna*, the *Gul Bakâolî* and *Ind. Ant.* xii. 177; and a couple more in my *Æsop*, p. 253: add Smeaton, *Karens*, p. 126.

Remarks.—Prof. Krohn comes to the conclusion that the majority of the oral forms of the tale come from literary versions (p. 47), whereas the *Reynard* form has only had influence on a single variant. He reduces the century of variants to three type forms. The first occurs in two Egyptian versions collected in the present day, as well as in Petrus Alphonsi in the twelfth century, and the *Fabulæ Extravagantes* of the thirteenth or fourteenth: here the ingrate animal is a crocodile, which asks to be carried away from a river about to dry up, and there is only one judge. The second is that current in India and represented by the story in the present collection: here the judges are three. The third is that current among Western Europeans, which has spread to S. Africa and N. and S. America: also three judges. Prof. K. Krohn counts the first the original form, owing to the single judge and the naturalness of the opening, by which the critical situation is brought about. The further question arises, whether this form, though found in Egypt now, is indigenous there, and if so, how it got to the East. Prof. Krohn grants the possibility of the Egyptian form having been invented in India and carried to Egypt, and he allows that the European forms have been influenced by the Indian. The "Egyptian" form is found in Burmah (Smeaton, *l. c.*, p. 128), as well as the Indian, a fact of which Prof. H. Krohn was unaware, though it turns his whole argument. The evidence we have of other folk-tales of the beast-epic emanating from India improves the chances of this also coming from that source. One thing at least is certain: all these hundred variants come ultimately from one source. The incident "Inside again" of the *Arabian Nights* (the Djinn and the bottle) and European tales is also a secondary derivate.

X. THE SOOTHSAYER'S SON.

Source.—Mrs. Kingscote, *Tales of the Sun* (p. 11 *seq.*), from Pandit Natesa Sastri's *Folk-Lore of Southern India*, pt. ii., originally from *Ind. Antiquary*. I have considerably condensed and modified the somewhat Babu English of the original.

Parallels.—See Benfey, *Pantschatantra*, § 71, i. pp. 193–222, who quotes the *Kama Jātaka* as the ultimate source: it also occurs in the *Saccankira Jātaka* (Fausböll, No. 73), trans. Rev. R. Morris, *Folk-Lore Jour.* iii. 348 *seq.* The story of the ingratitude of man compared with the gratitude of beasts came early to the West, where it occurs in the *Gesta Romanorum*, c. 119. It was possibly from an early form of this collection that Richard Cœur de Lion got the story, and used it to rebuke the ingratitude of the English nobles on his return in 1195. Matthew Paris tells the story, *sub anno* (it is an addition of his to Ralph D'isset), *Hist. Major*, ed. Luard, ii. 413–6, how a lion and a serpent and a Venetian named Vitalis were saved from a pit by a woodman, Vitalis promising him half his fortune, fifty talents. The lion brings his benefactor a leveret, the serpent "gemmam pretiosam," probably "the precious jewel in his head" to which Shakespeare alludes (*As You Like It*, ii. 1, *cf.* Benfey, *l. c.*, p. 214, *n.*), but Vitalis refuses to have anything to do with him, and altogether repudiates the fifty talents. "Hæc referebat Rex Richardus munificus, ingratos redarguendo."

Remarks.—Apart from the interest of its wide travels, and its appearance in the standard mediæval History of England by Matthew Paris, the modern story shows the remarkable persistence of folk-tales in the popular mind. Here we have collected from the Hindu peasant of to-day a tale which was probably told before Buddha, over two thousand years ago, and certainly included among the Jātakas before the Christian era. The same thing has occurred with *The Tiger, Brahman and Jackal* (No. ix. *supra*).

XI. HARISARMAN.

Source.—Somadeva, *Kathit-Sarit-Sagara*, trans. Tawney (Calcutta, 1880), i. pp. 272–4. I have slightly toned down the inflated style of the original.

Parallels.—Benfey has collected and discussed a number in *Orient and Occident*, i. 371 *seq.*; see also Tawney, *ad loc.* The most remarkable of the parallels is that afforded by the Grimms' "Doctor Allwissend" (No. 98), which extends even to such a minute point as his exclamation, "Ach, ich armer Krebs," whereupon a crab is discovered under a dish. The usual form of discovery of the thieves is for the Dr. Knowall to have so many days given him to discover the thieves, and at the end of the first day he calls out, "There's one of them," meaning the days, just as one of the thieves peeps through at him. Hence the title and the plot of C. Lever's *One of Them.*

I. THE CHARMED RING.

Source.—Knowles, *Folk-Tales of Kashmir*, pp. 20–8.

Parallels.—The incident of the Aiding Animals is frequent in folk-tales; see bibliographical references, *sub voce*, in my List of Incidents, *Trans. Folk-Lor Congress*, p. 88; also Knowles, 21, *n.*;

and Temple, *Wideawake Stories*, pp. 401, 412. The Magic Ring is also "common form" in folk-tales; *cf.* Köhler *ap.* Marie de France, *Lais*, ed. Warncke, p. lxxxiv. And the whole story is to be found very widely spread from India (*Wideawake Stories*, pp. 196–206) to England (*Eng. Fairy Tales*, No. xvii., "Jack and his Golden Snuff-box," *cf.* Notes, *ibid.*), the most familiar form of it being "Aladdin and the Wonderful Lamp."

Remarks.—M. Cosquin has pointed out (*Contes de Lorraine*, p. xi. *seq.*) that the incident of the rat's-tail-up-nose to recover the ring from the stomach of an ogress, is found among Arabs, Albanians, Bretons, and Russians. It is impossible to imagine that incident—occurring in the same series of incidents—to have been invented more than once, and if that part of the story has been borrowed from India, there is no reason why the whole of it should not have arisen in India, and have been spread to the West. The English variant was derived from an English Gipsy, and suggests the possibility that for this particular story the medium of transmission has been the Gipsies. This contains the incident of the loss of the ring by the faithful animal, which again could not have been independently invented.

XIII. THE TALKATIVE TORTOISE.

Source.—The *Kacchapa Jātaka*, Fausböll, No. 215 · also in his *Five Jātakas*, pp. 16, 41, tr. Rhys-Davids, pp. viii.–x.

Parallels.—It occurs also in the Bidpai literature, in nearly all its multitudinous offshoots. See Benfey, *Einleitung*, § 84; also my *Bidpai*, E, 4 *a*; and North's text, pp. 170–5, where it is the taunts of the other birds that cause the catastrophe: "O here is a brave sight, looke, here is a goodly ieast, what bugge haue we here," said some "See, see, ſhe hangeth by the throte, and therefor ſhe ſpeaketh not," saide others; "and the beast flieth not like a beast;" so she opened her mouth and "paſhte hir all to pieces."

Remarks.—I have reproduced in my edition the original illustration of the first English Bidpai, itself derived from the Italian block. A replica of it here may serve to show that it could be used equally well to illustrate the Pali original as its English great-great-great-great-great-great grand-child.

XIV. LAC OF RUPEES.

Source.—Knowles, *Folk-Tales of Kashmir*, pp. 32–41. I have reduced the pieces of advice to three, and curtailed somewhat.

Parallels.—See *Celtic Fairy Tales*, No. xxii., "Tale of Ivan," from the old Cornish, now extinct, and notes *ibid.* Mr. Clouston points out (*Pop. Tales*, ii. 319) that it occurs in Buddhist literature, in "Buddaghoshas Parables," as "The Story of Kulla Pauthaka."

Remarks.—It is indeed curious to find the story better told in Cornwall than in the land of its birth, but there can be little doubt that the Buddhist version is the earliest and original form of the story. The piece of advice was originally a charm, in which a youth was to say to himself, "Why are you busy? Why are you busy?" He does so when thieves are about, and so saves the king's treasures, of which he gets an appropriate share. It would perhaps be as well if many of us should say to ourselves, "*Ghatesa, ghatesa, kim kârana?*"

XV. THE GOLD-GIVING SERPENT.

Source.—*Pantschatantra*, III. v., tr. Benfey, ii. 244–7.

Parallels given in my *Æsop*, Ro. ii. 10, p. 40. The chief points about them are—(1) though the tale does not exist in either Phædrus or Babrius, it occurs in prose derivates from the Latin by Ademar, 65, and "Romulus," ii. 10, and from Greek, in Gabrias, 45, and the prose *Æsop*, ed. Halm, 96; Gitlbauer has restored the Babrian form in his edition of Babrius, No. 160. (2) The fable occurs among folk-tales

Grimm, 105; Woycicki, *Poln. Mühr.* 105; Gering, *Islensk. Æventh.* 59, possibly derived from La Fontaine, x. 12.

Remarks.—Benfey has proved most ingeniously and conclusively (*Einl.* i. 359) that the Indian fable is the source of both Latin and Greek fables. I may borrow from my *Æsop*, p. 93, parallel abstracts of the three versions, putting Benfey's results in a graphic form, series of bars indicating the passages where the classical fables have failed to preserve the original.

BIDPAI.

A Brahmin once observed a snake in his field, and thinking it the tutelary spirit of the field, he offered it a libation of milk in a bowl. Next day he finds a piece of gold in the bowl, and he receives this each day after offering the libation. One day he had to go elsewhere, and he sent his son with the libation. The son sees the gold, and thinking the serpent's hole full of treasure determines to slay the snake. He strikes at its head with a cudgel, and the enraged serpent stings him to death. The Brahmin mourns his son's death, but next morning as usual brings the libation of milk (in the hope of getting the gold as before). The serpent appears after a long delay at the mouth of its lair, and declares their friendship at an end, as it could not forget the blow of the Brahmin's son, nor the Brahmin his son's death from the bite of the snake.

Pants. III. v. (Benf. 244-7).

PHÆDRINE.

- - - A good man had become friendly with the snake, who came into his house and brought luck with it, so that the man became rich through it. - - - One day he struck the serpent, which disappeared, and with it the man's riches. The good man tries to make it up, but the serpent declares their friendship at an end, as it could not forget the blow. - - - -

Phæd. Dressl. VII. 28 (Rom. II. xi.).

BABRIAN.

- - - - - - - - - - - - -

A serpent stung a farmer's son to death. The father pursued the serpent with an axe, and struck off part of its tail. Afterwards fearing its vengeance he brought food and honey to its lair, and begged reconciliation. The serpent, however, declares friendship impossible, as it could not forget the blow - - - nor the farmer his son's death from the bite of the snake.

Æsop, Halm 96b (Babrius-Gitlb. 160).

In the Indian fable every step of the action is thoroughly justified whereas the Latin form does not explain why the snake was friendly in the first instance, or why the good man was enraged afterwards; and the Greek form starts abruptly, without explaining why the serpent had killed the farmer's son. Make a composite of the Phædrine and Babrian forms, and you get the Indian one, which is thus shown to be the original of both.

XVI. THE SON OF SEVEN QUEENS.

Source.—Steel-Temple, *Wideawake Stories*, pp. 98–110, originally published in *Ind. Antiq.* x. 147 *seq.*

Parallels.—A long variant follows in *Ind. Antiq.*, *l. c.* M. Cosquin refers to several Oriental variants, *l. c.* p. xxx. *n.* For the direction tabu, see Note on Princess Labam, *supra*, No. ii. The "letter to kill bearer" and "letter substituted" are frequent in both European (see my List, *s. v.*) and Indian Folk-Tales (Temple, Analysis, II. iv. *b*, 6, p. 410). The idea of a son of seven mothers could only arise in a polygamous country. It occurs in "Punchkin," *supra*, No. iv.; Day, *Folk-Tales of Bengal*, 117 *seq.*; *Ind. Antiq.* i. 170 (Temple, *l. c.*, 398).

Remarks.—M. Cosquin (*Contes de Lorraine*, p. xxx.) points out how, in a Sicilian story, Gonzenbach (*Sizil. Mähr.* No. 80), the seven co-queens are transformed into seven step-daughters of the envious witch who causes their eyes to be taken out. It is thus probable, though M. Cosquin does not point this out, that the "envious step-mother" of folk-tales (see my List, *s. v.*) was originally an envious co-wife. But there can be little doubt of what M. Cosquin *does* point out—viz., that the Sicilian story is derived from the Indian one.

XVII. A LESSON FOR KINGS.

Source.—*Rājovāda Jātaka*, Fausböll, No. 151, tr. Rhys-Davids, pp. xxii.–vi.

Remarks.—This is one of the earliest of moral allegories in existence. The moralising tone of the Jātakas must be conspicuous to all reading them. Why, they can moralise even the Tar Baby (see *infra*, Note on "Demon with the Matted Hair," No. xxv.).

XVIII. PRIDE GOETH BEFORE A FALL.

Source.—Kingscote, *Tales of the Sun.* I have changed the Indian mercantile numerals into those of English "back-slang," which make a very good parallel.

XIX. RAJA RASALU.

Source.—Steel-Temple, *Wideawake Stories*, pp. 247-80, omitting "How Raja Rasalu was Born," "How Raja Rasalu's Friends Forsook Him," "How Raja Rasalu Killed the Giants," and "How Raja Rasalu became a Jogi." A further version in Temple, *Legends of*

Panjab, vol. i. *Chaupur*, I should explain, is a game played by two players with eight men, each on a board in the shape of a cross, four men to each cross covered with squares. The moves of the men are decided by the throws of a long form of dice. The object of the game is to see which of the players can first move all his men into the black centre square of the cross (Temple, *l. c.*, p. 344, and *Legends of Panjab*, i. 243-5). It is sometimes said to be the origin of chess.

Parallels.—Rev. C. Swynnerton, "Four Legends about Raja Rasalu," in *Folk-Lore Journal*, p. 158 *seq.*, also in separate book much enlarged, *The Adventures of Raja Rasalu*, Calcutta, 1884. Curiously enough, the real interest of the story comes after the end of our part of it, for Kokilan, when she grows up, is married to Raja Rasalu, and behaves as sometimes youthful wives behave to elderly husbands. He gives her her lover's heart to eat, *à la* Decameron, and she dashes herself over the rocks. For the parallels of this part of the legend see my edition of Painter's *Palace of Pleasure*, tom. i. Tale 39, or, better, the *Programm* of H. Patzig, *Zur Geschichte der Herzmare* (Berlin, 1891). Gambling for life occurs in Celtic and other folk-tales; *cf.* my List of Incidents, *s. v.* "Gambling for Magic Objects."

Remarks.—Raja Rasalu is possibly an historic personage, according to Capt. Temple, *Calcutta Review*, 1884, p. 397, flourishing in the eighth or ninth century. There is a place called Sirikap ka-kila in the neighbourhood of Sialkot, the traditional seat of Rasalu on the Indus, not far from Atlock.

Herr Patzig is strongly for the Eastern origin of the romance, and finds its earliest appearance in the West in the Anglo-Norman troubadour, Thomas' *Lai Guirun*, where it becomes part of the Tristan cycle. There is, so far as I know, no proof of the earliest part of the Rasalu legend (*our* part) coming to Europe, except the existence of the gambling incidents of the same kind in Celtic and other folk-tales.

XX. THE ASS IN THE LION'S SKIN.

Source.—The *Sīha Camma Jātaka*, Fausböll, No. 189, trans. Rhys-Davids, pp. v. vi.

Parallels.—It also occurs in Somadeva, *Katha Sarit Sagara*, ed. Tawney, ii. 65, and *n.* For Æsopic parallels, *cf.* my *Æsop*, Av. iv. It is in Babrius, ed. Gitlbaur, 218 (from Greek prose Æsop, ed. Halm, No. 323), and Avian, ed. Ellis, 5, whence it came into the modern Æsop.

Remarks.—Avian wrote towards the end of the third century, and put into Latin mainly those portions of Babrius which are unparalleled by Phædrus. Consequently, as I have shown, he has a much larger proportion of Eastern elements than Phædrus. There can be little doubt that the Ass in the Lion's Skin is from India. As Prof. Rhys-Davids remarks, the Indian form gives a plausible motive for the masquerade which is wanting in the ordinary Æsopic version.

XXI. THE FARMER AND THE MONEY-LENDER.

Source.—Steel-Temple, *Wideawake Stories*, pp. 215–18.

Parallels enumerated in my *Æsop*, Av. xvii. See also Jacques de Vitry, *Exempla*, ed. Crane, No. 196 (see notes, p. 212), and Bozon, *Contes moralisés*, No. 112. It occurs in Avian, ed. Ellis, No. 22. Mr. Kipling has a very similar tale in his *Life's Handicap*.

Remarks.—Here we have collected in modern India what one cannot help thinking is the Indian original of a fable of Avian. The preceding number showed one of his fables existing among the Jātakas, probably before the Christian era. This makes it likely that we shall find an earlier Indian original of the fable of the Avaricious and Envious, perhaps among the Jātakas still untranslated.

XXII. THE BOY WITH MOON ON FOREHEAD.

Source.—Miss Stokes' *Indian Fairy Tales*, No. 20, pp. 119–137.

Parallels to heroes and heroines in European fairy tales, with stars on their foreheads, are given with some copiousness in Stokes, *l. c.*, pp. 242–3. This is an essentially Indian trait; almost all Hindus have some tribal or caste mark on their bodies or faces. The choice of the hero disguised as a menial is also common property of Indian and European fairy tales: see Stokes, *l. c.*, p. 231, and my List of Incidents (*s. v.* "Mental Disguise").

XXIII. THE PRINCE AND THE FAKIR.

Source.—Kindly communicated by Mr. M. L. Dames from his unpublished collection of Baluchi tales.

Remarks.—Unholy fakirs are rather rare. See Temple, Analysis, I. ii. *a*, p. 394.

XXIV. WHY THE FISH LAUGHED.

Source.—Knowles, *Folk-Tales of Kashmir*, pp. 484–90.

Parallels.—The latter part is the formula of the Clever Lass who guesses riddles. She has been bibliographised by Prof. Child, *Eng. and Scotch Ballads*, i. 485; see also Benfey, *Kl. Schr.* ii. 156 *seq.* The sex test at the end is different from any of those enumerated by Prof. Kökler on Gonzenbach, *Sezil. Mähr.* ii. 216.

Remarks.—Here we have a further example of a whole formula, or series of incidents, common to most European collections, found in India, and in a quarter, too, where European influence is little likely to penetrate. Prof. Benfey, in an elaborate dissertation ("Die Kluge Dirne," in *Ausland*, 1859, Nos. 20-25, now reprinted in *Kl. Schr.* ii. 156 *seq.*), has shown the wide spread of the theme both in early Indian literature (though probably there derived from the folk) and in modern European folk literature.

XXV. THE DEMON WITH THE MATTED HAIR.

Source.—The *Pancāvudha-Jātaka*, Fausböll, No. 55, kindly translated for this book by Mr. W. H. D. Rouse, of Christ's College, Cambridge. There is a brief abstract of the Jātaka in Prof. Estlin Carpenter's sermon, *Three Ways of Salvation*, 1884, p. 27, where my attention was first called to this Jātaka.

Parallels.—Most readers of these Notes will remember the central episode of Mr. J. C. Harris' *Uncle Remus*, in which Brer Fox, annoyed at Brer Rabbit's depredations, fits up "a contrapshun, what he calls a Tar Baby." Brer Rabbit coming along that way, passes the time of day with Tar Baby, and, annoyed at its obstinate silence, hits it with right fist and with left, with left fist and with right, which successively stick to the "contrapshun," till at last he butts with his head, and that sticks too, whereupon Brer Fox, who all this time had "lain low," saunters out, and complains of Brer Rabbit that he is too stuck up. In the sequel Brer Rabbit begs Brer Fox that he may "drown me as deep ez you please, skin me, scratch out my eyeballs, t'ar out my years by the roots, en cut off my legs, but don't fling me in dat brier patch;" which, of course, Brer Fox does, only to be informed by the cunning Brer Rabbit that he had been "bred en bawn in a brier patch." The story is a favourite one with the negroes: it occurs in Col. Jones' *Negro Myths of the Georgia Coast* (Uncle Remus is from S. Carolina), also among those of Brazil (Romero, *Contos do Brazil*), and in the West Indian Islands (Mr. Lang, "At the Sign of the Ship, *Longman's Magazine*, Feb. 1889). We can trace it to Africa, where it occurs in Cape Colony (*South African Folk-Lore Journal*, vol. i.).

Remarks.—The fivefold attack on the Demon and the Tar Baby is so preposterously ludicrous that it cannot have been independently invented, and we must therefore assume that they are casually connected, and the existence of the variant in South Africa clinches the matter, and gives us a landing-stage between India and America. There can be little doubt that the Jātaka of Prince Five Weapons came to Africa, possibly by Buddhist missionaries, spread among the negroes, and then took ship in the holds of slavers for the New World, where it is to be found in fuller form than any yet discovered in the home of its birth. I say Buddhist missionaries, because there is a certain amount of evidence that the negroes have Buddhistic symbols among them, and we can only explain the identification of Brer Rabbit with Prince Five Weapons, and so with Buddha himself, by supposing the change to have originated among Buddhists, where it would be quite natural. For one of the most celebrated metempsychoses of Buddha is that detailed in the *Sasa Jātaka* (Fausböll, No. 316, tr. R. Morris, *Folk-Lore Journal*, ii. 336), in which the Buddha, as a hare, performs a sublime piece of self-sacrifice, and as a reward is translated to the moon, where he can be seen to this day as "the hare in the moon." Every Buddhist is reminded of the virtue of self-sacrifice whenever the moon is full, and it is easy to understand how the Buddha became identified as the Hare or Rabbit. A striking confirmation of this, in connection with our immediate subject, is offered by Mr. Harris' sequel volume, *Nights with Uncle Remus*. Here there is a whole chapter (xxx.) on "Brer Rabbit and his famous Foot," and it is well known how the worship of Buddha's foot developed in later Buddhism. No wonder Brer Rabbit is so 'cute : he is nothing less than an incarnation of Buddha. Among the Karens of Burmah, where Buddhist influence is still active, the Hare holds exactly the same place in their folk-lore as Brer Rabbit among the negroes. The sixth chapter of Mr. Smeaton's book on them is devoted to "Fireside Stories," and is entirely taken up with adventures of the Hare, all of which can be paralleled from *Uncle Remus*.

Curiously enough, the negro form of the fivefold attack—"fighting with *five* fists," Mr. Barr would call it—is probably nearer to the original legend than that preserved in the Jātaka, though 2000 years older. For we may be sure that the thunderbolt of Knowledge did not exist in the original, but was introduced by some Buddhist Mr. Barlow, who, like Alice's Duchess, ended all his tales with : "And the moral of that is——" For no well-bred demon would have been taken in by so simple a "sell" as that indulged in by Prince Five-Weapons in our Jātaka, and it is probable, therefore, that *Uncle Remus* preserves a reminiscence of the original Indian reading of the tale. On the other hand, it is probable that Carlyle's Indian god with the fire in his belly was derived from Prince Five-Weapons.

The negro variant has also suggested to Mr. Batten an explanation of the whole story, which is extremely plausible, though it introduces a method of folk-lore exegesis which has been overdriven to death. The *Sasa Jātaka* identifies the Brer Rabbit Buddha with the hare in the moon. It is well known that Easterns explain an eclipse of the moon as due to its being swallowed up by a Dragon or Demon. May not, asks Mr. Batten, the *Pancavudha Jātaka* be an idealised account of an eclipse of the moon? This suggestion receives strong confirmation from the Demon's reference to Rahu, who does, in Indian myth, swallow the moon at times of eclipse. The Jātaka accordingly contains the Buddhist explanation why the moon—*i.e.* the hare in the moon, *i.e.* Buddha—is not altogether swallowed up by the Demon of Eclipse, the Demon with the Matted Hair. Mr. Batten adds that in imagining what kind of Demon the Eclipse Demon was, the Jātaka writer was probably aided by recollections of some giant octopus, who has saucer eyes and a kind of hawk's beak, knobs on its "tusks," and a very variegated belly (gasteropod). It is obviously unfair of Mr. Batten both to illustrate and also to explain so well the Tar Baby Jātaka—taking the scientific bread, so to speak, out of a poor folk-lorist's mouth—but his explanations seem to me so convincing that I cannot avoid including them in these Notes.

I am, however, not so much concerned with the original explanation of the Jātaka as to trace its travels across the continents of Asia, Africa, and America. I think I have done this satisfactorily, and will have thereby largely strengthened the case for less extensive travels of other tales. I have sufficient confidence of the method employed to venture on that most hazardous of employments, scientific prophecy. I venture to predict that the Tar Baby story will be found in Madagascar in a form nearer the Indian than Uncle Remus, and I will go further, and say that it will *not* be found in the grand Helsingfors collection of folk-tales, though this includes 12,000, of which 1000 are beast-tales.

XXVI. THE IVORY PALACE.

Source.—Knowles, *Folk-Tales of Kashmir*, pp. 211–25, with some slight omissions. Gulizar is Persian for rosy-cheeked.

Parallels.—Stokes, *Indian Fairy Tales*, No. 27. "Panwpatti Rani," pp. 208–15, is the same story. Another version in the collection *Baital Pachisi*, No. 1.

Remarks.—The themes of love by mirror, and the faithful friend, are common European, though the calm attempt at poisoning is perhaps characteristically Indian, and reads like a page from Mr. Kipling.

XXVII. SUN. MOON, AND WIND.

Source.—Miss Frere, *Old Deccan Days*, No. 10, pp. 153–5.

Remarks.—Miss Frere observes that she has not altered the traditional mode of the Moon's conveyance of dinner to her mother the Star, though it must, she fears, impair the value of the story as a moral lesson in the eyes of all instructors of youth.

XXVIII. HOW WICKED SONS WERE DUPED.

Source.—Knowles, *Folk-Tales of Kashmir*, pp. 241–2.

Parallels.—A Gaelic parallel was given by Campbell in *Trans. Ethnol. Soc.*, ii. p. 336; an Anglo-Latin one from the Middle Ages by T. Wright in *Latin Stories* (Percy Soc.), No. 26; and for these and points of anthropological interest in the Celtic variant see Mr. Gomme's article in *Folk-Lore*, i. pp. 197–206, "A Highland Folk-Tale and its Origin in Custom."

Remarks.—Mr. Gomme is of opinion that the tale arose from certain rhyming formulæ occurring in the Gaelic and Latin tales as written on a mallet left by the old man in the box opened after his death. The rhymes are to the effect that a father who gives up his wealth to his children in his own lifetime deserves to be put to death with the mallet. Mr. Gomme gives evidence that it was an archaic custom to put oldsters to death after they had become helpless. He also points out that it was customary for estates to be divided and surrendered during the owners' lifetime, and generally he connects a good deal of primitive custom with our story. I have already pointed out in *Folk-Lore*, p. 403, that the existence of the tale in Kashmir without any reference to the mallet makes it impossible for the rhymes on the mallet to be the source of the story. As a matter of fact, it is a very embarrassing addition to it, since the rhyme tells against the parent, and the story is intended to tell against the ungrateful children. The existence of the tale in India renders it likely enough that it is not indigenous to the British Isles, but an Oriental importation. It is obvious, therefore, that it cannot be used as anthropological evidence of the existence of the primitive customs to be found in it. The whole incident, indeed, is a striking example of the dangers of the anthropological method of dealing with folk-tales before some attempt is made to settle the questions of origin and diffusion.

XXIX. THE PIGEON AND THE CROW.

Source.—The *Lola Jātaka*, Fausböll, No. 274, kindly translated and slightly abridged for this book by Mr. W. H. D. Rouse.

Remarks—We began with an animal Jātaka, and may appropriately finish with one which shows how effectively the writers of the Jātakas could represent animal folk, and how terribly moral they invariably were in their tales. I should perhaps add that the Bodhisat is not precisely the Buddha himself but a character which is on its way to becoming perfectly enlightened, and so may be called a future Buddha.